THE KILLING FLOOR

David Fein, owner of Supreme Packing, a slaughterhouse in a grimy little town in Southern California, had a problem. He was a compulsive gambler. Lately, gambling had taken over his life. First he couldn't cover his losses at the plant. Then he got a quick loan and went into debt. By the time he took in Tortorello as a business partner—a clean-cut Harvard type with his own bookkeeper and some "Family" connections—he was in big trouble. Now he hasn't come home for four days and his wife is frantic.

Jacob Asch, ex-reporter turned private detective, hears the whole sad story from Jake Bloom, a former employee of Fein's. Asch figures that Fein is probably sleeping off a four-day drunk in a flop-house or he's in the sack with another woman. He's heard them all before; found them all before . . . the drunks, the deadbeats, the people bent on self destruction. David Fein would be like all the rest. Asch will take the job.

What he hadn't counted on was the body on the killing floor.

GN00356694

THE KILLING FLOOR

by

Arthur Lyons

NO EXIT PRESS

1988

No Exit Press
18 Coleswood Road
Harpenden, Herts AL5 1EQ
England

British Library Cataloguing in Publication Data

Lyons, Arthur. A Killing Floor. I. Title.
813'.54 [F]
ISBN 0-948353-35-X

9 8 7 6 5 4 3 2 1

Printed by William Collins

Vernon stinks. It always stinks.

The sharp, rancid smells of cattle and hogs and blood and manure hang together in a perpetual greasy cloud over the streets of the city.

And its odor is perfectly coordinated with its visual splendors. Slaughter houses line both sides of Soto Street, huge, rambling complexes, their shapeless hulks alternating intermittently with scrap metal yards and potbellied water towers and trucking yards and industrial smokestacks staining the sky with smudge.

It goes on like that for blocks, gray and faded and dismal, and then, after your eyes become accustomed to the opressive ugliness, they get assaulted by The Mural.

A few years ago the owner of Farmer John, the largest hog-killing operation on the West Coast, decided it would be good PR to beautify his Vernon plant. So he commissioned a well-known mural painter to cover the place with four square blocks of bright blue skies and fleecy white clouds and squealing pigs being pursued over rolling grasslands by smiling, freckle-faced farm boys. One of the owner's friends might have saved him the expense by letting him in on the secret that his proposed project would be like putting costume jewelry on string warts, but apparently nobody did, because the mural still stands, a grotesque monument to Vernon's civic pride.

It was Monday, December third and the air was crisp and cool, the sky a smoggy brown-blue. It had been three years since I had last been in Vernon and I was finding I hadn't missed it a bit. I was driving down Soto, breathing through my mouth, looking for Sam's Deli and wondering what the hell Nate Bloom could want to see me about.

I'd known Bloom for a total of one week three years ago, and in spite of the fact that our relationship had been for the most part a professional one, I had grown to like him in that time. He was a wiry little Jew with a tough, curt exterior and a dry, sarcastic sense of humor which I enjoyed immensely, even when I'd been the butt of one of his wisecracks. But beneath the tough, businesslike exterior, he was a marshmallow. He even wangled a nice bonus for me, which could have been part of the reason I remembered him so sympathetically.

Bloom had then been the credit manager for Supreme Packing Company and when sides of beef began disappearing regularly from Supreme's inventory, he had hired me to find out where they were going.

I found out, but with considerable help from Bloom. It had been an education working with him, I had to admit. He had been in the meat business for thirty-nine years, as a salesman, a cattle buyer, an accountant, and a credit manager. Twenty-one of those years had been spent with Supreme, first with the original founder of the company, Leonard Fein, and then with the son, David, who took over the business when the old man died. Bloom showed me the ropes, and one week later I caught the night watchman opening the back gates for a panel truck which turned out to be driven by his brother.

It had been somewhat of a surprise when I returned Bloom's call and found out he was now working for another outfit, Fulton Packing. I asked him when he had left Supreme, but he was rather vague about it, just as he was vague about why he wanted to see me. It was a "personal matter" he had said. A personal matter. I started to wonder what kind of personal matter a sixty-one-year-old married man could have that would require the services of a private detective, and then stopped myself. I was always doing that—wondering about things that I couldn't possibly find an answer for.

Relax, Asch, relax. You'll find out all about it soon enough. Probably more than you'd like to know. Just lean back and listen to the radio and take in the sights and smells of beautiful downtown Vernon. After all, it's not every day you get to see such magnificent artwork. The Sistine Chapel of slaughter houses.

Sam's Deli turned out to be a two-story box directly across the street from Farmer John's. Its front was mostly windows with a lot of the space occupied by signs advertising various breakfast and luncheon specials. I pulled into the lot and parked.

The inside of the restaurant was cleaner than the street, but that was about all I'd say for it. The linoleum floor was chipped and dirty and half the booths in the room were held together with duct tape. It was nine-thirty, and the eight people that constituted the breakfast rush were dispersed between the stools at the counter and the booths. Bloom was sitting in a booth by the window, staring out at one of the towheaded boys in the mural. He seemed startled when I said hello.

He had aged much more than the three years that had elapsed since I had seen him last. There were more lines around the watery blue eyes and the thin-lipped mouth, a few more hairs missing from the front of the receding gray wave—but that wasn't it. It wasn't anything physical that had aged him. It was something else, something intangible, something missing rather than something there. The spark of humor was gone from the eyes, there was a lack of spirit in the expression.

The expression momentarily changed when he grabbed my hand, smiling broadly. "How're you doing, Jake? Thanks for coming by. I know you must be busy."

"No problem, Nate," I said, and slid into the booth.

A dumpy, middle-aged waitress with a face like one of the kosher dill pickles she served, came sauntering over to the table with a coffeepot in her hand. "Coffee?"

"Please," I said, turning my cup over. Bloom already had a cup half-full and he took a warm-up.

The waitress put the pot down on the table and, shifting all her weight toward one hip, poised her pencil on her pad and stared at me. "Whaddya gonna have?"

I eyed one of the signs on the wall that said: One Egg, Three Buttermilk Pancakes, Coffee $1.49. "I'll take your breakfast special."

"It's over at nine."

"What time do you open?"

"Eight-thirty."

"It's a long one, huh?"

She didn't answer. She just stared at me indifferently.

"Tell you what," I said, "it sounds so good, I'll take it at the regular price."

"We don't sell it," she droned, "except as a special."

I snatched the menu out of its slot by the sugar jar and scanned it quickly. "Corned beef hash and a poached egg," I said. "And whole wheat toast."

"We ain't got whole wheat. Just rye. We're out of whole wheat."

"Rye, then," I said.

She wrote it down, stifling a yawn. "You want anything, Nate?"

"No, thanks, Mary," he said.

She nodded and left with her pot.

"Lovely woman," I said when she was out of hearing range. "What does she do, moonlight as a fire-eater or something?"

"She's been here twelve years," he said, some of the old amusement back in his eyes.

"Well, then, I don't blame her so much," I said, looking around the place. I took a sip of coffee. "So how have you been, Nate?"

He shrugged listlessly and gave me a battle-weary smile. "All right. Getting by." He paused and said: "You know my wife passed away—"

"No, I'm sorry. I didn't know."

He nodded. "Last year. Lung cancer. It was really bad there for a while, toward the end. It was actually a blessing when she died. For her, not for me. I've been lost without her. It's hard getting used to living alone again after thirty-four years."

"I'm really sorry," I repeated, feeling foolish but not knowing what else to say.

He nodded absently and looked out the window.

"So what's the new job like?"

"It's fine," he said. "John Fulton is a pretty good guy. He knows his business. We've known each other for years and when he heard I'd left Supreme, he gave me a call and made me an offer. It doesn't pay as much, but I'm not working as hard, either, which is all right with me. I don't seem to get the satisfaction I used to out of the work. It just seems like, I don't know, it doesn't mean that much anymore."

"What happened at Supreme? Why did you leave?"

He pursed his lips and said: "I was fired."

That one surprised me. "After twenty-one years?"

He nodded.

"What the hell happened?"

"A lot of things. Dave took in a partner two months ago, and the partner brought in his own controller. That let me and the accountant out."

"And Fein let it happen?"

"In all fairness to Dave, he had his back to the wall. Tortorello—he's the new partner—bailed Dave out of financial

· 5 ·

hot water on the agreement that certain changes would be made. I was one of the changes." He hesitated and said: "As a matter of fact, Dave is the reason I called you."

"Why? What do you mean?"

"He's disappeared."

"What do you mean?"

He shrugged. "He's disappeared. He hasn't been home or at the plant in four days. Barbara—Dave's wife—called me up last night and asked if I'd seen him. She was nearly out of her mind. I calmed her down the best I could and told her I'd get in touch with you, that you might be able to help."

"When was the last time you saw Fein?"

"Two months ago when I left Supreme."

"You got any idea where he might be?"

He looked at me steadily. "I've got an idea."

"Where?"

"On a binge."

"What kind of a binge?"

"Gambling."

"I didn't know Fein was a gambler," I said.

He nodded. "He started again about a year ago. Boozing, too. That's what got Supreme into trouble. He was dipping into the company accounts to pay off his debts. Over the past year we got into more than one argument about it. He told me to mind my own business, that it was his money and he could do anything he wanted with it. I tried to warn him, but he didn't want to listen. Then, when the shit hit the fan, he blamed it on me."

"How?"

He turned the palm of one hand toward me. "One of our biggest accounts, Big Boy Markets, went BK, sticking us for a nice chunk of dough. Normally, there would have been enough money in the bank to carry the loss over until the end of the year when it could be written off as a tax loss, but Dave had been drawing too much. He blamed me because

I was the credit manager. He said I should have kept closer tabs on Big Boy's credit. But hell, there was nothing on the surface to show they were in trouble. No slow-pays, nothing. Anyway, Dave managed to secure a loan for sixty thousand, but then we hit a couple of lean months over the summer and he had to take in Tortorello as a partner."

"You said Fein started gambling *again* about a year ago. He used to gamble a lot?"

He nodded. "Yeah. He was compulsive. The old man bailed him out of more than one scrape. He went to Gambler's Anonymous and even went to a psychiatrist for a while. None of that did much. The thing that cured him was marrying Barbara. He really loved that girl. He wouldn't have done anything to hurt her. I thought he was cured for good."

"What set him back?"

He shrugged helplessly. "I don't know."

"What kind of gambling did he do?"

He took a sip of coffee. "Any kind. He used to place bets through a book. Football, baseball, horses. It didn't seem to matter. He started playing cards at Gardena a lot. Once in awhile, he'd take a plane up to Vegas."

"When this Tortorello bought into the business, did he know about Fein's gambling?"

"I don't know," he said.

The waitress came over with my breakfast and more coffee. After she left the table, I asked: "It seems to me that Fein treated you pretty shabbily, Nate. Why are you so concerned about him now?"

"I'm not," he said. "It's Barbara I'm really worried about. She's a great kid—one in a million. She has deserved better than she's been getting for the past year. If Dave gambles away everything, I don't want to see her get stuck."

"You think there's a possibility of that?"

He scowled darkly. "Yeah. Given the right conditions and his frame of mind lately, I think there is."

"How long have they been married?"

"Six years."

"I take it the marriage isn't so good anymore."

He stared into his coffee cup. "No."

"What happened? He fall out of love with her or something?"

"I don't know what happened," he said.

"Another woman?"

He put his arm up over the back of the booth and turned sideways in his seat. "I don't know, Jake. It's possible, I guess. All I can tell you is that, as far as I know, he's never cheated on Barbara. If he's seeing another woman, he never let on to me about it. Probably because he knew he would get a lecture about it."

I remembered Bloom's long-winded, wistful recitals of the bliss of married life and his glowing descriptions of his own marriage. He had administered them to me after he found out I was divorced and living alone. A man isn't meant to live alone, he'd told me. What you need, Jake, is a good woman to balance you out. You've got too many rough edges in your personality. He was probably right, but I hadn't wanted to tell him so. I had had the feeling that he would have immediately combed the offices of Supreme Packing looking for one to fit the bill. I took a mouthful of corned beef and chewed it halfheartedly.

"Will you talk to Barbara?" he asked.

I looked out at the unabashed innocence of the towheaded farm boy across the street and sighed wearily. I wanted to tell Bloom I was tired. Tired of tracking down wandering husbands and unfaithful wives and runaway daughters and skip-payments who more often than not turned out to be bums who never should have been given credit at all. I wanted to tell him to forget about it, that David Fein would more than likely come home of his own accord in a day or two, that he was more than likely sleeping off a four-day drunk in a flop-house somewhere or sitting unshaven and smelling like a raccoon at a card table in Gardena or in the sack with another woman. I wanted to tell him that it probably wouldn't make a hell of a lot of difference if he was found or not because, if he was truly compulsive, he would gamble everything away next time or the time after that if he didn't do it this time. I wanted to tell him all that and a lot more, most of which had nothing to do with him.

I might have, too. Except that half of something is more than all of nothing and nothing was all I had going right now. For three weeks I had been sitting around my apartment, drinking beer and listening to my beard grow, and although that may be a thrilling way to spend your idle hours, it doesn't pay the rent.

Besides, like I said before, I liked Bloom.

The poached egg pinned me with an accusing cyclopean stare from the top it its mountain of hash. I poked out its yellow eye and said: "When does she want to see me?"

"I can give her a call from here."

I nodded and shifted my gaze out the window again. The towheaded boy was still smiling indefatigably. You poor, dumb ignorant kid, I thought. You really don't know what it's all about, do you?

· 2 ·

THE HOUSE WAS in Pacific Palisades on a luxuriously green street lined with jacaranda trees, thick carpets of lawn and precisely trimmed hedges and shrubs. The air was cool and moist, laced with a hint of salt, but the sea was still two or three miles to the west, visible only to those farther up the hill who had paid for the view.

The Fein house had not quite made heaven. It was in purgatory, about halfway up the hill. It was a long, pink, one-storied house with a large expanse of brown shingle roof and lots of ferns growing in flagstone planters out front. I parked behind the powder-blue Mark IV in the driveway and went up the stone walk.

There was a brass mezuzah tacked to the front door frame. It must be nice to know your roots, I thought, as I rang the doorbell. My own Jewishness was a loose, disjointed tangle of feelings. Having been the product of a mixed marriage—a Jewish father and an Episcopalian mother—I'd grown up schizoid. It was true that I did feel a strong cultural bond to Judaism, but the faith part of it had never really taken hold any more than my mother's unshakable belief that we had all been cleansed of sin through the blood of Christ. I don't know, maybe I was just plugged into some common pool of paranoia shared by all Jews, a paranoia engendered by the number six million. And I'd come to the conclusion years ago that if there was a God up there watching over us, he had to be dressed in black leather.

My thoughts were broken by the woman who answered the door. She looked in her early thirties, trim, tennis-tanned, with sun-streaked blonde hair and pale eyes the color of green ice. Her mouth was wide with a sensuously swollen lower lip. All in all, she was a striking woman. The only thing I didn't like about her face, in fact, was her nose; it was too retroussé and the nostrils had a pinched, molded look, as if it had been shaped from clay and stuck on. It was ironic, I thought, that her single unattractive feature was probably the only one she had paid for. She wore a red sweater and a white skirt cut above the knee.

"Mrs. Fein?"

"Yes," she said. "Are you Mr. Asch?"

I said I was, and she smiled and offered her hand. Her hand was warm and soft. Her smile was, too, even though it looked a bit forced. She stepped back and asked me to come in.

The house was a split-level, the dining area two steps up from the living room. The dining room wall was almost entirely glass and looked out onto a swimming-pooled yard, the far side of which was bordered by a hill of ivy. A huge fig tree stood just outside the door, sheltering part of the red brick patio.

"Would you like some coffee?" she asked. "I was just going to have some."

"That sounds great," I said with false enthusiasm.

I didn't really want any coffee, but sometimes accepting a cup helped break the ice. Some people I have found have an easier time spilling their personal secrets when their hands are occupied. I didn't know if Mrs. Fein was one of those or not, but I didn't figure it could hurt anything.

She told me she would be right back and went up the stairs into the kitchen. I sat down in a thickly stuffed chair and looked around.

The furniture in the room was expensive and heavy, right

down to the cream-colored baby grand piano in the corner. Cut-crystal and silver knickknacks were carefully arranged on various coffee and end tables. Both the thick carpeting and the walls were an off-white, giving the room an aura of cold indifference. The house didn't care who owned it or whether David Fein was right now gambling away the mortgage. Scouring my own conscience, I couldn't say truthfully that I did, either.

She came out of the kitchen carrying a tray on which sat a coffeepot and two cups. I got up to help her, but she told me to sit down and I obeyed. She set the tray down on the coffee table, sat on the couch and poured out two cups.

She handed me one, and I stirred cream and sugar into it and took a sip. I had to make an effort not to wince. She may have been a hell of a nice-looking woman, but Mrs. Olsen she wasn't. I put the cup and saucer down on the edge of the table and took out a notepad.

The woman was obviously tense. She was sitting on the edge of the couch, her cup balanced precariously on the end of her lap. Her knees were locked tightly together and her back was rigid, but there was something in the way she held her head, a graceful line in the neck and chin, that softened the stiffness of her pose.

"When was the last time you saw your husband exactly, Mrs. Fein?"

"Thursday evening," she said in a quiet voice. "He came home from work and had dinner and then went out again."

"What time was that?"

"About eight, I guess."

She picked up her cup and lifted it to her lips. Her hand trembled slightly, but she didn't make a face when she tasted the coffee. She was probably used to it.

"He didn't say where he was going?"

She shook her head. "He doesn't tell me much of anything anymore. I—he just said he was going out and not to wait up for him."

"Has he ever done anything like this before?"

"No. Never." Then, less definitely: "He's stayed out all night once or twice, but he's never stayed away for days before."

"What kind of a mood was he in when he went out?"

She put the cup down suddenly on the coffee table and lifted the lid of an ornate ceramic cigarette case beside it. She took out a cigarette and lit it with the case's matching lighter. She exhaled a blue smokescreen between us. "We had an argument."

"What about?"

"I asked him to stay home," she said. She took a nervous puff from her cigarette and tapped it on the edge of a glass ashtray, even though there was no ash on it. "He'd been in a good mood before dinner, and I told him I thought it would be nice if he'd stay home and relax for a change and we could watch television or something. I don't remember what got him started, but he turned nasty and then we started arguing and he stormed out."

"Had he been drinking?"

She looked down at her lap. "Yes."

"A lot?"

"He'd had about three martinis before dinner."

"Is he a heavy drinker?"

"Lately, yes."

"Does he explode like he did often?"

She nodded. "Over the past few months, it seems like every time I've tried to get into a conversation with him, it's ended in an argument. Usually over nothing." She stopped, her face thoughtful, as if she were carrying on an inner search for the right words. "David was, I don't know, he isn't the same man I married six years ago. There isn't any communication between us anymore. It's like he's drawn up a wall around himself and won't let anybody in. When we first got married, he used to discuss his problems with me all the time. But now, he doesn't seem . . . he. . . ."

Her voice trailed off as if someone had turned down the volume inside somewhere, and she looked away self-consciously. She was obviously having a difficult time with it, and I felt sorry for her.

I didn't say anything and that seemed to make her more nervous. She mashed her cigarette out in the ashtray and went on, as if hearing herself talk was easier than just sitting still. "We'd discussed divorce, but David asked me to hold off. He said he couldn't afford a divorce right now and asked me to wait until he could get himself straight financially. But he hasn't shown any signs of getting himself straight. He's just been digging himself a bigger hole."

"I understand he's had a gambling problem for some time," I said.

She nodded. "From what I understand, for a few years before we were married, he really got into debt. His father sent him to psychiatrists and everything to try to cure him. Then, when we got married, the problem just seemed to go away by itself."

No, Mrs. Fein, I thought. Compulsions don't just go away by themselves. People bury them and they lie dormant below the surface, ready to reemerge when the reason to hold them in check disappears.

"Mark—" she went on, "that's David's brother—is a doctor. We have been trying to get David to go again. Mark made arrangements for David to see a friend of his who's supposed to be very good, but David refused to see him. He just kept saying that psychiatrists were the ones who were crazy and there was nothing wrong with him."

He could be right, I thought. I began nibbling my lower lip. "You've checked with the brother, I take it."

She nodded. "I've checked with everyone. Nate was my last resort. David would never admit it, not in words, anyway, but he felt guilty about what had happened to Nate. I thought he might try to contact him, but he hasn't."

"Can you think of anyone else—friends, relatives—that he might try to get in touch with?"

"No," she said. "There's just Mark. David's mother and father are dead, and he doesn't have any other relatives in California that I know about. And he doesn't have any close friends to speak of. He really isn't very much of a social person. He's always been too wrapped up in the business. Until last year, that is."

"Have you notified the police about this?"

"Yes. They said they couldn't do much about it. They said he'd probably come home . . ." Her cheeks flushed with color and her voice clogged with emotion. "I—I just keep having visions of David lying in an alley somewhere, the victim of a mugging or something—"

"That isn't likely," I told her. "The police would have notified you by now if something like that had happened." *If* there was identification on the body, I thought, but did not say.

"What kind of a car was he driving?"

"A 1974 LTD. Gold. With a tan vinyl top."

I wrote it down. "Do you know the license number?"

"PRIME," she said.

"Pardon me?"

"P-R-I-M-E," she repeated. "Like prime meat."

I gave her a smile she didn't return. "That's an easy one to remember."

"Yes."

I closed my notebook and sat tapping it in the palm of my hand. I found myself staring at her legs. They were very nice legs, like the rest of her, evenly tanned with smooth, well-molded calves and neat, trim ankles. I began to fantasize and had to force my mind back on the narrow path. That was one of my firm "Rules to Live By": Never Defecate Where You Eat. Another one was: If You're Going to Chew Tobacco, Always Wear a Brown Suit. I had a million of them.

I sighed and sat back on the couch. "Mrs. Fein, an investigation of this nature can be very expensive. I think it's only fair to warn you right now. My fees are $150 a day plus expenses. Plus fifteen cents a mile."

She took the news calmly. "Nate told me."

"I'll also need a retainer."

"How much?"

"Three hundred dollars."

"I'll make you out a check," she said, standing up.

It wasn't that I was hardhearted, but I had learned the hard way about getting money up front in missing persons cases. I'd had more than just one in which I'd run around for days looking for somebody only to find out they had come home the night before of their own accord. Trying to convince your clients they should pay you what they owe you often turns out to be worse than the job you were supposed to do. Pay you?

I stood up with her. "I'd like you to make out a list of everyone you can think of whom your husband knew—friends, relatives, business associates."

"I'll do my best."

"I'd also like to look through your husband's things. His clothes, his desk—"

"Sure," she said. "You can follow me, if you like."

"WHERE WOULD you like to start?"
"I might as well start with his desk," I said.
We moved down a narrow hallway and turned off into a small den in the front of the house. Sunlight streamed in through the large picture window that looked out onto the front lawn, bleaching out the room.

The room was occupied by a small, flower-print love seat, a mahogany end table and a free-standing reading lamp. One wall was bookshelves filled with best sellers and a lot of *Reader's Digest* condensations. The desk was a built-in that ran underneath the length of the bookshelves.

On the top of the desk was an electric portable typewriter, a container of pens and pencils, a telephone, and a stack of unopened letters and bills. One of the envelopes had been torn open and the letter was sitting on top of it. It was a note from the Auto Club notifying David Fein his membership would expire January 1. The middle drawer contained a black, bound, three-ring checkbook. Mrs. Fein said it was the household account, so I just glanced through it and put it back. The side drawers held the usual stuff, stationery, paper clips, carbon paper, a stapler. The bottom drawer was a filing drawer for the household business. Fein had everything neatly separated in manila folders, the colored tabs of which were marked: Insurance, Contracts, Mortgage, Auto. The last drawer contained nothing but several phone directories for different parts of the city.

I turned and looked up at Mrs. Fein, who was standing behind me with her arms crossed. "Did your husband have another checking account?"

"Yes."

"Do you know what bank?"

"Security Pacific, I think. I'm not sure."

"Would you happen to know where the checkbook would be?"

She shook her head and began rubbing her arms as if she were cold.

"You think it might be in his office at the plant?"

"I don't know. Maybe."

"Do me a favor," I said. "Call your husband's partner— what's his name—Tortorello, and tell him I'll be coming by this afternoon to talk to him. Tell him I have your permission to look through your husband's office."

"All right."

I stood up and waved a hand at the desk. "I'm through here. May I take a look at his clothes now?"

We went back down the hallways and into a large bedroom. The room was done in yellows and creams. The king-size bed had a brass headboard and was covered with a canary yellow antique satin spread. On either end of the bed was a brass and glass bedstand on which were matching antique lamps. Over the bed was a large painting featuring amorphous blotches of color. It took up almost the entire wall, and if it was supposed to represent something, it eluded me just what it was. Two velour chairs and another glass table finished the room.

On the glass table was a framed picture of Barbara Fein, in shorts and a halter top standing on a sandy beach with her arm around the waist of David. Fein had on a pair of swim trunks and looked darkly handsome, a broad smile set into his square-jawed face.

Barbara Fein noticed me looking at the picture and offered: "That was taken in Hawaii six years ago. On our honeymoon."

There was a distant sadness in her voice, as if she wished she were back there now but secretly knew those days were probably gone for good. She shook herself loose from the memory and walked abruptly to the double sliding closet doors at the far side of the room and pulled one of them open. "David's things are in here."

Hanging in the closet were several dozen dress shirts and a dozen more short-sleeved shirts, assorted suits, sports jackets and individual pairs of slacks. Most of the clothing was conservative, although there were a few jackets that had a bit of flash to them. Below the suits was a shoe tree that held eight or nine pairs of shoes and a pair of galoshes. Beside the shoe tree was a large cream-colored suitcase. If Fein had planned on a trip, he was traveling light.

I started going through the pockets of the coats and pants. About three-quarters of the way down the rack, in the pocket of a gray-checked sports jacket, my fingers touched a piece of paper. I plucked it out and unfolded it.

It was a rent receipt for $275 from the Casa Loma Apartments, 29871 Golding Street, West L.A. It was made out to David Fein and was dated October 2, 1975. Someone had scribbled in ink across the top that it had been paid with check #78. I put it in my pocket and went on with the search.

The other side of the closet housed a large built-in bureau. After going fruitlessly through countless sweaters, T-shirts, pairs of underwear and socks, I gave up and stepped out of the closet.

I took the paper out of my pocket and showed it to her. "That mean anything to you?"

She stared at it uncomprehendingly. "No. What is it?"

"It's a rent receipt. Your husband has apparently been keeping an apartment at this place."

Her cheeks colored with the possibilities the little slip of paper contained. "I don't know anything about it."

"I'll check it out," I said and put it back in my pocket. "Do you have a picture of your husband I could use? Preferably wallet-size."

"I have one that was taken when we went sailing in Santa Barbara. It's a couple of years old."

"As long as it's a good likeness," I said.

"He hasn't changed too much since it was taken," she said. "I'll get it."

She started out of the room, and I said after her: "Also, I'd like that list of names—"

"I'll do the best I can," she said, stopping in the hallway and turning around. "I thought David might have left his address book around the house somewhere, but I haven't been able to find it. I guess he must have taken it with him."

I went out into the living room, and she came in a little while later. She gave me the list and the picture, a small color photograph of David Fein sitting in the back of a sailing boat, holding the rudder in one hand and a can of beer in the other. She also gave me a check for $300, which I was relieved I wasn't going to have to ask her for.

I went to the front door and opened it. "I'll be in touch with you later," I told her as I stepped out onto the front porch. I took out a business card and wrote my home number on it. "If you need to reach me for any reason, no matter what time, you should be able to get me at one of these two numbers."

"Thank you," she said.

She closed the door slowly, and I went down the driveway and got into my car. My mind kept repeating images: that sensuous lower lip, those pale green eyes, those smooth calves, those trim ankles. I wondered why it was that the good ones were always taken. And being dumped on by the likes of David Fein. If I was married to something like that, I sure as hell wouldn't be spending my time in some stale-smelling, smoke-filled card room. There just wasn't any justice in the world.

To hell with it, Asch. You've got her check. What more do you want, for chrissakes?

I didn't wait for the obvious answer. Instead, I backed out of the driveway and coasted down toward Sunset.

· 4 ·

THE CASA LOMA WAS a huge, four-story apartment complex with swirled plaster walls and an arched entryway leading into a red tile courtyard. All that, I guessed, was supposed to add a bit of atmosphere to go along with the Spanish name. It had all the atmosphere of a Taco Bell.

Fein's name was on the alphabetical listing by the locked front gate, apartment 301. I pressed the buzzer to 301 and when I got no answer, I started pushing buttons at random until a metallic female voice came through the squawk box asking me who I was. I told her I was from the telephone company and that I had to check her phone. I got to the front gate as it buzzed and pushed it open.

I took the elevator up to the third floor and started down a maze of narrow corridors looking for 301. There must have been a logical pattern for the sequence of apartment numbers, but whatever it was I couldn't make it out. Finally, I stopped a blonde girl carrying a basket of laundry and asked directions and she directed me through another archway and across an open catwalk.

Joni Mitchell's falsetto wafted through the door of 300 across the hall from Fein's. She didn't seem to be quite making all the notes.

I rang the bell to 301 three times before I slipped my plastic lock-picking card out of my wallet and went to work on the door. Luckily, there was no traffic in the hallway, and I managed to get inside without being seen.

The apartment was a furnished one-bedroom that smelled of dust and stale cigarette smoke. The carpeting was a thick green shag, the furniture all greens and browns and darkly stained wood. A wrought iron chandelier hung over the breakfast table near the kitchen, and I noticed that four of its little flame light bulbs were burned out. It didn't look as if David Fein ate a lot of breakfasts here.

Two empty glasses and a half-empty bottle of Dewar's White Label stood on the drainboard in the kitchen. There was a lipstick smear on the rim of one of the glasses. I picked it up and stuck my nose in the glass. Scotch. Jesus, I was a clever one, all right. Couldn't put anything over on me.

The bedroom confirmed the picture the kitchen had already painted for me. Whoever had used the double bed last had not bothered to make it. On the night table beside the bed was another glass, also marked with a lipstick smear of the same shade as the one in the kitchen.

There was an open book of matches beside the glass. I picked it up.

It was from some restaurant called the Crow's Nest, Marina del Rey. There was a drawing of a clipper ship on it, rolling full-sail over a choppy sea. I dropped it in my pocket and started to go through the rest of the room.

The chest of drawers was empty, as was the closet. There was nothing under the beds. I went back out to the kitchen and went through the cupboards. Assorted fifths of Scotch, bourbon, gin, and vodka, all at various stages of consumption. The icebox was empty except for a quart bottle of tonic and one of club soda.

I stepped into the hall and closed the door. I searched my pockets for a stick of chewing gum and finally found one. I usually had one somewhere, almost always stale. This one was no exception. It broke into dry pieces in my mouth, but soon I worked it into a moist wad. I took it out of my mouth and pressed it between the very top of the door and the jamb, working it with my thumb until I was sure it was stuck. Then I stepped across the hall to 300.

Joni Mitchell quieted down immediately when I knocked. The door was pulled open by a young man dressed in a striped T-shirt and jeans and no shoes. He was tall and skinny and had long blonde hair that he kept brushing out of his eyes with a quick, jerky flick of his wrist. He looked me over and said in a slightly defensive tone: "Yeah?"

"Pardon me," I said, smiling diplomatically, "but have you lived in this apartment long?"

"A year and a half," he said. "Why?"

"Have you ever seen the man who lives across the hall in 301?"

He shrugged suspiciously. "A couple of times."

I nodded. "I'm really sorry to bother you, but I'm a friend of his from out of town and I've been trying to get hold of him for days. I've got to leave town again on Thursday and I really wanted to see him before I left. Dave and I used to room together in college and we were really close, you know, we were on the football team together, and I haven't seen him for years. My name is Jake Asch, by the way——"

I pushed my hand at him. He seemed stunned by the verbal onslaught and stared at my hand dumbly for a few seconds before taking it. "I didn't get your name," I said, still smiling.

"Bartowski. Tom Bartowski."

"No relation to Steve Bartowski, the quarterback, by any chance?"

"No."

"There's a hell of a quarterback," I said wistfully. "Going to be a superstar. I'd like to see somebody make a Polish joke about him."

"Yeah, well, look, I'm really bu——"

"Like I said, Tom," I cut him off, "I'm really sorry to bother you, but I've phoned and phoned and gotten no answer over there. Have you seen Dave—the guy across the hall—lately?"

He shook his head and brushed back a wisp of blonde hair from his forehead. "I've only seen him a few times, total. I work nights and I'm usually leaving for work when he's going in."

"But you haven't seen him lately?"

"The last time I saw them—him was about two weeks ago."

He was still a little suspicious of me and seemed embarrassed by his slip. I leaned toward him conspiratorially and said: "Tell me something; Was she good looking?"

"I—" He hesitated, then said: "Yeah."

I smiled knowingly. "Yeah, that's old Dave, all right. In college he was always the one with the broads. I'd hang around him just to get the leftovers. Was she a redhead? Dave always had a thing for redheads."

"No," he said. "She had long, black hair."

"Wait a minute," I said urgently. "I may know who that is. Is she a real short gal?"

"No," he said. The suspicion had left his eyes now, and he seemed caught up in the spirit of the thing. He had to be; he wasn't questioning how I could know who Dave was dating if I hadn't seen him in four years. "She wasn't so short. Maybe five-seven or so. Real sexy looking."

"How old?"

He shrugged. "Twenty-one, twenty-two." He cupped his hands about two feet in front of his chest and leered. "Really tremendous tits."

If his description was accurate, it wouldn't be hard to find the girl at all. She would be lying facedown most of the time. "Was he with the same broad a lot?"

"Every time I saw him."

"You ever talk to either of them?"

He shook his head. "Like I said, I usually only saw them when I was leaving for work."

"You didn't happen to hear a name or anything?"

"No."

I nodded and pushed my hand at him again. "Well, thanks a lot, Tom. And if you see Dave in the next couple of days, tell him Jake was by looking for him and to stay put, for chrissakes, so somebody can get hold of him."

"Okay," he said. "Will do."

He closed the door, and Joni Mitchell filled the hallway again. She sounded like I felt—uninspired and about a half a tone flat.

· 5 ·

THE ADDRESS Barbara Fein had written down for Mark Fein belonged to a seven-story glass and steel medical building on the corner of Linden Drive. Since I was in the area anyway and since Mrs. Fein was paying me fifteen cents a mile, I decided to stop by and talk to him first.

The metal letters on the walnut door to Suite 704 said: Mark Fein, M.D., Internal Medicine.

The waiting room was sedately luxurious with pale grass-cloth walls, thick, dark-brown carpeting and heavy Mexican lamps adorning the teak end tables. Waiting patients sat quietly on the two couches that lined the walls, like birds on a telephone wire.

The young dishwater-blonde nurse behind the sliding glass receptionist's window smiled and said: "May I help you?"

"I'd like to see Dr. Fein."

"Do you have an appointment?"

"No, but—"

"Are you one of Dr. Fein's patients?"

To save time, I handed her a card: She studied it, then looked back at me uncertainly.

"Tell him it's about his brother," I said. "It will only take a few minutes of his time."

"If you'll take a seat, Mr. Asch, I'll see if Doctor Fein will see you."

It was always "Doctor." Never *the* doctor. It drove me crazy. I took the only available space on one of the couches next to a fat woman. The woman eyed me with expectant antagonism, waiting to see if I got in to see "Doctor" before she did.

The nurse poked her head out of the door next to the glass window and told me to come in. I shrugged helplessly under the livid glare of the fat woman and went through the door.

After a short journey down an antiseptic-smelling corridor, I was led into a paneled office whose walls were lined with medical books. I sat down in the brown leather chair across from the desk and was left alone to wait.

Mark Fein was probably a big hit with his female patients. He was tall, tanned and leanly handsome, and the strong bone structure of his face—the high forehead, the prominent bone ridge above the eyes, the firm line of the jaw—all gave the immediate impression of decisiveness and confidence. There were traces of David Fein there, particularly in the eyes and mouth, but the physical resemblance between the two was not striking by any means. Despite the fact that he was graying slightly around the temples, he looked younger than his brother by quite a few years.

He stepped forward, frowning, and pulled a slender hand out of the pocket of his white smock and offered it to me. Then he took a seat behind the desk.

"Now," he said, "what exactly did you want to see me about?"

"I'm working for your brother's wife," I said. "I understand she told you about your brother—"

"Yes, I know, I know," he said impatiently. "But I told Barb that Dave hasn't contacted me. I don't really see what help I could be."

"You may be able to help without even realizing it," I said.

He scowled. "I suppose you're right. But let's get this over with quickly. I have patients to see."

"You don't sound too concerned about the whole thing, Doctor."

He waved a hand in the air. "Of course I'm concerned. I just don't see what I can do about it, that's all. I've tried, God knows—" He started to go on, but then shook his head at some idea he was not willing to vocalize.

"You're talking about the gambling now?"

He nodded. "I've had it. I tried to talk him into seeing a friend of mine, Dr. Herman Factor. Factor is one of the foremost psychiatrists in the state, for God's sake, and only agreed to see Dave in the first place because he's my brother. I made an appointment for him, and he never even showed up for it. That was the last straw for me."

The tone of betrayal in his voice made it sound as if that were the ultimate sin, causing a doctor to have a blank hour in his schedule. At sixty bucks an hour, it probably was.

"You make it sound as if he's a hopeless case."

"I'm afraid he is," he said, sighing regretfully. "It's a sad thing to say about your own brother, but I don't see what can be done about it. If Barb was smart, she'd get out now before she winds up with a nervous breakdown. But she has some sort of twisted sense of loyalty. She says she can't leave him while he's in trouble. It's noble of her, I suppose, but I've told her that two lives being destroyed instead of one isn't going to solve anything. Dave's suicidal, that's all there is to it."

"You think he might try to do himself in?"

He shook his head grimly. "I didn't mean it literally. I just meant he's trying to punish himself. All gamblers are self-destructive. They know they're not going to win. They play to lose."

"Do you have any idea what he's punishing himself for?"

He shrugged. "I talked to Herman Factor about it."

"What did he say?"

He picked up a pencil from the desk top and grasped it with both hands. "I don't see what bearing that could have on finding out where Dave is."

"The more I know about the man, the easier it's going to be to find him," I said.

He thought about it and said: "If you really want to know, Dr. Factor said it sounded to him like Dave was suffering from a severe case of mother rejection."

He stopped and we stared at each other silently. Finally, he gave up the battle, blinked, and looked away.

"I'm sorry if I'm getting too personal, Doctor," I said. "If it makes you feel uncomfortable, don't talk about it."

"If it made me feel uncomfortable, I wouldn't, don't worry," he said in a tone that was at once defensive and clinical. "There's nothing to feel uncomfortable about. Facts are facts. Our mother was a bitch is about it in a nutshell. She was a narrow, self-centered woman who discouraged any sign of affection from Dave or myself. Dave took it hard. To compensate for those feelings of rejection, he transferred all his affections to our father. He worshipped Dad. That's the only reason he went into Supreme, because Dad wanted him to."

He paused thoughtfully and went on: "The one thing that our father respected was money. That's what drove Dave to work like a demon. He was going to be a millionaire come hell or high water to make Dad respect him. He dreamed a lot of unrealistic dreams when he went into the business—he was going to double the volume of Supreme, all sorts of fantasies like that to make Dad proud of him. When those dreams didn't materialize, he started trying to make a million in other ways. That's when the gambling started."

He smiled a dry, tight, humorless smile, his eyes focused on some point on the desk. "It's ironic. All the time he was trying to win Dad's love, and Dad was the one who had to keep bailing him out of the scrapes he got into."

"You seem to have come through it all right," I said.

He shrugged. "I was less impressionable than Dave. I was always the analytical type." He raised a skeptical eyebrow and looked at me. "Now. After that, you know just where to start looking for Dave, right?"

His superior attitude was beginning to get on my nerves. I threw a jab of my own. "For having such a good grasp on the crux of your brother's problems, you seem awfully willing to give up on him."

He looked at me steadily and put the pencil down carefully on the top of the desk. "Dave burned me a couple of times to feed his obsession. To tell you the truth, Mr. Asch, I simply can't afford to indulge him anymore."

"He borrowed money from you?"

"Yes."

"How much?"

"Ten thousand dollars."

"That's a lot of money."

"I wouldn't have loaned it to him if I had known what he intended to use it for," he said. "He told me he had some stock options he wanted to pick up. He said we could go fifty-fifty and both make a lot of money. He always had the head for business and he'd made me money in the market before, so I said okay. I only found out later that he gambled it away on the horses."

"When was that?"

"About ten months ago."

"Did he ever pay you back?"

"Three thousand of it."

"He still owes you seven?"

He nodded, not looking too happy about it.

"When was the last time you saw him?"

"Three weeks ago," he said. "He came in to have his blood pressure checked. He complained about feeling a little giddy."

"Could there be a problem there?"

"Not as long as he takes the medicine I prescribed for him. Even if he doesn't, there isn't any real physical danger. His blood pressure has always been high."

"Can you think of anybody he might try to contact or stay with? Relatives or friends?"

He shook his head. "We have no relatives in L.A. And as

far as friends go, Dave has none. A friend to Dave is someone he can borrow money from, and he has none of those left."

"You don't sound as if you like your brother very much, Doctor."

As I watched his face, the features suddenly softened. "I don't like what he has become," he said helplessly. "I don't know, but as you get older, you tend to look at people more as people and less as brothers or sisters, mothers or fathers. Dave is a very, very sick man and he needs help. As a doctor and his brother, I'd like to help him, believe me I would, but I just don't know how."

The condescending pose was gone; he was just another human being. I felt my own opinion of him softening. I could understand his bitterness about what his brother had done to him. I would have probably felt the same way. And as far as his superior manner toward me went, I put that down to insecurity. A lot of people are defensive when being questioned; it was just a face they wore to protect themselves. He probably wasn't such a bad guy at all, just bewildered by the events of his life. Like all the rest of us.

"If I need to get in touch with you," I said, "can I reach you at home?"

"Certainly." He wrote down his phone number on a prescription pad and handed it to me.

We shook hands and said good-bye, and I went out into the waiting room. The fat woman was still there. She gave me the Evil Eye as I passed her, but then the nurse stepped out of the door and said, "Mrs. Evans," and beckoned her in.

The hostility in her face broke up like a clearing storm, and she stood up, smiling. She was going to get to see Doctor.

MARK FEIN'S TALK of his brother's suicidal tendencies, even in a figurative sense, spooked me. Missing Persons had probably already run Fein's description through the county coroner's office—that was usually the sum total of what they did—but I thought I'd double-check, just to make sure.

The clerk there took the photograph I had and, after running it downstairs, told me that they had no John Does come in during the past four days that even faintly resembled the picture.

For the next hour I dropped coins into a pay phone and recited Fein's description to officious-sounding hospital personnel. All it got me was a hot ear and a list of $5.25 worth of toll calls to add to Mrs. Fein's expense sheet. It also gave me a feeling of relief that at least I wasn't going to have to break *that* kind of bad news to the woman.

I took the freeway to Soto and drove back into Vernon.

Supreme Packing was a blocky, olive-green complex of buildings that wandered away from the boulevard with no apparent purpose or design. I turned down the narrow side street that ran alongside it and parked in a muddy dirt lot across from the back gates.

A large refrigerated truck was backed up to the elevated loading dock, and several men dressed in long, bloodstained white coats and plastic billed hats were loading sides of beef into its back end. The foreman was checking off the meat on a clipboard he had cradled in his left arm. I stepped up to him and asked where I could find Mr. Tortorello.

He looked me over like I was one of the sides of beef he had on his list. "Mr. Tortorello is busy."

"He's expecting me," I said, handing him a business card. "It's about Mr. Fein."

He looked at the card, then at me again. Then he scratched his head and signalled to one of the loaders, a young Chicano with shoulder-length black hair. He came over, holding a vicious-looking meat hook.

"Take this man to see Mr. Tortorello," the foreman told him. "He's on the killing floor."

The Chicano handed his meat hook to one of the other loaders and told me to follow him. We went up the concrete stairs of the loading dock. He disappeared through a doorway and came back out holding a clean white coat and a plastic cap. He handed them to me without saying anything, and I put them on.

I followed him down a narrow alley that ran between two wooden-frame buildings, underneath a series of pipes and rusted catwalks, through a wall-less welding shop where several goggled workmen were spot-welding pieces of broken equipment. Then we were in an open cement courtyard, passing by the feeding pens, through the stench of cowshit and the din of mooing cattle, to a short flight of stairs that led into another, larger building.

My guide opened the door at the top of the stairs, and we stepped onto a long, narrow landing that was flanked on one side by a low concrete wall. A large black man, dressed in a coat like the ones we wore, stood by the wall in front of us, his pose nonchalant and casual, a smoking .22 in his right hand. Something crunched underneath my feet and I looked down. Empty cartridge casings.

On the other side of the wall was about a six foot drop into a blood-spattered steel pen. The black man didn't look up at us, didn't even seem to know we were there. His eyes were watching the steer that was bellowing in protest at the electric prodder poking him in the rump and moving him up the long chute and into the pen.

The Chicano started to move on down the landing, but I stopped, watching in mute horror and fascination as the steer reached the end of the line and the rear flap slammed shut from behind, sealing him in. The animal bellowed in terror and tried to stampede but there was nowhere to go. The beating of its hooves against the metal floor reverberated off the walls in an almost deafening clatter, and the animal responded with even more fear to its own noise.

Just as its terror seemed to reach a maximum, the black man put the pistol to the animal's head and pulled the trigger. The steer's legs collapsed instantly, as if it had been struck by lightning, and the animal folded into an inert mass at the bottom of the pen.

The man turned to me and smiled a broad, white smile as an introduction. "Just blanks in the gun," he said slowly, seemingly eager to teach now that he had a pupil. I must have looked like a novice. "It only stuns 'em."

He pulled a lever beside him that made the back wall of the pen fall open, and the steer rolled unconscious into the room behind it. The killing floor.

The concrete floor was covered with blood, but it looked artificial, too red, like paint. It could have been paint—the scene looked surreal, like a scene from a work by Dali—but the warm, humid smell of death hung in the air, a heavy almost palpable mist, reminding me immediately that it was not paint.

Three Chicanos, all dressed in sleeveless smocks, rubber aprons and high rubber boots, went to work on the animal as it rolled toward them. One of them bent down and hooked one of its back hooves with a thick iron chain that was attached to a conveyor system in the ceiling, and the steer was hoisted up by its hind leg. One of the others swung a huge funnel attached to the end of a long metal pipe underneath the animal's throat, getting ready for the kill.

The man with the knife stepped forward and slit the animal's throat. A rush of hot, black blood gushed out of the wound, most of it going into the funnel, but some of it overflowing onto the floor.

"Come on, man, let's go," my guide said, and I tore myself loose from the scene and followed him down the landing.

I followed him outside again, and we went down a series of steps and entered the building through another doorway.

Perhaps sixty or seventy people worked on the floor of the large, high-ceilinged room. Steer carcasses, suspended from their hind legs by chains, passed overhead in various stages of disassembly.

In front of us half a dozen men were working on one of the carcasses with air knives, removing the hooves and head and cutting away part of the hide. They all had their jobs down expertly. Once they had the feet removed, the hoof-men tossed the hooves into a long metal trough on the floor beside them that ran the entire length of the room to the outside. The trough housed a huge metal corkscrew that was constantly turning, drawing the hooves under and pushing them outside into a separate tank.

The head-men, in the meantime, were cutting the tongues from the heads and hanging them on a separate conveyor belt above them—a head, a tongue, a head, a tongue. The procession of heads stared down at their decapitators with accusing, dead eyes, but the workers didn't seem to notice and kept right on cutting, efficiently, mercilessly.

The headless carcass turned a corner and into the arms of a waiting machine which stripped off the rest of the hide. Then it was placed on a moving, steaming, stainless steel table, where a group of men gutted it and laid out the organs separately for the federal inspector who stood at the end of the table watching for some sign of disease.

A man wielding a huge power saw, hanging from the ceiling by a chain, split the carcass into sides, and the process was nearly complete.

Torquemada was probably watching all this from wherever he was, I thought, and kicking himself in the ass. All the Inquisition lacked was a little efficiency. With the right equipment, think how many souls could have been saved.

My Chicano, Virgil, told me to wait while he approached a sandy-haired man who was issuing instructions to two men working at a table on cattle heads. One of the men was taking off the cheek meat with a sharp knife, while the other man split the skulls neatly with a guillotinelike machine and removed the brains.

The sandy-haired man listened to my young guide, then came over to me. "I'm Steve Tortorello," he said, offering his hand. "Mrs. Fein called me awhile ago and told me you'd be coming by."

Tortorello was in his early thirties, I judged, and would have been good looking if it hadn't been for the acne scars that marked his cheeks. He had a round face with a narrow, pointed nose and a small mouth that was turned down at the corners. His smile was friendly enough, but his eyes were dark and the only expression in them was mathematical—they seemed to be constantly weighing, measuring. They reminded me of the cold, black background of a pocket calculator; the only trouble was that the numbers were being flashed on the inside where I couldn't see them.

"It's really a shame about Dave," he said, shaking his head sadly. "It looks like he's gone off the deep end this time."

"You haven't heard anything yet, I take it."

"No." He brushed a hand across the side of his head, smoothing down a few strands of brown hair. A topaz cuff link peeked out of the end of the sleeve of his bloodstained white coat, almost as if it were embarrassed by its own ostentation. "I just hope he's all right, that's all."

"Do you have any reason to think he wouldn't be?"

He seemed surprised by the suggestion. "Me? No, why?"

"Just the way you said it."

"No," he repeated.

"Would you mind if I asked you a few questions, Mr. Tortorello?"

"No, of course not, if you think it might help. I've got to go back to my office. Would you like to talk there? It'd be a little more private." He waved a hand at the room.

"Sure. That would be fine."

We left the man operating the guillotine and started wending our way back up the disassembly line. The floor was wet in spots from the steam-cleaning guns that were being used by several workers to clean pieces of equipment and we had to walk carefully.

As we passed the men throwing the hooves into the revolving corkscrew, I tapped him on the shoulder and pointed to the trough. "What does that do?" I yelled, trying to make him hear me over the noise of the air knives.

"The hooves, unusable bones and waste are thrown in there and pushed down the trough to a truck outside. We sell the stuff to renderers. Some houses around here sell the hooves separately, but we don't. There's a big demand for them in the Mexican community, from what I gather, but we don't bother with them here."

"Really?" I remarked, genuinely surprised. "What do Mexicans use them for?"

He shrugged. "Soup, I suppose. I don't really know."

We passed beneath the moving line of heads to the door. As we got there, he turned to me and said: "That's the great thing about the packing business. It's the most economical business in the world. Nothing goes to waste. Everything in the animal is used for something. The blood we sell to pet food companies, the hides to tanneries, the intestines to medical supply houses to make surgical twine. We even tried making walking sticks out of dried bulls' pricks once. It didn't catch on, though. Let the goddamn oil companies employ a little of that same economy in their operations and the price of gas would drop twenty cents a gallon."

He looked back over my shoulder at the killing floor as if he were seeing a sunset in Bryce Canyon and opened the door. At least he was enthusiastic.

I followed him outside, and we took the long way around, bypassing the shooting pen. We walked in silence past the stench of the feeding pens and through the welding shop. At the loading dock, he took off his coat. He draped the coat over one arm and reached out with the other. Underneath, he was wearing a blue pin-striped dress shirt and blue slacks, with a gray silk tie. "Here, let me take that for you—"

I peeled off my own, and my hat, and he handed them to a long-haired kid who had come running up to take them. Tortorello gestured to a glass door in the side of the big building, and we went inside and up a flight of steps.

We passed through a large rectangular room filled with desks, most of which were empty. The three that weren't were manned by a trio of middle-aged, overweight secretaries, listlessly pecking at their typewriters.

Tortorello's office was a small, depressing affair off the main room. Its walls were painted an atrocious high-gloss yellow-green and its brown linoleum floor was badly scuffed. The desk wasn't in much better shape. He offered me a seat and sat down himself behind the desk.

"Now," he said, rubbing his hands together, "we can talk. What did you want to ask me?"

I cleared my throat and began. "Has Fein been coming in regularly? Every day?"

His mouth turned down at the corners and he shrugged. "Most every day, I guess."

"His wife says he came from work Thursday night. Were you around that day?"

He thought about it. "I saw him on Thursday morning.

We talked for a few minutes about a contract I've been trying to negotiate with the Army. They want to buy dressed beef from us, and I've been trying to work out the details—"

"He didn't mention anything to you about any plans he might have to leave town, or anything like that?"

He shook his head. "No. As far as I remember, all we talked about was the Army deal and the chance of it going through."

"He didn't tell you that he wasn't going to be in for the next few days?"

"No."

"What do you know about David Fein, as a man?"

He swiveled around in his chair, took a package of cigarettes from his coat pocket and lit one. "Smoke?"

"No, thanks."

He exhaled and shook the match out. "I don't know much about Dave's personal life at all, if that's what you mean. When we talk, it's usually about the business. I never ask him what he does after he leaves here and he never asks me."

"It doesn't sound like a very friendly relationship."

"I wouldn't say that. We get along fine. From what I know of him, he's a great guy. But our relationship has been basically business, at least up to this point. I mean, that's why I'm here. He liked my ideas about how to improve the business and so far things have worked out fine."

"How did you hear about Fein wanting to take in a partner in the first place?"

He made a noncommittal gesture with his cigarette. "Word gets around. I knew Fein had taken a beating when the Big Boy Market thing went down, so I approached him about buying in."

"How much of this place do you own, may I ask?"

"Thirty percent."

"Do you mind me asking how much you paid for it? Just for my own curiosity," I quickly amended. "It has nothing to do with my looking for Fein."

He smiled thinly. "I don't mind. I paid seventy-five thousand."

"That seems like a pretty good deal."

"For both of us." He leaned toward me conspiratorially and said: "Just between the two of us, if I hadn't stepped in here, Fein would have gone into receivership for sure. The management practices around here were really abominable. The payroll was at least ten percent too high. It's taken me two months just to get the place operating back in the black again. In another two months we should see the major change."

He spoke with cool confidence, yet his attitude was not arrogant. I had the genuine impression that he believed in himself and his methods totally, and I could see where that belief would be contagious, especially to someone like Fein, who had started to lose his belief in himself. "Is that why you fired Nate Bloom?"

"Nate is a nice guy, but he has some antiquated ideas about the meat business. Besides, I brought in my own controller. He took the place of both the credit manager and the accountant, for the same goddamn salary Bloom was getting. That's what I've been saying: You've got to consolidate. Especially with the high cost of labor today."

I shook my head in admiration. "For such a young guy, you really sound as if you know what you're doing. What business were you in before this?"

"Restaurants. I still am in the restaurant business, actually."

"Really? Whereabouts?"

"The Golden Steer on La Cienega," he said.

"I've seen it," I said. "Looks like a nice place. I haven't eaten there I'm sorry to say. I'll have to try it one night."

I paused, trying to gather my thoughts. "It doesn't really seem like the restaurant business would prepare you for a business like this—"

"Management is all figures," he said flatly. "You know

figures, you know business. It's just a matter of how to in-
crease profits and minimize loss. I learned the theory in Harvard Business School, but the application I learned running a
restaurant. I could have learned it in just about any other
business, too."

"You're from back east?"

He tapped the cigarette on the edge of the copper ashtray
on the desk. "St. Louis, originally."

"You still work at the restaurant, then?"

"About five nights a week," he said.

"You've got a tough schedule."

He shrugged. "It's not that bad. I'm not here all day. I usually leave around noon. Actually, it's lucky Mrs. Fein called
me up and told me you were coming by. Otherwise, I would
have been gone."

"From what I hear, Fein gambled a lot," I said.

He regarded me with the same cool stare, but just for a
split second I thought I had seen something flicker behind
the dark eyes. "I wouldn't know. Like I told you, I don't keep
tabs on his personal life."

"You wouldn't happen to know who his bookie was, by any
chance?"

"I didn't even know he had one," he said casually.

I didn't know how far to take that one. I didn't know how
much Tortorello knew about Fein's compulsive gambling and
I didn't know how much trouble bringing it to light might
stir up in the business. My job was to find the man, not lose
him a business partner.

"One more thing: Have you ever heard Fein mention the
name of any friends—male or female—he might have had?"

He shook his head and blinked, slowly. "No."

"I'd like to look in Fein's office now, if it'd be all right."

"Sure," he said. "I just wish I could be more help."

"Thanks for the help you have given me," I said. I started
to stand up when a stocky, gray-haired man came through
the door and halted abruptly.

"Oh, sorry, Steve, I didn't know you were busy." The man spoke with a pronounced eastern accent. New York or New Jersey. He started to back out, when Tortorello halted him with a hand motion. "Come on in, Al. Al Schwartz, my supervisor, this is Mr. Asch."

We shook hands stiffly.

"Mr. Asch is the detective Mrs. Fein called about earlier. Show him Dave's office, will you, and let him look around."

"Sure, boss," Schwartz said.

Tortorello stretched his hand across the desk in a friendly thrust. "Listen, Mr. Asch, I hope you find Dave safe and sound. I've really got to run now. I'm supposed to meet my wife and I'm already late. She'll butcher me like one of those steers. You know how it is—"

He smiled, showing me a lot of even, white teeth. "And come into the restaurant one night. Just let me know in advance and I'll make sure you're taken care of."

"Thanks, I'll do that," I said and was ushered out the door by Schwartz.

Schwartz led me down the hall two doors to another tiny office, almost identical to Tortorello's. He stood watching as I went through the drawers of the desk.

It didn't take long. Fein's checkbook wasn't there. Neither was anything else that was of any help. Business files, bulletins from the U.S. Department of Agriculture, paper clips, stationery, staples, an old copy of the *Racing Form*, but no hint of where David Fein might be. There was a correspondence file, but all the letters were strictly of a business nature, nothing personal.

"Okay," I said to Schwartz, who regarded me nonchalantly with heavily pouched eyes.

"That's it?"

"That's it."

He turned out the light and followed me out. I thanked him and told him I knew my way out.

I went across the street to my car and drove up the street

to a pay phone. I called Fulton's Packing, and after about three minutes of paging, Bloom finally picked up the phone.

"This is Jake, Nate."

"Right, Jake. What's up?"

"I saw Barbara Fein," I said. "She hired me."

"I'm glad," he said, sounding relieved. "Have you found out anything yet?"

"I just started, for chrissakes. I'm not Peter Hurkos, you know. Anyway, the reason I'm calling is maybe you can help me—"

"Sure. Anything."

"You said Fein places a lot of bets through a book."

"Yeah, that's right."

"You remember his name?"

"The book? Yeah, it's Chico. I'm pretty sure that's his name."

"You know where I can get hold of this Chico?"

"No, I sure don't. But I can ask around. I know a few guys around here who bet the ponies pretty regular. I think they use him, too."

"Good," I said. "And listen, Fein has to be using a code name to call in his bets. You know what it is? You ever hear him call one in?"

"No. Jesus, I'm sorry, but I don't, Jake."

"That's okay. Don't worry about it. One more thing: You told me Fein plays cards in Gardena a lot. You know what clubs he plays in?"

"No," he said. "Christ, I'm sorry I can't be more help. I'd like to do something—"

I suddenly thought of something else.

"You know what hotel Fein stayed at when he went to Vegas?"

"That I know," he said. "Caesar's Palace. Either there or the Dunes. You think he's gone to Vegas?"

"I don't know," I said. "When do you think you can find out about that book for me?"

"I'll get on it today."

"You got my home number?"

"No, I don't think so."

I gave it to him and told him to call me there. I said good-bye and stepped out of the phone booth.

My watch said four-thirty. There was a sharp chill in the air and the gray buildings facing the street were bleeding slowly into the thickening dusk. It was getting dark early lately, but that was okay. Vernon was one town that looked better in the dark anyway.

· 7 ·

THE CROW'S NEST SAT on the water's edge, long and sleek, all distressed wood and glass. The ceiling in the cocktail lounge was striped with heavy beams and a fireplace crackled warmly in the corner.

The windows behind the polished mahogany bar looked out onto the harbor and the lights from the moored boats, and the harsher neon signs of the restaurants and night clubs that lined the bar side of the Marina shone double, firm in the night air, wavering and unsteady in the black water.

It was still early for the swinging singles crowd that would fill the place in a few hours, but the advance scouts were already strategically entrenched, nursing their drinks and sweeping the room with watchful predatory eyes.

I took a stool at the bar, and the bartender, an unsmiling young kid with a thick handlebar mustache, put a paper coaster in front of me and asked what I'd have. I told him bourbon and water and watched him as he poured it.

He rang up the check and put it down beside my drink, and I said: "Hey, has what's her name been in tonight? Aaah. . . ." I snapped my fingers repeatedly. "Jesus Christ, isn't that dumb? I can't remember her name. . . . Oh hell . . . long black hair, big tits—"

"Terri?"

"Yeah, that's right—Terri. She been in tonight?"

He shook his head and started to wash some highball glasses that were lined up on the top of the bar.

"When was she in last?"

He shrugged. "A couple of nights ago. Who remembers?"

"Was she with anybody?"

He picked up a bar towel and wiped out one of the glasses. "I don't know. Could be."

I nodded and took a sip of my drink. I pulled Fein's picture out of my pocket and showed it to him. "Ever see this guy in here before?"

He took the picture and bent down to examine it in the light of the backbar. He straightened up and handed it back to me. "Maybe. I don't know. He looks kind of familiar, but who the hell knows? A lot of people come in here every night."

"You ever see him with Terri?"

"What are you?" he said irritably, "A cop or something?"

"Private investigator."

"What are you looking for this guy for?"

I smiled. "His wife got kind of used to having him around."

He glared at me disdainfully and went back to wiping his glass.

I waited. I had the distinct impression I would be waiting a long time. "You wouldn't happen to know Terri's last name, would you?"

He stared at me steadily and said in a hard voice: "No."

I nodded and took a ten out of my wallet and put it down on top of the check. "Keep the change."

Even that didn't make him smile. "Thanks." He reached for the money, but I trapped it under my hand.

"You know where I might be able to find Terri?" I repeated.

He glanced down at the bill and thoughtfully moistened his mustache with the tip of his tongue. His head snapped quickly toward the end of the bar. "You see that blonde down there?"

I broke eye contact with him and looked down the bar. A

long, willowy blonde in a loose-fitting and very abbreviated muslin dress was checking out the room from her stool at the end of the bar. "Yeah?"

"Ask her. They come in together all the time."

"What's her name?"

"Cee Jay."

I let go of the bill, and he stuck it in his tip glass.

The girl's searchlight eyes finally got around to me and when she saw me staring at her, she parted her lips in a professional smile and dropped her gaze coyly to her drink. But not before she telegraphed the invitation.

I slid off my stool, picked up my drink and sauntered down to the end of the bar, hoping she hadn't seen me handing the bartender Fein's photograph.

She looked as if she would have been more at home on a surfboard than a barstool. Her blonde hair was long and straight, and she had that tanned, outdoorsy, salt-scrubbed, beach-bunny look. Except her eyes were no beach-bunny's eyes. They were steely-blue and there was a cold, hard light in them that no white-toothed smile could soften.

"Hiya doin', Cee Jay?" I said, taking the stool next to her.

Her smile turned puzzled. "Do I know you?"

"You probably don't remember me, but I met you in here one night with Terri." I motioned to her nearly empty glass. "Can I buy you a drink?"

"Why not?" she said and finished off the rest of it.

I beckoned to the bartender, who came over wearing a surly expression. She ordered a vodka collins, and I told him to keep the rest of two dollars this time. He went away, his mouth set hard beneath his handlebar mustache.

"Cheers," I said, clinking her glass with mine.

"Cheers."

I took a swallow of my drink and said casually: "Where's Terri tonight?"

"Working."

"Oh yeah? Where?"

"The New World Spa," she said. Her eyes narrowed suspiciously. "I thought you said you were a friend of Terri's."

"Naw. I just met her once, the same night I met you."

The suspicion died and she said: "What's your name?"

"Al. Al Grambling."

"You from around here, Al?"

"El Segundo."

She nodded.

"Say, what the hell is Terri working tonight for? That's really a drag."

"Yeah, well, she usually works the day shift, but one of the night girls is sick and the boss asked Terri to fill in. We both gotta alternate nights until the girl gets better."

"You work with Terri?"

"Yeah. We're both masseuses."

I picked up one of her hands and examined it critically. "I'll bet you're really good at it, too."

She leaned her breasts against my arm. "You've never had a massage until you've had one of my specials."

"I'll bet," I said and took a sip of my drink. "You and Terri pretty good friends?"

"Yeah. Real good." The suspicion was there again. To dispel it, I asked: "You ever do outcalls?"

"Sometimes," she said. "It depends."

I tried to look eager. I didn't have to try too hard. "On what?"

She shrugged and took a sip of her drink. "The guy. There are some real creeps running around out there, believe me. A lot of people have weird ideas about a girl just because she's a masseuse, you know?"

"I can imagine," I said disgustedly. "You girls must see it all."

"You don't know the half of it."

I probably knew at least half of it. It was Al Grambling that didn't know half of it. Al Grambling was straight as an arrow. An arrow that shot around corners. "I'll have to come by the New World sometime and ask for you, Cee Jay. Where's it at, anyway?"

"12349 Santa Monica Boulevard." She poked the pink tip of her tongue between her teeth and held it there. I guessed that was supposed to be sexy. It wasn't bad, once I thought about it. "What are you doing now, Al? You look real tense." She reached over and gently squeezed the back of my neck. "Ooooh, yeah, I can feel it. You *are* tense. I could take out a few of those knots for you—"

"I'm sure you could, honey," I said. "But I haven't got time tonight as much as I'd like to. But I will come by the New World. You work days?"

She nodded, then put her hand on top of mine on the bar. It was dry and warm. "Why don't you stick around, Al?"

"I can't. Really. I'd love to, but I can't. Maybe I'll see you around here some night this week, though, if you're going to be around."

She shrugged. "Thanks for the drink, anyway," she said. Her eyes had already left me and were scanning the room once more.

"My pleasure," I said, getting off my stool. I don't even think she heard me.

· 8 ·

THE NEW WORLD SPA OCCUPIED a corner on a palm-lined stretch of Santa Monica Boulevard on the eastern edge of the city of Santa Monica.

It had a false brick front and a wood shingle facade extending down from the roof, and below the shingles a lighted yellow sign ran the length of the building, casting a jaundiced glow over the street. The windows were heavily curtained and a small sticker in the corner of one of them said Master Charge was welcome.

A bell dingdonged in the back somewhere when I opened the door and stepped into the empty waiting room. It was small, but not as seedy as I had expected. It had paneled walls and naugahyde couches and even a coffee table with some magazines on it. The most noticeable piece of furniture in the room was a small desk, the most conspicuous thing about it being that there was nobody behind it.

The curtains hanging from the doorway beside the desk were parted by a pale young girl with a frizzy red Afro. She took her place behind the desk and smiled. "Can I help you?"

"I'd like a massage."

"Fine." She handed me a card with their rates on it, and just in case I couldn't read, she said: "We have a regular half-hour massage for $15, or an hour for $25. Or we also have a half-and-half for $25."

"What's a half-and-half?"

She blinked and said: "You get massaged for half the time and you get to massage the masseuse half the time."

"That's just for the use of the hall, right? The extras all cost more?"

She tried to look confused, but it didn't quite come off. She still didn't know if I was from the vice squad. "Pardon me?"

"Never mind," I said. "I don't want to massage anyone; I'll take the half hour."

"Fine," she said again. "That will be $15."

She took my money and made out a bill. "Your first name?"

"Jake," I told her, and she wrote it on top of the bill. "A friend of mine recommended this place. He said you've got a really good masseuse here—Terri."

She looked up. "Terri's got another customer right now—"

"I'll wait."

"Just a minute," she said and went through the curtains again. She came back a few seconds later. "Terri will be through in a couple of minutes. You can take a sauna, and by that time she should be ready to take you."

"Sounds good," I said, and we completed our business transaction.

The room on the other side of the curtains was long, divided by a high paneled partition that had five doors cut into it. All the doors were closed. She opened one and told me I could undress inside and left me.

The room was a tiny cubicle with just enough floor space to accommodate the sheeted massage table in the middle of it. A nightstand beside the table was piled high with towels, baby oil and powders of various kinds, and on it, a cheap red plastic light burned, staining the white sheets pink. The wall behind the pillowed end of the table was mirrored, and my face floated there, strange and unfamiliar.

I sat down on the edge of the table and waited. Someone

moaned in the next stall. The place smelled of baby oil and desperate loneliness, and I wasn't sure if some of the odor wasn't coming from me.

Ten minutes dragged by. Then the door opened and she came in.

She had on a pair of short-shorts and a tight-fitting pink top that would never be the same after she took it off. Her breasts stuck straight out from her chest like two bullets, the nipples visible through the fabric, pointed and hard.

The long, black hair framed her pale face and gathered around her shoulders. Her whole being, in fact, was dark and primitive, a wild and dusky image of sex. That's what she was—sex. She exuded it from her pores like some animal musk, and the effects of it were instantaneous and overwhelming. It didn't even matter that she carried the knowledge of it mockingly in her large, dark eyes. Or even the knowledge that she sold it. Its availability only made the need for it that much more urgent. Like a kid with his face pressed against a candy store window. All you had to do was dig through your pocket and come up with the change.

"Hi," she said smiling. "I'm Terri."

Her voice was dusky, too, and full of smoke.

"I'm Jake."

"Don't you want to get undressed, Jake?"

"I'd love to, but I can't."

She looked at me strangely. "I can't massage you if you don't get undressed."

"Let's just talk then."

She shrugged. "It's your half hour," she said, obviously irritated she was not going to be making any money for extras for the next half hour. "What do you want to talk about?"

"We can start with David Fein," I said.

Her body stiffened and her face looked angry in the red light.

"What is this? Who the hell are you?"

"A private investigator. I'm working for Fein's wife. He hasn't been home in four days, and she's worried about him."

"Four—" she started, but her mouth dropped open, and her voice trailed off like rainwater running off a roof.

She stepped back and one of her arms jerked upward, as if it had been pulled by a string. "Look, just because this guy's old lady can't hold him at home, don't come around hassling me about it. I don't even know who this dude is, man. We have a lot of customers. You can't expect me to remember all of them."

"I don't," I said. "But Fein has been a special customer of yours, Terri. He's been keeping an apartment at the Casa Loma where you've been giving him special therapeutic massages. Does that refresh your memory a little?"

"You're out of your tree, man," she growled, backing up toward the door.

I knew she was lying, and she knew I knew. What I didn't know about was the fear in her face. She looked like a cornered animal, snarling but afraid. "Come on, Terri. I know you two were meeting—"

"I don't give a shit what you know," she said, her voice shrill, almost frantic.

Before I could say anything else, she had opened the door to the cubicle and stormed out. I started to follow, but the doorway was swallowed up by a huge hulk of a man.

The man was big shouldered and thick waisted, but I didn't feel like being the one to test out how much of it was fat. He had thinning hair and a face like a well-worn catcher's mitt. His nose was flat and pushed slightly to one side of his face and his eyes stared expressionlessly from beneath a ledge of scar tissue that had been deposited through the years, layer by layer, round by round, like the building of some calcareous reef.

"Okay, creep," he croaked in an almost-whisper. "Out."

He hadn't taken everything in the face in his career. He had taken at least one in the throat.

"That's just where I was going," I said, putting on my best smile. I wanted no part of this one. I had done some boxing in college, not much, but enough to know that the best amateur in the world didn't stand a chance with the worst pro. And this pug's face looked as if he could take a lot more than I could ever give.

He let me by. Terri was standing by the wall, her arms folded over those magnificent boobs, glaring at me narrow-eyed.

The bouncer gave me a little shove through the curtains. There were several men waiting now, thumbing through magazines on the couches. They all looked up, startled, as I came flying through the curtains.

"And *stay* out," the pug croaked after me. "We don't want your kind around here."

The men stared at me curiously, trying to determine just what kind I was. Probably one of those *preverts* who put ads in the *Free Press*: Bi wht male, into leather, looking for discreet wht-blk cpl for fun and games. B & D (no pain), French Pastry, Over the Mountain. Must be sincere.

Well, hell, nobody could accuse me of not being sincere.

I went down the street to my car, wondering what I was going to do now that I had blown it. I hadn't expected the violence of her reaction and I wondered about the reasons for it.

I got in the car and consulted my watch. Nine-ten. I sat there watching men go in and out of the front door of the New World, and after twenty minutes or so I felt my eyes starting to droop. It was like counting sheep.

I tuned in to the Laker game. Abdul-Jabbar, Goodrich and Allen were kicking ass on the Golden State Warriors, and Chick Hearn was going crazy announcing. He even managed to communicate some of his enthusiasm to me, and I found I was wide awake again. It was the third quarter and the Lakers were up by twelve, but then they started playing their usual game and by the middle of the fourth they were down by fifteen. To keep my blood pressure down, I turned it off, and by eleven I was having a hard time keeping my eyes open again.

At eleven-twenty they snapped open automatically when they caught a glimpse of Terri coming out the front door. She was wearing tight-tight blue jeans, a short jeans jacket and knee-high leather boots. She started down the block, and half a block up she unlocked the door of a new brown Cougar and got in. The engine roared as she pulled out into traffic. The engine of my Plymouth wheezed asthmatically as I followed.

At Lincoln she signaled and made a left. I got caught at the light and banged the steering wheel impatiently with the palm of my hand, waiting for it to change. I kept my eyes on the stream of traffic ahead, trying to separate her tail-lights from the others, and when the light turned green I punched the accelerator.

I closed the distance between us steadily and finally caught her at Venice Boulevard. She turned right on Washington, heading toward the Marina. For a minute I thought she might be going to the Crow's Nest to see what the action was like, but right before Pacific her left blinker flashed ruby-red and she swung onto a narrow street that ran alongside a cement canal filled with brackish water.

The street was lined with modern two-story stucco apartment buildings and she turned into the driveway of one of them. I slowed down and went past and parked up the street.

When I got back to the driveway, she was climbing the outside stairs of one of the buildings. She stopped in front of the door of apartment 6, rummaged through her purse looking for her keys, unlocked the door and went in.

The mailbox said that Wenke lived in apartment 6. Just to make sure Wenke wasn't the name of some gorilla Terri was shacked up with, I went across the courtyard to the garage to do a little cross-checking. No luck. The car was locked, the windows rolled up tight, no registration visible. I'd just have to take my chances.

I went up the stairs to number 6 and knocked. There was a delayed reaction, and then I heard a voice behind the door ask: "Who is it?"

"Miss Wenke?"

"Yes?"

"This is the manager. I've had a complaint about you."

Indecipherable muttering. "Talk to me about it in the morning—"

"I'm afraid it can't wait, Miss Wenke—"

"Oh Jesus Christ." There was a fumbling of the lock and the door opened just enough for me to get my foot inside. "Hey, what the hell is—YOU!"

I put my shoulder into the door and walked in. The apartment was a one bedroom. The furniture was nice—not the typical junk that comes with a furnished apartment. She had a quality stereo system, color TV, original canvases on the walls, several fluffy sheepskin throw rugs on the floor. It looked as if she were doing all right for herself.

I walked quickly through the living room, my ears and eyes alert for any movement, past the kitchen and up the one stair that led into the bedroom.

The queen-size bed was unmade, the bedroom disarray being in sharp contrast to the neatness of the living room. She had followed me into the bedroom and stood now in the doorway. "You dirty sonofabitch."

"That's me," I conceded, smiling.

"You're a real asshole, mister."

"I'll let that one go," I said. "My father always taught me to turn the other cheek."

The humor of the remark seemed to elude her. She sneered and pushed her sharp dagger of a chin at me. "Get the hell out of here—"

"Where's Fein?"

"I told you I don't know any Fein."

I wagged a finger at her. "Your nose is going to grow. Where's Fein?"

Her upper lip curled under, exposing a row of even, white teeth. "I've got some friends who could really do a number on your head, you know that?"

I held up my hand in an exaggerated tremble. "You're frightening me, Terri. Please stop."

"Get out of here," she growled. "Now."

"Let's hear about Fein first."

She pursed her lips angrily, then exhaled loudly and made a helpless shrugging motion with her hands. "All right, all right. So Fein is a customer. So I've been to his place a couple of times. Big deal. What are you trying to do, make a big thing out of it? So his wife doesn't get his rocks off anymore. I do. So what?"

"Where did you two meet?"

She stared at me, a dark, cold stare. "He came in the New World."

She never broke eye contact with me, never looked away, but something in her eyes told me she was lying. "Where is he now?"

She threw up her hands in disgust. "How the fuck am I supposed to know? We got it on a few times a month. He'd call me up and tell me to meet him at the Casa Loma and I'd go. I don't keep track of him, man. He's a trick, that's all."

"Why doesn't he go to the New World anymore?"

She shrugged. "He doesn't like it there. He likes privacy. And that's okay with me. I can make more money outcalling anyway. It's all free and clear. I don't have to give anybody a percentage."

"So why were you so scared when I told you he'd been missing for four days?"

"Look, I don't need any hassles, man, with the cops or some John's wife, or private detectives, or nobody. I just don't need to get involved with shit like that, you know, man? But I don't know where Fein is, and that's the truth."

I wasn't sure I accepted it, but there was not much I could do about it. "Okay, Terri. But if you really don't want to get hassled, I suggest you tell Fein to call home. If he happens to call you, that is."

I went past her, back through the living room to the front door. She followed me. I stopped at the door and took one last look at her.

Even now, facing the brittle, cold core of her personality, I felt something totally animal inside me responding to her. She was a succubus that came on the night air and there was no real defense against her, except to just get out. So I got out. "I'll see you around, Terri."

"Don't bother."

"It's no bother."

She smiled, but there was no warmth in it. "It could be, asshole, if you're not careful."

I smiled back. "I'm always careful."

"That makes me feel good," she said and slammed the door.

I was glad that made her feel good. I was glad something was still able to make her feel good. She didn't look as if she felt good too often.

On the way down to the car I started whistling for no reason at all.

· 9 ·

I WOKE UP exhausted.

Johnny Carson had interviewed his usual parade of pinheads next door until one, and then Bela Lugosi had chased some helpless screaming ingenue through *The Ape Man* or *Devil Bat* or one of his other monumental PRC epics. No wonder he'd been a junkie; I probably would have been, too.

I must have fallen asleep sometime before Bela had the perennial stake put through his heart, although I didn't remember when or how.

The bull dyke who lived in the next apartment had been doing that a lot lately, ever since we had gotten into an argument over her late-night record playing and I had called her a "fucking truck driver," or words to that effect. Now, whenever she knew she was going to be out all night, she would roll her TV snugly up to the cardboard wall that separated us and turn it on.

I would have gone into the other room to sleep, but there was no other room, unless you were willing to count the bathroom, which I wasn't. Yet.

The manager had been very sympathetic when I told him about it and had talked to the woman, but she'd just given him her innocent teamster stare and said petitely: "Fuck him. I turn the tube off when I leave. He don't like it, tell him to move."

The manager wasn't about to tell me to move, but he wasn't about to tell her to move, either, and I could see the writing on the wall. It was going to be war. If the owner of the biggest newspaper on the West Coast couldn't force me to leave town, I'd be damned if I was going to let some ugly butch broad force me out of my own apartment.

I coffeed and shaved myself and called Nate Bloom at home. He told me he had a line on Fein's bookie and also something else that he wanted to talk to me about. He suggested we meet again at Sam's at noon, and I told him I would see him then.

I had another cup of coffee and showered and was getting dressed when the phone rang. It was Barbara Fein.

"I'm sorry to call you so early," she apologized. "I didn't wake you up, did I?"

"No. As a matter of fact, I was just going to call you."

"Have you found out something?" Her voice sounded anxious.

"Something."

I took a deep breath and told her about the Casa Loma and Terri. There was a dead space on the line and she said softly: "I see. Is that where you think he's been for the last five days? At the apartment?"

"I don't know. The girl denies it. At least she claims she hasn't been with him. His neighbors haven't seen him there. I'm going to do some more checking today, though."

There was a pause. "Well . . . let me know what, if you find out anything."

"I will," I said. "Good-bye, Mrs. Fein."

I decided Mark Fein was right. It was out of some twisted sense of loyalty that Barbara Fein was sticking to her husband. But it was a twisted sense of loyalty I felt envious of. I wished somebody felt it for me.

The rest of the morning I spent phoning Mrs. Fein's list of possibles. None of them had seen or heard from David Fein in the past five days and most of them had not seen him in months. I placed two long-distance calls to Las Vegas, one to Caesar's Palace and one to the Dunes, person-to-person to David Fein. Neither hotel had a David Fein registered. I thought about trying some of the other hotels, but decided to hold off. If need be, I could always call an operative I knew in Vegas to check around the town for me. But I wanted to run out all my L.A. leads first.

On my way to Vernon I stopped at the Casa Loma. The chewing gum was still lodged like a wad of sealing wax against the door.

Bloom had his same booth by the window when I got there.

As soon as I sat down, he leaned across the table eagerly and said: "Have you got any leads yet?"

This whole detective business must have agreed with him. He still looked tired, but he looked two hundred percent better than he had yesterday.

"A couple," I said. "Nothing very solid."

"What?"

I shook my head. "Sorry, Nate, but I can't discuss it with you."

He looked disappointed. "Sure. It was stupid to ask. Let's order some lunch and I'll tell you what I've found out."

Mary the fire-eater took our order, with the same exuberant enthusiasm she had displayed yesterday. She went away and he said: "Chico conducts his business in a Mexican joint down the street called Enrique's. He's there every Tuesday and Friday, all afternoon usually."

"He'll be there this afternoon, then," I said, more to myself than to him.

His gray head bobbed in confirmation.

"Chico's just an agent, right?"

He looked at me questioningly. "An agent?"

"A guy who pays out and collects."

"Yeah, I guess so."

"Anybody know whose money he's using? Who the book is behind him?"

"I doubt it," he said. "To tell the truth, I never asked the guy I got the information from. But I'll tell you one thing, he's doing a hell of a business with these packing house workers. A hell of a business."

I nodded, and he leaned across the table and gently touched the sleeve of my coat. "There's something else I want to talk to you about," he said.

I waited. He pinched his lower lip between two fingers, then said. "Something strange is going on at Supreme."

"Like what?"

He shrugged. "You know how it is in the business. Talk circulates. You hear things. Well, two weeks ago Tortorello started buying cattle from the Palo Verde Valley. A lot of cattle. He started trucking them in for slaughter yesterday."

"So?"

"So, it doesn't make any sense. The past couple of months have been slow. The demand is down. What happened is that a lot of the growers have been holding their beef off the market to try to drive the price up. They've done it, but they've also cut down the demand. People aren't buying that much beef and all the packers around here have been slaughtering half the number of cattle usual for this time of year."

I shrugged. "Maybe Tortorello anticipates the demand for beef is going to go up."

He glowered at me. "Then he'd be the wisest man in the market, because nobody—and I mean *nobody*, from the growers to the packers to the Department of Agriculture— thinks the demand is going to go up for at least two or three months."

"Why the hell would he buy the cattle then?"

"That's what I'd like to know," he said, then hesitated.

"Look, Jake, I haven't said anything about this to anybody, because a lot of people would think it's just sour grapes with me, but something stinks with this Tortorello."

"What do you mean?"

"I think he's a *goniff*."

"Why do you think that?"

"I don't know," he said, slouching back in the booth. "It's just a feeling I got. I've gotten it before with other people, and I haven't been wrong a hell of a lot of times. You met the guy. What did you think of him?"

"He seemed pretty sharp to me," I said.

"Yeah. Maybe too goddamn sharp."

"Do you have any evidence to back up your suspicions?"

He shook his head. "No. Like I said, it's just a feeling I got that something isn't kosher with him. Like how the hell did he happen to show up just at the right time to buy into Supreme?"

"He told me he heard about the deal from a mutual friend of his and Fein's."

He nodded knowingly. "I tried to pin Dave down a couple of times about where he'd met the guy, but he never gave me a straight answer."

"So what do you think is going on, Nate? All this must be leading somewhere."

"I don't know," he said. "I wish I did. But I've been in this business a long goddamn time, Jake. I know when something smells. And something smells at Supreme, I'm telling you."

I didn't know if his suspicions were wishful thinking or dreams produced from eating too many sour grapes, like he said, or if they had some foundation in fact. What I did know was that I couldn't do much about them. Not on the information I had.

Our lunch came and we fell into a mouth-stuffed silence. I grudgingly had to admit that the sandwich I had was good. It was good as long as I didn't have to look at Mary's smiling face.

After we finished, Bloom pushed his plate away and asked: "How is Barbara taking the whole thing, anyway? I only talked to her that once."

"She'll be all right," I said. "She's under a lot of strain, but she'll live. I've seen people in worse shape."

He shook his head sadly. "Sometimes, Jake, I look at all our lives and wonder what it's all about, you know? I mean, look at Dave and what he's got—a good business, a great kid like Barbara for a wife—and he goes out and screws it up for himself. Sometimes I wonder just what we're all trying to do, where we're going."

"Nowhere."

An expression of faint surprise came over his features. "Huh?"

"It's all an underwater bicycle race, Nate."

He nodded slowly and looked out the window. I picked the check up off the table and stood up. He reached out a hand. "Let me get it—"

"You got the last one," I said.

I paid the check at the cashier, and we went outside to the parking lot. "Let me know what happens with Chico," he said.

"I will. And you find out anything more about Tortorello's mysterious cattle shipments, give me a jingle. Need a lift?"

"No, that's all right," he said. "It's just a couple of blocks. I'll walk."

"You're sure?"

"Yeah. Thanks anyway."

He waved and headed up the block, his head bowed as if there was a great weight sitting on his shoulders. By the time I got to be sixty-two—if I ever made it—I was sure my head would be lower than that.

I opened the car door and got in.

· 10 ·

Enrique's was a soot-streaked burrito and beer joint a few blocks from Sam's. The lunch hour was going full blast, and the place was filled with packinghouse workers, smoke and the jabber of border Spanish. A staccato chorus of mariachi trumpets blared from a jukebox in the corner like a pack of yapping dogs. The lighting inside was mercifully dim, and I was sure that when the health inspectors came around it got even dimmer.

I stepped up to the bar and ordered a bottle of Suprema from the bartender, a pale, chubby man wearing a soiled apron. He started to reach for a cloudy glass that was sitting on the backbar, but I told him I didn't need it and he shrugged, brutally decapitated the bottle and set it down in front of me. All I was short of was a mild case of hepatitis to make my life complete.

I gave him a buck and told him to keep the change. He started to walk away and I asked casually: "Chico around today?"

He head-feinted over my right shoulder toward a table in the back, where a nattily dressed man sat talking to a Chicano in work clothes. The man wore an expensive gray-and-maroon check sports jacket over a lighter gray turtleneck sweater. He was sleek and well groomed, with a sharp, ferret-like face and black, oily hair that was combed straight back from his forehead. He reminded me of a rat that had just climbed out of the sewer, dark and shiny and wet.

They talked for a few seconds, then got up and went through a doorway that led to the rest rooms. They came back out a short time later, and Chico went back to his table while the other man drifted back into the crowd and rejoined his friends. I took my beer over to Chico's table and pulled up a straw-seated chair, straddling it casually. "Hi, Chico. How's business?"

He looked at me. His eyes were definitely unfriendly, but they were also uneasy. "Do I know you, man?"

"We've never met, no. But we have mutual friends."

"Yeah? Who?"

"David Fein," I said, giving him a second to digest it. "You seen him around lately?"

He leaned back in his chair. The flimsy wooden back creaked loudly in protest. "Who?"

"David Fein."

"Never heard of him."

"How could you forget one of your best customers?"

The muscle twitched at the corner of his eye, but his voice was flat and steady, like a dial tone. "I didn't catch your name."

"Asch."

"Okay, Asch. So who are you?"

"A close friend of the family."

"Oh yeah?"

"That's right," I said. "Fein hasn't been home in a few days."

"So? What's that got to do with me?"

"Maybe nothing," I said. "Maybe a lot. How much does Fein owe?"

His face went blank. "I don't know what you're talking about."

"Okay," I said, sighing. "I guess I'll have to go to the cops, then. I was sincerely hoping we could get this thing straightened out without having to call in a third party, but I guess I was hoping for too much."

He studied me intently and as I stood said: "How do I know you're not a cop yourself?"

I brought out my wallet and showed him my photostat. "Private detective," I said, looking down at him. "You want to talk, or do I go get some cops?"

He balked, then said grudgingly: "I ain't seen Fein in a week or so."

"Did he place a bet with you?"

"Yeah."

"How much?"

"He bet on a trotter in the third at Hollywood Park. He couldn't make it out there that night and wanted to put down three hundred to win on the horse. Out of Nowhere."

"The horse lose?"

He nodded. "Wasn't even in the money."

"Then Fein owes you money?"

He shrugged. "Yeah, but he's good for it. There's no problem there."

"Does Fein owe you more than three hundred?"

I waited for an answer. I had the definite feeling my beer would be warm and flat before I got one. I shrugged. "Okay. I guess I'll have to go to the cops—"

"Wait a sec, man. Look, before I talk to you, I gotta get the okay. Know what I mean? I gotta make a call first."

"Okay. Make it."

He stood up. "You wait here, man. I'll be right back."

His forward motion was toward the front door.

"There's a phone in the back," I said, pointing toward the sign over the doorway leading to the rest rooms.

"That one's out of order," he said. "I'll be right back."

I nodded, and he went through the crowd to the front door and into the white light of the afternoon. I got up, went through the doorway and picked up the receiver on the pay phone in the hall. I deposited a dime and got a dial tone and then dialed the number of my answering service.

"7712."

I hung up and stood there, thinking. A huge roach skittered across the dirty linoleum floor in front of me and disappeared under the door of the bathroom. For a second I thought it was pulling a little cart behind it, but quickly put that down to my overactive imagination.

The exit sign glowed green above the back door, and I went to it. The smells of grease and frying tortillas hung in a heavy aura around the outside of the place, overpowering the other odors of the street. I went around the side of the building and saw Chico briskly walking up Soto. At the next block, he turned left and disappeared.

I crossed the street and watched from the other side, shielded by a parked car, as he came back around the corner trailed by two men.

One of them was tall and lanky, dressed in blue jeans, a Windbreaker and heavy boots. The other was short and beach-tanned and had curly, bleached-blonde hair. Despite his height, that one was impressive. He was wearing sneakers and jeans and a blue muscle T-shirt that looked as if it were doing its best to keep from disintegrating. His arms and chest were huge, his waist tiny and he had a thick steel pipe for a neck. All in all, he had the glow of health about him.

I waited until they had gone through the door of Enrique's, then jogged across the street to my car.

I'd pulled up to the driveway and was waiting for a break in traffic when they came out the front door. Chico pointed at me and yelled: "Hey!" That was all Pipe-neck had to hear. He sprinted to the car.

The traffic had not let up, but that was a moot point now. I punched it just as he got one of his meaty hands on my door handle. The acceleration spun him like a top and flung him across the sidewalk as I launched across Soto, my tires smoking.

The driver of the car I cut in front of had good reflexes. He stomped on his brakes and jerked his wheel, missing my rear end by a foot or two. But my mind wasn't on him. It was on the cattle truck that was bearing down on me from the opposite direction with his air horn blaring.

My car was fishtailing badly over the double yellow line, almost out of control, but the lane on the other side of the truck was filled and he had no place to go. I felt no panic; there wasn't time for it. I put my foot to the floor and pulled the wheel, hard, and my rear end came around just as the truck passed, his horn still bellowing angrily.

The blaring of the air horn merged with the screaming of the huge tires and I caught a glimpse of the truck in my rear-view mirror as it screeched to a stop in the middle of the street.

I kept my foot glued to the floor. I had a feeling that if I stuck around, Pipe-neck and his friend would have a little help from the Teamster's Union.

· 11 ·

I HAD ORIGINALLY PLANNED to spend the rest of the day in Gardena and at Hollywood Park, but Bloom's revelations about Tortorello and his mysterious cattle purchases had made me curious. The trotters would not be running at Hollywood until evening and Gardena stayed open all night, but the county offices closed down at five. I headed downtown.

The California State Corporations Commission's file on Supreme Packing was a fat one and it took quite awhile to get through it. The operation was owned by Supreme Land and Cattle, Inc., incorporated in Los Angeles in 1942. There had been several major reorganizations in its officers and stockholders in the past thirty-four years. At the time of its incorporation, the president had been Leonard Fein, the vice-president, Elwood Wengraf, and the secretary-treasurer, Herbert Greenbaum. Leonard Fein had apparently bought out the other two in 1962 and put his son in as vice-president. In 1970 David Fein moved up to president, and Leonard Fein was out of the picture. At that time, Barbara Fein was installed as secretary-treasurer, and five percent of the company's stock was put in her name. I assumed that move had been merely to comply with California law, which states that there must be at least two partners in order to form and sustain a corporation. Three months ago, Steven Tortorello had purchased thirty percent of David Fein's stock and had filled the vacant vice-president slot. Fein, his wife and Tortorello were the only present stockholders.

The yearly balance sheets were in the file, and although the last two years showed a steady decline in net profits, on paper at least, Supreme looked as if it were in pretty good shape. The last balance sheet, however, didn't take in the collapse of Big Boy Markets.

Tortorello's restaurant, the Golden Steer, was owned by T.T.A., Inc., the letters, I assumed, standing for the initials of its three officers, Tortorello, president, Sam Triolo, vice-president, and Albert Aarons, secretary-treasurer. Its balance sheets looked healthy with a fat bank balance and six figures in the assets column.

The microfilmed tax rolls in the County Assessor's office showed that the land on which the Golden Steer sat, 45125 La Cienega Boulevard, was owned by a Los Angeles based corporation, Amway Investments.

I don't really know what made me trudge all the way back to the Corporations Commission office and have the clerk pull Amway's file. Maybe it was just a kind of inertia. Sometimes I get like that, I've found. I start digging, and like a badger, I get locked in on it, fixated and it's hard to stop. Whatever it was that kept me going, when I opened the cover of the Amway file I knew I had dug my way into something I was not sure I wanted to be in.

If you didn't read the papers, Amway would probably just look like an ordinary corporation that dealt in real estate. Its officers and primary stockholders were Nick D'Augustino, Mario Brocato, Philip Schwartz, and John Donaldson. The last three names meant nothing to me, but the name D'Augustino did.

Nothing had ever been proven, of course, but there was a lot of speculation by L.A. law enforcement, public and private, that Nick D'Augustino was the Southern California representative of Joseph Bruno's Newark Family and was the kingpin of the local gambling and porno industries. When questioned about such things, Mr. D. was always at a complete loss for words. When subpoenaed to appear before a congressional hearing on crime that was being held in L.A. a few years back, Mr. D. had proclaimed in astonished tones that he knew "nothing about no organized crime," that he was just a "real estate investor." The good senators questioning Mr. D. couldn't argue with that. He did indeed invest in real estate.

I had a hunch. I had the clerk pull the DBA file on the New World Spa. It was owned by Happytime Corporation, an outfit that also owned three other massage parlors and two movie theaters in various spots around town. Its principal officers were Abe Klugman, president, Arthur Browne, vice-president, and Moe Simonoff, secretary-treasurer. The parcel of land on which it sat was owned by Amway Investments.

It was close to five and the clerk at the County Assessor's office told me he was closing up. I drove down Broadway in a daze, the circuits of my mind jammed with thoughts, none of them coming together in any compelling pattern. I spotted a coffee shop on the corner of Seventh and decided to stop and get a bite to eat. I wanted to do some thinking, and it would also give the rush-hour traffic out to Gardena a little time to ease up.

The coffee shop had no parking lot, so I parked down the street in a pay lot and walked back the block and a half. Since the restaurant was not crowded, I took a booth in the back. I ordered a chef's salad and coffee, and tried to piece it all together in my mind. D'Augustino's name coming up twice was too much to be a coincidence, but just where he fit into the whole mess and whether he was connected with Fein's disappearance, I didn't know. What I did know was that his presence, even in the background, made me nervous.

The daylight was completely gone when I stepped outside forty minutes later. The street had a dead, haunted look. The sidewalks were almost deserted and the fronts of the pawn-shops and clothing stores that lined the street were all barred and padlocked for the night, a testimonial to the neighborhood's clientele. The dirty brick buildings looked old and lonely, their darkness only occasionally reclaimed by the tired flicker of a neon sign.

I walked back to the parking lot and the attendant, a small, olive-skinned kid who looked like Sirhan Sirhan, took my ticket and punched it in the time clock. He told me in a thick accent that I owed ninety cents; I paid it and went across the lot to the car. I had just put my key into the door when I heard a scuffling sound behind me. I started to turn, but didn't quite make it.

A fist that felt like a frozen ham ripped into my kidneys, and I sucked air involuntarily from the paralyzing pain. A hand grabbed the back of my neck and squeezed, then propelled me forward. My face hit the rain lip above the door of the car and I tasted blood; then I was yanked backward. I felt like a rag doll in the crushing grip and tried to struggle free, but my coat was jerked down over my arms, pinning them, and the pain ripped into my kidneys again and again. My knees buckled and I started to fall, but one of the men thoughtfully held me up while the other one worked me over.

He worked methodically, his fists moving like pistons, tearing into my gut again and again, but finally the hand at my neck let go and I slid down the comforting solidity of the car, gasping loudly for breath.

I was close to passing out. I thought it was over, that they would leave then, but I was wrong. A heavy foot pinned my neck, pressing my face into the asphalt and then they gave me dessert. The bastard must have thought he was George Blanda kicking from the sixty. His foot caught me just below the ribs and lifted me off the ground.

The chef's salad came up and the pressure from the boot at my neck eased up. A voice, above me and far away, said very softly: "Maybe you'd better go back to divorce work for a while, shit-face. It might be safer."

Then a different voice: "Come on. Let's get the fuck out of here."

Their footsteps crunched rapidly away, and with great effort I lifted my head and took a blurred look thorugh the tears of pain that filled my eyes. They were about fifty feet away, jogging now, but there was no mistaking that pair.

You stupid asshole, Asch, I thought. Don't you ever look behind you, for chrissakes? They must have been following you all the way from Enrique's. You're real sharp, kid, no doubt about that.

I rolled over and braced myself against the rear tire of the car. I heard a strange voice repeat "Jesus, Jesus," as if in invocation, and then realized it was me. Forget it, I thought. *He's* not going to help you, kid. Not an agnostic half-Jew. Quit making appeals to deaf ears and get your ass up. GET UP.

I struggled to my feet and fell back against the car, holding my aching sides. It was lucky that kick hadn't been placed a little higher; otherwise I might have wound up with a punctured lung. As it was, I wasn't sure my spleen wasn't ruptured.

As I stood trying to regain my breath, I became vaguely aware of a figure standing a dozen yards away, staring at me. The parking attendant. His eyes and mouth were wide open.

"You . . ." my voice came out in a ragged whisper. "You saw . . . you saw them."

He shook his head violently. "No. I see nothing. I see nothing."

"You little bastard," I wheezed. "You saw them."

"I see nothing," he repeated.

The more I looked at him, the more he looked like Sirhan Sirhan. He's probably a Syrian, I thought. You can't trust those Arabs anyway. They're all terrorists. The little sonofabitch probably has a grenade under his valet's jacket.

I waved a hand at him in disgust and got into the car. The drive to County General seemed as if it took an hour.

The doctor in Emergency took X-rays, but everything came out negative. He asked me what had happened, and I told him I fell off my roof while trying to adjust my television antenna. He gave me a prescription for Percodan and sent me home with a disbelieving look.

The label on the bottle said to take one every four hours for pain, so as soon as I got back to the apartment, I took two. Then I got undressed and slipped into the shower, letting the warm water run soothingly over my wounded body. Purple bruises had already started to form on my sides and back.

By the time I'd toweled off and eased myself into bed, the Percodan had started to work. My face was numb. The places where they had punched me still hurt, but my face was numb. The wonders of modern medicine, I thought, and waited in the dark for the numbness to creep into my brain and put me to sleep.

· 12 ·

PIPE-NECK WAS misinformed. Divorce in California was now called "dissolution" and it did not take a private detective popping a flashbulb in a motel room to accomplish it. All you had to do was contact your lawyer, file some papers and agree on a property settlement, and *voila!* it was done. I had done some work in my time that had eventually resulted in divorce, but I had never done the kind the worthy gentleman who had stepped on my face had suggested. The million-dollar question still lingering in my mind when I woke up was who had suggested to him that he make the suggestion to me.

I walked around in a zombielike state, thanks to a Percodan hangover. I threw the pills in the wastebasket and shaved, then made myself a strong pot of coffee. After I'd killed off most of it, I got dressed, groaning painfully every time I felt something in my side pull, and called Mrs. Fein.

I told her I had something important I wanted to talk to her about, and she said to come up anytime. It was after eleven by the time I pulled up in front of the house.

She answered the door dressed in a flower-print blouse and a pair of pale blue slacks. She looked tired. There were dark circles under her eyes and for the first time, I noticed tiny crow's feet etched at their corners. That was okay. She could have circles and crow's feet and anything else and I'd still take her, anytime, anywhere.

As soon as I had sat down in the living room, she pounced on me. "What is it? Have you found out something?"

"A few things," I said, and then laid it out for her. I told her about D'Augustino and what I had learned about Terri, and Nate Bloom's suspicions concerning Tortorello and about my meeting with Chico. Her eyes grew wide when I told her about being worked over by Chico's goons. She leaned forward in her chair and anxiously looked me over. "Did—did they hurt you?"

"They weren't playing patty-cake," I said, "but they could have done a whole lot worse if they'd wanted to."

"But . . . I don't understand. Why would they want to hurt you at all?"

"That's a good question," I said. "Chico obviously didn't like the questions I was asking."

She bit her lip nervously. "You mean, they beat you up because of David?"

"I don't know. Maybe Chico just doesn't like people asking him questions, period."

She thought about that for a few seconds. Her eyebrows bunched together above her too-perfect nose. "Are you trying to tell me that David is mixed up with gangsters?"

I shook my head and shifted uncomfortably in my chair. My left side was starting to ache. "No. But the fact is that your husband has been gambling a lot. I don't know who he owes money to or even if he owes money at all. All I know is it's damn funny that this Tortorello showed up at such an opportune time. And I don't like the fact that he has connections—no matter how incidental—with one of the biggest racketeers on the Coast. I think it's also damn funny that your husband's been mixed up with a girl who works in a place that's also connected to the same man."

"You think Mr. Tortorello is a gangster?"

"I don't know," I told her. "It could all be a coincidence—"

"But you just said you don't think it is a coincidence," she interrupted me.

"No. I don't."

She looked past me with a glazed expression. "I can't believe that David would let himself get involved with those kind of people—"

"Those people are hyenas, Mrs. Fein. They prey on the weak and the sick. Your husband's gambling is a sickness that makes him a likely target."

"I suppose so." She closed her eyes and nodded weakly. When she opened them again, there was fear in them. "Do you think David could be in trouble? You think they could have hurt him in some way?"

"They hurt me and I didn't owe them a cent," I said.

She moistened her lips with her tongue and looked away. She shivered involuntarily as a chill ran up her back.

"I didn't come over here to alarm you, Mrs. Fein," I said in the most soothing voice I could muster. "Like I said, I don't even know if your husband owes anybody any money. I just felt that you should know what I've found out and wanted to ask you what you want to do about it."

She locked stares with me. "What do you suggest?"

"Going to the police. I have a friend in the Organized Crime Division of the D.A.'s Office—"

"No," she said, a little too forcefully. Thoughts moved rapidly behind her eyes. "I don't want to do that. Not yet. Not until you find out something conclusive."

I could not really blame the woman. She didn't want to accidentally blow the whistle on her husband, just in case he was mixed up in some shady business deal. I just hoped the conclusive something she wanted didn't turn out to be her husband's body.

"Have you exhausted every lead you have?" she asked.

"No."

"Then keep looking. David is all right. I'm sure he's all right." Her voice didn't sound sure at all.

I stood up. "I'll keep you informed of what I find out."

"Yes," she said, but her eyes were staring blankly at the carpet. She stood up mechanically and showed me to the door.

I had gone halfway down the driveway, when she called from the front porch. "Mr. Asch—"

I turned. "Yes?"

Her hand was raised to her chin, the polished nail of her index finger touching her lower lip. "Nothing," she said. "Nothing."

I got in the car. She was still standing on the front porch, watching me as I drove away.

· 13 ·

I'VE HEARD a lot of people mispronounce Gardena "Gardenia," but all it takes is one look and you know that the town has nothing to do with that flower or gardens or, for that matter, anything else that has the faintest hint of natural beauty. It is a spread-out, one-story city of wide streets, adult bookstores, topless bars and stores selling building supplies and vinyl floor coverings. Its main industry, however, is poker—lo-ball and draw—and, indicatively, the only buildings in town that have any elegance at all are the four clubs that specialize in those inspired arts.

The Horseshoe Club was closest to the freeway. I started with it.

It was three in the afternoon and the casino was packed. Every chair around the thirty green-felt tables in the pit was occupied. Prospective players were stacked three-deep against the wall—old men with alcoholic-seamed faces, young blacks, their huge Afros surmounted by black leather hats, slovenly housewives in wrinkled tent dresses that had obviously been thrown on in one hell of a hurry, and women with more ice on their fingers than an Amana freezer has cubes—all waiting anxiously to hear their initials being called by the half-dozen red-jacketed floormen who strolled between the tables, watching for any sign of a chair emptying. Those waiting loosened up their fingers and cracked knuckles, knowing that today was going to be their day. I hoped it was going to be mine.

In the hatcheck room a gray-haired woman sat at a table washing cards for reuse. I washed out with her, too. She couldn't identify Fein's photograph, but pointed to a white-haired security guard standing in the casino and told me to ask him.

The security guard's name was Clem. I showed him my I.D. and then the photograph. "That's Mr. Fein," he said nodding. "He comes in all the time. Three or four days a week."

I took back the picture. "Seen him lately?"

"Not in the past, oh, five days maybe."

I felt a little tingle of excitement. "He was in five days ago?"

"About that, I guess. Maybe six. I don't know exactly."

"What time was he in? Do you remember?"

He rubbed his chin and rolled his eyes toward the ceiling. "Early evening, I'd say. Toward the end of my shift. Maybe nine, nine-thirty. He lost quite a bit playing lo-ball—he must have, because he was over his credit limit. He was quite upset about it. He said he was going to go get some more money and come back."

"What was his limit?"

"You'd have to talk to the credit man about that," he said. He leaned toward me conspiratorially and said softly, "I know they'd lowered it lately. He used to have a $20,000 limit, but he must have had a few slow-pays or something, because they cut him back. I don't know what to, but it must have been quite a bit because he raised all sorts of hell about it when it happened."

"He never came back that last night he was in?"

"No," Clem said, "He'd been drinking pretty heavy, too. I told him he'd better call somebody and have them pick him up, because he wasn't in any shape to drive. But he said, no, he was okay."

"Do you know if he did call anybody?"

He tilted his hat back and scratched his forehead. "I don't know. I don't think so. I think he took his own car, but I'm not sure. You can ask the valet outside—George. He was on that night, I'm sure. He'd probably know."

I thanked him and he said: "Say, is Mr. Fein in some kind of trouble?"

"No trouble," I said. "He just hasn't been home in a few nights. His wife is worried."

He nodded knowingly.

"You must see a lot of that around here," I said.

"You can say that again."

I gave him one of my cards.."Well, if you do happen to see Fein around here, I'd appreciate it if you'd give me a call."

He looked at the card and pocketed it. "Sure thing."

I went out and talked to George. George was a young kid with muttonchop sideburns and a sallow complexion. He confirmed that Fein had been in five nights before and that he'd left around nine-thirty. He said he had been loaded to the gills and had driven off the lot peeling rubber. It was all very clear in George's mind because usually Fein left him a buck and that night he hadn't tipped him at all.

I checked out two of the other clubs, but came up with nothing there. Apparently Fein was a steady at the Horseshoe and didn't frequent the others much.

The last stop was the Normandie. It was the most elaborate of the four, all red-brick and marble facade, the architecture pseudo-English Tudor. A couple of the floormen inside thought they recognized Fein from the photograph, but none of them could say for sure. All of them were sure that he hadn't been in lately.

I consulted my watch as I cut across the jammed parking lot. Four forty-one. Just enough time to get some dinner and get out to Hollywood Park for the first race. I was trying to determine where I was going to eat when something caught my eye. The license plate on the gold LTD across the aisle said PRIME.

The excitement was back again. The doors of the car were locked. I stood, trying to gather my thoughts. The Normandie was crowded, and it was altogether possible that Fein was in there now. I had not seen him, but that didn't mean much; I could have missed him, he could have been in the bathroom or in the restaurant—any number of things could explain that. And the floormen, hell, they didn't look at faces, just bodies, filling and vacating chairs.

I turned and started to go back toward the building when the smell anchored me in my tracks. I squatted down behind the car and smelled around the trunk and my head was knocked back by the stench.

Something jumped around in the pit of my stomach and my hands started to tremble. I didn't want to open that trunk; I just wanted to walk away from it, but I knew I had to do it.

I went to my own car and got a crow bar out of the trunk and brought it back. Several men standing by the entrance to the club watched me work on the lock of Fein's trunk, but none of them made any attempt to interfere. They were more curious than anything. A cross-section of Gardena's model citizens.

The lock gave way with a loud bang, and as the lid popped up, I was pushed backward by the putrid, suffocating smell that rushed out and wrapped its foul arms around me. I turned away, fighting the urge to heave, then jerked my mind back into line, and thought, breathe through your mouth, breathe through your mouth. . . .

When I had my breathing regulated, I stepped back up to the trunk and looked inside.

The body was bloated and discolored, but not so badly that I could not recognize David Fein.

I walked over to the men standing by the front door and asked them where I could find a phone. One of them gave me an indifferent stare and waved a thumb inside. The phone was right by the front door. I got out my notebook and looked up Mark Fein's number.

"Hello?"

"Dr. Fein?"

"Yes?"

"This is Jacob Asch. I'm afraid I have some bad news. Your brother is dead. He's been murdered."

Silence flooded the line. "Jesus Christ," he said in a weak voice. "How. . . ."

"I don't know how or why or even when. I just found the body."

"But—"

"Listen, I can't answer any questions right now," I snapped. "I'll try later. I called you because I thought you'd better break the news to your sister-in-law. It might be better if you were there with her, just to make sure she's all right. Once I call the cops, I won't be able to get away for awhile."

"Jesus Christ," he repeated. It sounded as if we were talking long-distance.

"I'll try to make it up to the Palisades after I'm through with the police. I know it's a bad time, but there are a few things I have to talk to Mrs. Fein about, if she's up to it."

He sighed in an audible attempt to pull himself together. "Right. I'm leaving now."

I hung up and searched my pockets for another dime. All I had were bills. One of the men outside had change for a dollar. I used it to call the police.

· 14 ·

THE DETECTIVE-SERGEANT was named Marinko. He had a lantern jaw, short brown hair and dark, fuzzy eyebrows that wriggled and squirmed like two woolly caterpillars while I talked.

I had told it to him once in the parking lot of the Normandie—about finding the body, about searching for Fein there because of his gambling habit—while the coroner's men loaded the body into a plastic bag for transport downtown. Marinko had watched them complete the job, then suggested in a rather ho-hum tone that we drive down to the Gardena P.D. and go over it once more for the record. So there I was, telling it into a tape recorder microphone.

I finished it up, verified that the preceding facts were true to the best of my knowledge, and put my name to it. Marinko punched the STOP button and took a sip from the Styrofoam cup of coffee in front of him.

He sat thoughtfully for a moment with the cup tilted toward him and stared into it as if trying to read the future in the black residue at the bottom. "I talked to Mrs. Fein a little while ago," he said finally.

"You didn't tell me that."

"I wanted to get your statement first."

"What did she say?"

"About the same thing as you." He paused. "I also talked to her brother-in-law. He was up at her house. He answered the phone, as a matter of fact. Said you'd called him."

"Yeah. I did."

"Before or after you called us?"

"Does it matter?"

"I don't know," he said, as if he thought it really might.

"Mark Fein is a doctor. I thought it might be a good idea to have somebody up there in case Mrs. Fein had a hard time handling it. She's been under a lot of strain the past few days."

He pursed his lips, but didn't say anything. He pointed to the Styrofoam cup in front of me on the table. "You want some more coffee?"

"That would be grounds for police brutality."

He smiled vaguely. "Yeah, the stuff is pretty bad." He must have been used to it, because he got up and poured himself another cup from the coffee maker on the ledge. He came back, dropped into the chair and sighed loudly.

"We've been getting so much of this shit lately," he said. "It's really getting out of control."

"What kind of shit, Sergeant?"

"Muggings."

"That's what you think it was?"

"That would be my first guess. No money on the body. The back of his head was split open. We've had so many muggings in the parking lots of those fucking clubs in the past two years, we can't even handle it. We just had to ram through a city ordinance to force the clubs to pay for security police to patrol their own parking lots. Unfortunately, the law doesn't go into effect until the first." He took a sip from the cup. "Hell, those assholes just wait around for a winner so they can hit him over the head and take his money. It's an easy night's work."

"Fein was losing," I said.

"He was losing at the Horseshoe. That doesn't mean he wasn't winning somewhere else. I intend to check that out tomorrow."

"I checked around the other clubs tonight. Nobody remembers Fein being in."

"Maybe they'll remember a little better when I ask them," he said.

I conceded the point in my mind. "Why the hell would muggers kill him?"

He shrugged. "Things could have gotten out of hand. They had to get rid of him, so they dumped him in the trunk of his car and left him on the lot."

"Why would they leave him on the lot where they might attract attention?"

"The lot would be the least likely place they'd attract attention. The Normandie is open twenty-one hours a day. There are always cars on the lot. If they wanted to make sure the body wasn't discovered for a while, that would be a pretty damn smart place to drop it."

"It could have been that way," I admitted.

"But you don't think it was."

"I didn't say that."

He leaned forward belligerently. "You didn't have to. It's written all over your face." He leaned back again and smiled smugly. "Okay. Let's hear your ideas on the subject."

I told him about getting worked over by Chico's goons. His eyebrows recoiled as if they'd been touched by a lighted match. "Did you swear out a complaint on those guys?"

"No," I said.

His mouth turned down at the corners. "Why the hell not?"

"Because it would just result in more hassle than it was worth. They'd produce a dozen witnesses who'd swear in court they were playing cards twenty miles away at the time. The parking lot attendant wouldn't testify against anybody. He was scared shitless. Besides, a good lawyer would tear my identification apart in court. It was dark that night, I only really saw them from the rear—you know the routine, Sergeant."

He looked away and rolled his eyes. "Well, hell. That's really a wonderful attitude. No wonder law enforcement is such an easy job with attitudes like that."

I stared silently at the ends of my fingers, which were resting on the top of the table.

"You never i.d.'d those two clowns?" he asked.

"No."

"I'll want you to look at some pictures tomorrow," he said. "Make yourself available."

"Okay. Am I free to go now?"

"Yeah, you can go."

I stood up. He scrutinized my face. "You're sure you haven't left anything out?"

"Like what?"

"I don't know. If I knew, I wouldn't be asking."

I wrestled with my conscience. I'd left a hell of a lot out. I'd left out Terri and Tortorello and D'Augustino. Not that I intended to hold any of that back. It was just a matter of protocol—I had to clear it with Mrs. Fein first. But I also wanted to make damn sure I told it to the right people. Marinko struck me as an honest cop—even a fairly capable one—but I wasn't sure if he was really equipped or motivated to conduct an investigation of the activities of Nick D'Augustino. And I felt strongly that that should be done before Fein's murder went into the books as an overzealous mugging. "I may have something for you in the morning."

He looked at me curiously. "What?"

"I have to do some checking first."

"Don't get any ideas about working on this thing on your own, Asch," he warned. "This is police business now."

"I have no intention of working on it," I said. "As a matter of fact, I intend to tell Mrs. Fein tonight that I'm off the case. I just have to check some things over in my files, that's all."

"Can't you remember what's in your files?"

"No."

He gave me a doubting look.

"You've got to have faith in human nature, Sergeant," I said. "Trust me."

"Shit," he said, "I don't even trust my own wife."

"I've never met a cop that did," I said. "Good night."

· 15 ·

THE HOUSE WAS ablaze with lights when I pulled up and turned off my motor. A gray BMW Bavaria was parked behind the blue Mark IV in the driveway.

Mark Fein stood in the doorway, silhouetted by the living room lights, then glanced over his shoulder and stepped out onto the porch, pulling the door closed behind him. "I got here just before the police called," he said in an undertone. "She's taking it pretty well, everything considered. I've given her a strong tranquilizer, so if she seems a little, well, a little vacant, that's the reason. Just watch what you say, that's all."

I assured him I would and we went inside. Mrs. Fein was sitting on the couch. She had on the same outfit she had been wearing this morning. She looked at me through heavily lidded eyes.

"I'm sorry, Mrs. Fein," I said, taking a nearby chair.

She nodded. "What happened? I want to know what happened." Her voice was steady, drained of emotion. The tranquilizer, I assumed.

I told it in general terms, editing out anything I thought might be too upsetting for her. When I finished, she asked: "You're sure it's David?"

"Yes."

"The police asked me to come down to the morgue tomorrow and make a positive identification," Mark Fein cut in. He made a head-motion toward Barbara Fein. "They said there was no need for both of us to go, so I said I would."

I nodded.

Mrs. Fein looked down at the hands in her lap. "Who killed him, Mr. Asch?"

"I don't know. It's a police matter now. They'll find out."

"Do you think those people you were telling me about this morning had something to do with it?"

"I don't know," I said. "But that's something I want to talk to you about. I haven't told the police about those people."

I stopped and looked over at Mark Fein. She caught my glance and said: "It's all right. You can talk freely in front of Mark. He knows everything."

I nodded. "I haven't told them about Tortorello or the girl yet, but I'm going to have to. I can't withhold information in a murder case. And the sooner they know it all, the better. The girl may know something that could crack the case, and they should get to her as fast as they can. I just wanted to explain the situation to you, so that you would understand. I know this morning you said you didn't want to inform the police—"

She shook her head. "I thought David was alive then. It doesn't matter now. Nothing matters anymore except to find out who did this. Tell them anything you want." She stopped and her eyes drifted away from me glassily. "It all seems like some terrible nightmare . . . it doesn't even seem real. . . ."

Her grief broke through the tranquilizer-dam. She leaned forward and buried her face in her hands. Her shoulders shook violently as it poured out of her in half-choking, sobbing gasps.

Mark Fein rushed over and wrapped his arm around her shoulders tenderly. He looked up and his expression told me to leave.

I wanted to go to the woman and touch her, comfort her, put my hand on her head and stroke her hair and tell her it was all right. But it wasn't all right. I knew it wasn't all right.

We had no common emotional ground, and I was impotent to help her. I found myself disquieted by her grief, helpless because I felt none myself. David Fein was not even really a person to me. I'd met him once alive and once dead and that was all. Two days ago, he had been a job to me, a puzzle to solve, and I could not truthfully say he was anything more now.

I stood up, without another word, left.

As soon as I got home, I stripped off my clothes, stuffed them into the hamper and got into the shower. My nose was playing me flashbacks of the smell of Fein's body, and I turned the water on as hot as I could take it in an attempt to scald it away. I washed my hair and used the brush on my nails and scrubbed myself pink with the washcloth, then slipped into a terry cloth bathrobe and went out to the kitchen to make myself a stiff drink.

All the drink succeeded in doing was to make me feel claustrophobic. My insides were seething, churning, and the thought of facing the plasterboard walls of my apartment for the rest of the night was intolerable. I needed a kind word and the touch of sympathetic hands. The kitchen clock said 10:02. It was late and I stood debating with myself, back and forth, yes and no, before I picked up the phone and dialed Sarah's number.

"Hello?" Her voice was thick with sleep.

"Sarah?"

"Who's this?"

"Jake."

There was a pause.

"Hello? Sarah?"

"Oooh—Jake. I'm sorry. I'm half-asleep. I couldn't figure out who it was for a second."

I suddenly saw what a stupid idea this was in the first place.

"Hey, look, I'm sorry to bother you. Go back to sleep."

"No, that's okay. I have an early class in the morning and I was kind of tired, so I went to bed early. Where are you?"

"Home," I said. "Go on back to sleep."

"No, what did you want?"

I hesitated. "I—I, uh, I just needed to talk to somebody, that's all. It's been one of those days. I just thought you might like some company, that's all. It was stupid. Forget it and go back to sleep. We'll make it some other time."

I started to hang up, but she said: "Wait—"

I kept the phone pressed against my ear, hoping.

"Listen, come on over if you want. Really, it's okay. I'm awake now and probably wouldn't be able to go back to sleep anyway."

I didn't say anything.

"Okay?"

"Okay," I said. "I'll pick up a bottle of wine on the way over."

"I'll see you when you get here," she said.

Sarah was a short, cute, twenty-four-year-old high school teacher. She was lightly overweight, had long, chestnut hair, and magnificent breasts. A recent transplant from Ohio, she had hopped into her battered VW van the day after graduating from Kent State and stopped driving when the land ran out. Now she taught special classes for slow learners at Hollywood High, and at night, took extension courses at USC in television writing.

Her aspiring screenwriting career was one of the reasons we hit it off right away when introduced several months back by a mutual friend. She apparently had had some vague notion that as a private detective—especially as an ex-newspaperman-turned-private-detective—I would turn out to be a gold mine of plots for "Cannon" and "Barnaby Jones." Only self-discipline was not one of Sarah's strong points and the scripts never materialized, except out of her mouth. Pretty soon, she'd stopped asking me questions about "interesting cases I had had" and our relationship had settled down into one of casual comfort.

Not that we had grown close. In many ways we remained almost total strangers. But we did fulfill certain immediate needs in each other, needs that went beyond sex, although that was very good, too. We were totally relaxed around one another and there was some psychic thread that connected us—temporary, we both knew, but none the less real for that. We would not see each other for weeks and then the need would come again, like a cycle of the moon, and I would call her up. I often wondered what that thread was, but never hard enough to come up with an answer. I was just damn glad she was there.

I pulled on jeans and a sweater and a pair of loafers, and left the apartment. Outside Hollywood, I stopped at a liquor store and bought two bottles of Liebfraumilch.

Sycamore Drive, Sarah's street, was a narrow, tortuous, densely foliated street that wound like a snake into the Hollywood Hills and reached its summit in the Yamashiro.

From its hilltop perch, the Yamashiro had witnessed all the transformations of Hollywood, from orange groves and dirt roads to the concrete and neon jungle it was today, and handled them with typical Oriental stoicism. It had been built at the turn of the century by a wealthy Japanese immigrant, who for some reason had wanted to live in a scaled-down model of the Japanese Imperial Castle. After his death, some capitalist-minded heirs had decided the land was too valuable to lay fallow, so they made it into a Japanese restaurant and erected a block of apartments just below it on the hill. Sarah's was number 35.

She answered the door in a T-shirt that said "Bobby Womack" on it and a pair of faded blue jeans. Her hair was pinned up. "Hi," she said cheerfully.

"Hi."

The apartment was a studio, the bedroom separated from

the living room only by a Japanese-style partition. The floor was natural wood, and behind the far wall that was completely glass, the lights of the city burned like smouldering embers.

The kitchen, if a sink, a half-size refrigerator and a two-burner stove could be considered a kitchen, was squeezed into a three-foot area by the front door. I set the wine on the edge of the sink and pulled the bottles out of the paper sack. "I got Blue Nun. That okay?"

"Sure," she said.

"Got a corkscrew?"

She took one out of the drawer, and I went to work on one of the bottles while she put the other in the icebox.

"So what happened today that was so terrible?" she asked.

The cork slipped out of the bottle with a pop. "I've been working on a missing persons case the past few days, a husband that hadn't come home. I found him a few hours ago, murdered and stuffed in the trunk of his car. I just came from his wife."

"Jesus, Jake, I'm sorry."

"Yeah, well, that's the way it goes," I said. "I just feel sorry for the wife. She's a nice lady."

I wondered if sympathy was all I was feeling. Maybe a twinge of jealousy mixed in, that what Barbara Fein was feeling was not for me. I didn't know what it was about the woman, but she had struck something in me, some faint but resonant chord.

Sarah got out two wine glasses that did not match; I poured the wine and we sat on the couch.

There were only two lights on in the place, one in the kitchen and one over my head. I reached up and turned off the one above me. We sat in the semi-darkness, not saying anything, listening to the soft-rock coming out of her FM tuner. David Gates was singing "It Don't Matter to Me," stirring up old and nameless emotions in me and for some strange reason I felt like crying. But then, I often cried at all sorts of inappropriate times. During sad movies and happy movies and beautiful songs. I was a tough sonofabitch, there was no doubt about it.

I looked out at the lights. "I'm sorry if I seem down tonight."

"That's all right," she said reassuringly. "You don't have to say anything if you don't want to talk."

"It's just, sometimes, I don't know, I just wonder what it's all about," I said, echoing Bloom's words. "The funny part of it is that most of the time it doesn't really matter. You just go on living, doing whatever it is you do and it's not that bad. It only gets bad when you wonder about what it all means, why you're doing this and why you're doing that. Then you have to look at it and face the fact that none of it means a fucking thing."

The song ended and something else came on I didn't like so well. "I probably shouldn't have come over tonight," I said. "I'll just depress you."

"No, you won't."

I tried to break my own mood by pointing at the pen-and-ink drawing on the wall of a reclining female nude. "You know, you're hung up on asses."

"What?"

"Just about every piece of art you've got in here has a female *derriere* as a central theme. Even your bathroom wallpaper."

She laughed. Her laughter was soothing, like gentle, cool waves on a lake. "I never noticed before. What do you think it means?"

"I don't know," I said. "Maybe you like to sit down a lot."

"As long as it's nothing more ominous than that."

We lapsed back into a wine-sipping silence and I said: "How are things at school?"

"Fine," she said. "I'm teaching an extra class now in remedial reading. It's a hassle, but I'm getting paid for it, so it's okay."

"How's the screenwriting coming?"

She shrugged. "I'm taking a course at Valley State now. I got to meet Paul Newman last week. That was a thrill. He was speaking at the class."

I nodded, feeling like a stranger now, wondering what the hell I was doing here. But then she put her hand on my arm and the feeling went away.

I touched her hair. She put her glass down on the table, took a pin out from the back somewhere and shook her head so her hair tumbled down around her shoulders. I ran my hand over it, stroking it gently, feeling its softness, and she smiled. There was pleasure in the smile, but there also seemed to be a faint hint of pity in it, too, that I didn't like.

But who the hell was I to like or not to like? I was just thankful for Sarah and all the other Sarahs who had enabled me to make it to age 35. She was one more Band-Aid applied to a life that had been held together with Band-Aids, gauze, splints and adhesive tape. We all make it through the best way we can.

I pulled her face toward me and kissed her lightly on the lips, tentatively exploring the warm, moist inside of her mouth with my tongue, then pulled away. I wanted to make this last, to wipe any trace of tolerance off her face.

We stared at each other for a few brief seconds and then came together more hungrily. I set my drink down, never breaking contact with her mouth and put my arms around her. Her back felt solid and comfortable beneath my hands, as I slid them down and around and up underneath her T-shirt, up the tanned silkiness of her flesh, to her hard nipples.

She awkwardly unzipped my fly, then stood up suddenly and reached a hand out to me. I took it and stood up, and she peeled me down and dropped to her knees on the floor.

There we were, back-lit from the kitchen, putting on a live stag show for all of Hollywood. Fuck you, Hollywood, I thought as she went to work with her tongue. I closed my eyes and tried to shut down everything else except the pure, physical sensation. Fuck you too, world. . . .

Later, I lay in the darkness, watching the lights. She slept softly, the warm heaviness of her body pressed against me, her head resting on the crook of my arm. Still, the awareness of her next to me did nothing to lessen the feeling of loneliness—no, not really loneliness, but *alone-ness*—that filled me. The feeling was poignant and deep, but not altogether unpleasant, as if everyone and everything in the world was a product of my imagination and if I ceased to imagine them would simply cease to exist. I even closed my eyes and willed a section of the lights off—after all, you couldn't expect to do everything at once, you had to take it a little at a time—but when I opened them up again, the lights were still there, a blanket of icy fire. You're not concentrating, Asch. I closed my eyes and tried again, but got the same result.

I stayed awake like that for quite awhile—I'm not sure how long—but I finally managed to drift off, drugged to sleep by exhaustion and the soothing music coming from the stereo tuner.

· 16 ·

I WAS AWAKENED by the sound of running water. I sat up in bed and looked at the digital clock on the dresser. Quarter to seven.

Sarah came around the partition and looked surprised to find me awake. She was dressed in a pink blouse and brown skirt. "Hi," she said. "I tried not to wake you. You were sleeping so soundly."

"That's okay."

"You want some coffee?"

"Definitely."

I got out of bed and went into the bathroom to throw some water in my face. I brushed my hair and used some of her mouthwash and when I came out, she was standing by the bed, holding a cup of steaming coffee. She handed it to me.

"Cream and one sugar, right?"

"Perfect."

"There's some more on the stove," she said. "Stay as long as you want. I've got to get to school."

She plucked a jacket from the closet and picked up her purse. Then she came over to me and touched my face gently. "I'm really glad you came over."

"So am I."

She smiled and gave me a quick peck on the mouth and left.

I sat on the couch with another cup of coffee and watched the smog settle like sludge out of the morning sky. I called the Gardena station and asked for Marinko, but the receptionist said he was not expected until the afternoon, so I left my name and answering service number. I got dressed and left the apartment, turning off the burner under the coffee as I went out.

I stopped at Coffee Dan's on Hollywood Boulevard and read the morning edition of the *Times* over two soft-boiled eggs and toast. David Fein had made the edition, a two paragraph column on page four, headed "Meat Packer Found Slain." The article didn't tell me anything I didn't know. It gave a brief description of the murder scene and a quote from Sergeant Marinko—whom the reporter gave credit for finding the body on a "tip" from a citizen—attributing the deed to muggers.

It was after nine-thirty when I stepped out of the elevator onto the seventeenth floor of the Criminal Courts Building. A uniformed sheriff sat at the desk at the end of the marble-walled hallway. He took my name and after getting back the okay, directed me down a narrow corridor.

Jim Gordon's office was a tiny cubbyhole whose black glass windows afforded a breathtaking view of the downtown freeway interchange and the railroad yards and beyond that, the *barrio* of East L.A. A desk, two chairs, and a filing cabinet were crammed into the space, leaving little room to breathe, and stacks of legal briefs were piled everywhere. The walls were completely nude except for one blown-up, black-and-white SLA poster of Patty Hearst, submachine gun in hand, in her famous "Make-war-not-love" pose.

Jim was leaning back in his chair when I walked in, his small hands resting on the paunch that was swelling over the top of his pants. He looked as if he'd lost some more hair since I'd seen him last, but he'd spread the rest of it around to try to conceal the fact. He smiled over the stub of the cigar that was clamped firmly in the corner of his mouth and offered his hand. His small, gray eyes watched me from behind the thick-rimmed glasses.

Jim was short and built like a small bear, but the bear metaphor went beyond his physical appearance—there was a little bear in his personality, too. He had a truly outrageous sense of humor, completely off-the-wall, but below the surface you could sense an unpredictable aggressiveness, hard, intractable. I'd often wondered how many defense attorneys had blown their clients' cases having been taken in by the myth of Gentle Ben.

Gordon was one of the most able prosecutors in the D.A.'s Organized Crime Division. On the side, he owned part of a gymnasium and three apartment buildings. He drove a Porsche Targa that gave him nothing but trouble and smoked dollar cigars—illegal contraband from Cuba. He stayed in the D.A.'s office instead of going into private practice where he could make a hell of a lot more money because, as he put it, he was "having too much fun to quit."

We had originally gotten to know each other when I was working for the *Chronicle*, covering a "chicken-flicks" case he was prosecuting. The case involved the making and marketing of "chicken-flicks," homosexual porno movies that employed eight and nine-year-old boys as their stars. Some prominent people were involved—several judges, a multimillionaire oil tycoon, the thirty-year-old son of one of Hollywood's most celebrated female stars of the 40s and 50s—and the case drew a lot of attention in the media. Jim and I spent long hours discussing the case and had planned to do a book on it, which never panned out. But in the meantime, we had taken a liking to one another and become friends. We found we had a lot in common. We were both thirty-five, both Capricorns, and were both fanatical boxing fans. I had done some boxing in college, and Jim had been a Golden Gloves titleholder at one time. He'd even once sparred several rounds with Emile Griffith.

I sat down in the chair across the desk and pointed at the poster on the wall. "William Randolph Hearst may not like that," I said.

He looked at the poster, then at me. He shrugged. "If he can't take a joke, fuck him."

I laughed and he smiled. "Looks like you've put on some weight," I told him.

He took off his glasses and rubbed his eyes, then set the glasses on top of the desk. "I'm down, man. You should have seen me a month ago. I got up to one-eighty, for chrissakes. It got so bad I finally went back to my old boxing coach and told him to get me back in shape. 'Shape for what?' he says. 'For fighting,' I tell him. He tells me I'm crazy, that I'm too fat to do road work, so he sticks me on this diet—one meal a day—so I can start running again. I've dropped fifteen pounds and I start running next week."

"I should probably go with you," I said, slapping my own stomach.

"Sure," he said. "We can push each other. If one of us doesn't feel like running in the morning, the other one will browbeat him until he gets his ass in gear."

I nodded.

"I'm serious," he said.

"It's okay by me."

"Good," he said with a self-satisfied expression. "I'll call you and we'll get it set up. Now, what's up?"

"A murder," I said.

His expression changed. "Who got murdered?"

"A guy named David Fein. He owned Supreme Packing in Vernon."

"Where did it happen?"

"In Gardena. Last night."

"Nice town," he said. "A case of yours?"

"Up until last night. It was a missing persons case until I

happened to find the body. Now the Gardena P.D. is handling it."

"What do you need from me?"

"I wanted to apprise you of the facts. It may be too big for them to handle on their own."

"Why? What's the big deal?"

"You know anything about a Steven Tortorello? He owns a restaurant on La Cienega called the Golden Steer."

He ran a hand over his head, smoothing down some unruly strands of thin hair. "No, why?"

"How about a bookie's agent named Chico? He operates around Vernon."

"Chico Orduno," he said. "I know him. I nailed him a few times."

"You know who he works for?"

"We've never nailed it down. He keeps his mouth shut pretty tight. Consequently, he always gets the best legal representation. He never stays in the joint too long."

"Could he be working for Nick D'Augustino?"

He slipped his glasses back on, as if to screen off the thoughts that moved in his eyes. "It's possible. Why?"

I told him why. I laid it all out for him, from Fein's disappearance to the run-in with Chico's muscle to Fein's involvement with Terri. I gave him names, addresses, the whole shot. Several times, he told me to go slower as he scribbled furiously on a notepad on the desk. When I finished, he sat back and tossed the pencil down on the top of the desk. "You know who those goons were who worked you over?"

"No."

"You want to take a look at some pictures?"

"Sure."

He held up a finger. "Just a minute. I want to make a call first." He looked up a number in his phone book, then picked up the phone and dialed. "Hello? Yeah, this is Gordon from the D.A.'s office. Let me speak to Herb . . . Herb? Jim Gordon. Good . . . Say, listen, what have you got on a Steven Tortorello? T-O-R-T-O-R-E-L-L-O. He owns a restaurant called the Golden Steer. Nothing, huh? He might be connected with Nick D'Augustino in some way. How about a T.T.A. Inc.? Or a Triolo? Okay . . . well, look, thanks. If you happen to dig up anything let me know, will you? It might be something. I don't know . . . yeah, right . . . okay. Bye."

He hung up. "That was the F.B.I. As far as their local agent knows, Tortorello is clean. No connections. That doesn't mean anything, though."

"What about Happytime Corporation? Klugman and Simonoff?"

He took the cigar stub out of his mouth and inspected the end of it. It was out. He relit it with a pocket lighter and said: "I didn't have to ask about them. I already know all about those assholes. Klugman and Simonoff are both shysters. Simonoff was disbarred last year for trying to bribe a juror in a bribery case, if you believe that one. Mr. Browne, the third member of the corporation, owns a couple of film labs that develop porno. They also develop some of Walt Disney's stuff, which is why we don't bother to move on them."

"Think they're connected to D'Augustino?"

"Not directly. They're strictly second-level hoods. What the setup usually is, is this: Say an outfit like Happytime wants to open up a massage parlor. They approach one of D'Augustino's people and ask for a location. They get one for a thousand a month, but they pay another thousand a month in cash to a bagman who shows up like clockwork every month. That extra grand gives Happytime permission to operate in D'Augustino's territory and also fringe benefits —like muscle, if it's needed." He paused. "Where do you think the girl fits into the whole thing?"

"I wish I knew. Fein was balling her, but if you saw her, that's not hard to understand. I wouldn't mind it myself. But it's a little too much for me to accept that her showing up just when she did was a coincidence."

"You think D'Augustino was the one Fein was losing

money to all along, right? And that D'Augustino called in the debts by putting his own man into the business?"

"That's what I've been thinking."

"Then why would they kill him?"

"Maybe he objected to what was going on." I told him about Tortorello's mysterious cattle purchases.

"What do you think that means?"

"I have no idea. Neither does Bloom, Fein's ex-credit manager. He's the one who told me about it. Are you getting any cases lately of organized crime trying to muscle in on legitimate businesses?"

"Some. One group tried to do a little organizing in the rendering business a few months ago. But that business is a natural for that kind of activity. There's no union or anything to stand in their way. They dynamited a few grease trucks, beat up a few drivers. We put a stop to that, though. I just sent up one of the big boys behind the whole thing for five to ten."

"Yeah, I read about that in the papers," I said.

He leaned forward and picked up the pencil again. "What did you say the sergeant in charge of the case's name was again?"

"Marinko."

He wrote it down. "I'm going to give Sergeant Marinko a call and see if he might like some assistance on this thing."

"You think he'll get pissed off that I came to you with it?"

He screwed up his face and waved a hand in the air. "Hell, no. He'll be tickled pink. What've they got down there? Three detectives working homicide? He'll shit for joy when he finds out I'm going to send down some of the staff." He stood up. "Let's go down the hall and see if we can i.d. those two scumbags."

The investigator's room was past the guard's desk out front and through two sets of glass doors. It was a large room filled with desks and there was a separate, smaller adjoining room stuffed with filing cabinets. D.A.'s investigators sat or stood around the desks engaged in casual conversation, the snatches of which I heard having nothing to do with their work. Most of them were young, in their late twenties or early thirties, and, according to county hiring policies, the ethnic percentages correspond almost exactly to those of the population at large. Jim headed to the back of the room, toward Frank Capek, who was standing by the water cooler talking to a Japanese.

Capek must have been close to fifty, although his age was hard to pin down with any exactitude due to his robust build and the fact that he shaved his head. He had originally come to America in the 1930s, when he and his parents had fled Czechoslovakia to escape the Nazi tide, and he still spoke with a noticeable Czech accent. He had been a D.A.'s investigator for thirty years and knew L.A.'s streets and everybody on them by their first name, from bookies to pickpockets to the members of the County Board of Supervisors. He also knew me by my first name, although we had only met a couple of times before.

"Jim," Capek said, looking up from his conversation. "Just the man I wanted to see." He held out his hand to me and smiled. "Hello, Jake. How are you?"

"Fine, Frank. How about yourself?"

"Fine, fine," he said. "Still in the private detective business?"

"Yeah."

He nodded and the Japanese excused himself and moved away with a paper cup full of water. Capek leaned toward Jim in a conspiratorial manner, but he didn't seem to mind if I heard what he was going to say. "Listen Jim, I need a small favor. I was contacted by this fellow a few days ago who has some guns he wants to get rid of. A grease gun and a Russian AK-47. He wants to be a good citizen and turn the things in, you know, but he wants to do it anonymously. He doesn't want his name to appear on any reports or anything."

"Where'd he get a AK-47?" Gordon asked.

Capek shrugged. "Who knows? Listen, I'm just glad to get those damn things off the street. What I need is to book the stuff in without going through channels. If this guy finds out his name's going to be put on a report, he'll back off. You think you can handle it for me?"

"Sure," Gordon said, his tone friendly. "I'll take care of it, Frank. Don't worry."

Capek smiled. "Thanks, Jim. I knew you were the man to talk to about it."

"Don't thank me," Gordon said. "You're going to do me a reciprocal favor. I need a little information."

"Sure," Capek said, nodding.

"Who works as muscle for Chico Orduno? Big, blonde guy who looks like a fugitive from Muscle Beach? And another tall, dark guy who wears boots."

He thought about it. "Jeez, I don't know. The blonde fellow could be Harvey Gierak. I don't know about the other one."

"Let's take a look at Gierak's file," Jim said.

We went into the adjoining room, and Capek started going through one of the filing cabinet drawers. He pulled one file and opened it. Pipe-neck stared at me glassily from the photograph, his eyes half-shut and showing mostly whites, like some tranquilized wild animal.

"That's him," I said.

Capek nodded seriously. "Harvey's been around awhile. We've never been able to get him on much. He's smart. And as mean as they come."

"He and another guy worked Jake over a couple of nights ago," Gordon said.

Capek looked at me with a new interest. "Yeah? What for?"

"I was asking Chico some questions. I guess they didn't like that."

Gierak's rap sheet had a nice variety of arrests on it—assault and battery, possession of narcotics, mayhem, attempted murder—but he'd only been convicted twice for assault. All the other charges had been dropped—"In the Interest of Justice."

"You got no ideas about the other one, huh?" Gordon asked.

Capek shook his head. "I sure don't, Jim. I'll ask around, though. It shouldn't be any problem to find out."

"Why don't you do that," Gordon suggested. "What are you working on now?"

"A narcotics case."

"Whose?"

"Belson's."

Jim nodded. "Got it about wound up?"

"Just about," Capek said. "Why?"

"I may want you to do a few things for me. I'll get it authorized. It could be big."

Capek looked definitely interested now. "What is it?"

"A murder."

Capek pointed at the file in Gordon's hand. "Gierak have something to do with it?"

"Maybe. That'll be one thing I'll want you to do—find out."

Jim told Capek he would talk to him later about it, and we went back down the hall to his office. He sat behind his desk, put his feet up and took one of his dollar Havanas out of his shirt pocket and meticulously snipped off its end with a pocket-size cutter. After inserting it in his mouth, he said: "The first thing I'm going to do is have Capek go out and shake down that hooker and see what she knows."

"For what it's worth, he'd better shake damn hard. She doesn't appear to be the nervous type."

"Don't worry," he said, as if enjoying the thought. "Capek is very good at leaning on people. The reason I want to use him on this is because he should be able to get the scam on Fein—whether he owed Chico a lot of money. The sonofabitch knows everybody."

"He may also know somebody who knows Tortorello," I said.

"I'm going to do some more checking on that myself." He

took his feet off the edge of the desk and came forward in his chair. "Where are you going to be later?"

"At home probably."

"Give me your number again. I've got it somewhere, but give it to me just in case."

I gave it to him. He put the pencil down and stared at me grimly. "I'd stay out of this from now on if I were you, Jake."

"Don't worry. I'm out. I told Mrs. Fein last night I was off the case."

He nodded. "I'm just telling you, because if there is something in all this, you don't want to be in the middle of it. The Mafia isn't a nice, close-knit little family. The Godfather image everybody's got is a crock of shit. I'm not trying to scare you, I'm just telling you how it is. There was a case in Chicago a little while ago. There was this bagman for a shylock who'd been skimming off a little bit of the collection money for himself. Some people found out about it. They took him out and stripped him and hung him in a tree on meat hooks. One of them sliced pieces off his ass with a butcher knife while another guy cauterized the bleeding parts with an acetylene torch. The guy died of shock."

"Nice."

He nodded. "They are. They're all nice guys. The Feds got a taped phone conversation between the one who was using the torch and a friend of his. They were both laughing like hell about it. It seems that the bagman weighed around three hundred pounds and the guy with the torch thought he looked an awful lot like a pig being butchered. Real nice people."

"For not trying to scare me, you're doing a pretty good job of it."

"Good," he said. "I hope you're good and scared. Because these people are animals and they don't mind hurting others at all."

I stood up to leave. "I know. I already got a little teaser."

"I'll call you tonight," he said.

· 17 ·

I USED THE PAY PHONE in the lobby downstairs to call
my answering service. "7712," an incredibly sexy
voice said.

"You're new," I said.

"Yes," she said breathlessly. "I just started today."

"I'm Jacob Asch," I said. "411 to you. What's your name,
by the way?"

"Penny."

"Welcome aboard, Penny," I said. "Any messages?"

"Just a minute, Mr. Asch, and I'll check."

My spine was melting but I stiffened my resistance. I have
learned over the years to beware of sexy voices on the phone
—they invariably turned out to belong to dogs. Like blind
people whose other senses become more acute to compensate
for their lack of vision, so the uglies always seem to develop
the most fantastically lewd voices.

There was a shuffling of paper and then she was back on
the line. "Oh, yes, Mr. Asch. There was one call that just
came in a little while ago. A Terri Wenke. She said she'd call
back in a little while."

My melting spine stiffened suddenly. "Did she leave a
number?"

"No. She just said she'd call back."

"Thanks, Penny," I said. "I'll be talking to you."

I hung up and dialed Jim Gordon's number upstairs. His secretary said he was out of the office at the moment and she didn't know when he would be back. I gave her my office number and told her to have him call me there when he got in.

My office was on Seventh, in the middle of L.A.'s garment district. It was not far from Civic Center and I figured it would be the best place to wait for the call. I was there in eight minutes.

The office itself was a narrow wallboard cubicle that would have been a dead-ringer for the inside of a Rice Krispies box if it had not been for the scuffed desk, two chairs, filing cabinet and safe that filled it and the window that let light through one wall.

I seldom conducted any business out of the place. Actually, I only rented it as a mail drop and to give my name a little substance in the Yellow Pages. People like that little extra bit of security when they hire a private detective; I suppose they figure that if you have an office, you can't pick up everything and run in the middle of the night. That was a good one on them.

There was a package sitting outside in the hallway, and I picked it up and looked at it. It was addressed to me, no return address. I unlocked the door and scooped up the three letters on the office floor and dropped everything on the desk. I opened the letters first. I always liked to leave my big treats until last.

There was a Union Oil credit card bill for $38.25, a catalogue from Frederick's of Hollywood, telling me they had a special this month on women's crotchless underwear, and a letter with lightning bolts all over it from the United States Purchasing Exchange that said my "Magic Number"—entitling me to redeem a gift item for only 99¢ when I ordered $4,500 worth of merchandise from their catalogue—was inside. I threw it into the wastebasket without even finding out what my Magic Number was.

The package was a carefully wrapped shoe box containing a half-pound of smelly hamburger meat. It had an accompanying note from a Mrs. Bonita Selicio, in an almost-illegible scrawl, saying that she had bought the meat at Lucky's Market and that she "thought it was spoiled." She wanted me to investigate the matter. I didn't have to. I could tell by the smell she was right.

I threw everything into the wastebasket except the Union Oil bill. I made out a check for it, stamped the envelope and set it neatly on the edge of the desk for mailing. Then I swiveled around in my chair and put my feet up on the window ledge and made daydreams out of the white, wispy trails of steam that curled up from the presses of Silverline Slacks on the floor below. The visions I kept shaping out of the steam were not very nice; they had to do with Jim's acetylene torch bedtime story. I kept hoping he would return my call.

The phone rang, startling me. I snatched up the receiver. "Asch," I said.

Silence. Then the smoky voice said: "This is Terri."

I didn't know what she wanted me to say, so I said nothing. Neither did she. Finally, I asked: "What do you want, Terri?"

"I have some information you might be interested in," she said.

"Oh yeah? What kind of information?"

"About David Fein."

"Fein's dead, Terri."

There was no hesitation this time. "I know. You asked me some questions before. If you want some answers, like who killed him, meet me in the parking lot of Ralph's Market on Olympic, by Century City. One hour. Come alone. You got it?"

Her voice was hard and steady, but unnatural. It sounded as if she were trying hard to hold it under control, like a guitar string that was tuned too taut. It sounded as if it were going to crack any second. "Look, Terri, I'm downtown. I don't know if I can make it there in an hour. It depends on traffic—"

"I'll wait twenty minutes," she cut me off.

"But listen—" I tried to say, but it was too late. She'd already hung up.

I tried Jim's office once more, but the secretary said he was still out of the office and had no idea where he was. That was it then. There wasn't time to do anything else. I slipped on my coat and left the office.

Traffic on the freeway was light, and I reached Ralph's with half an hour to spare, which was about what I'd planned on. The lot was about three-quarters full and I circled it, looking for Terri's brown Cougar or any sign of Gierak or his buddy. Nothing but shoppers pushing wire baskets or carrying armloads of brown paper bags filled with food. I parked at the east end of the lot, angled toward the driveway, and waited.

About twenty minutes later, a brown Cougar slowed down in the turning lane and signaled. I saw Terri through the glare of the windshield as she turned into the driveway and swung into a parking space nearby. I had not seen anyone else in the car with her, but I wanted to make damn sure before I committed myself. I started my engine and pulled out of my space and drove around in front of her slowly, making sure she saw me. Then I backed into a space about three rows away and kept my motor idling.

She waited for me to come to her and when it dawned on her finally that I wasn't going to, she got out of her car and walked briskly over to mine. She was wearing a pair of tight, white jeans and a blue, tight-fitting stretch top with silver sequins arranged like an exploding star on her chest. A blue scarf held her black hair away from her pale forehead and she was wearing huge, round, rose-tinted shades. In the bright noon sunlight, she looked even more pale, like some stunning ectoplasmic emanation. She pulled open the car door and slid into the front seat.

"Why don't you shut off your engine?" she asked, making an annoyed gesture at the dashboard. Her voice still had that taut, tense quality.

"I'll keep it running," I said, looking past her out the window for any sign of movement from her car.

She shrugged.

"So what have you got to tell me?" I asked.

"That'll depend."

"On what?"

"Things," she said.

"How did you hear about Fein being dead?"

She didn't move her head, but I could see her eyes behind the glasses move away from me. "The papers."

I shook my head. "It wasn't in the papers."

"No?" she asked, half-sneering, half-smiling.

"No."

"Somebody told me about it."

"Yeah? Who?"

"Never mind who," she said. "You want to know who killed Fein?"

"Do you know?"

She nodded.

"How?"

"Because I was paid to keep Fein company, that's how. Certain people wanted to make sure he was out of the way for a while. I was supposed to keep him occupied—" She started to say something else, but thought better of it and shut up.

"Did Fein know you worked at the New World?"

She shook her head. "No. Fein was a nice guy but he was really lame. I told him I was a secretary, and he believed me. It was set up so that it'd look like an accident that we met. We were both in a bar and I sort of made a play for him. He never knew what was going on. But nobody said nothing about it turning into murder."

"Legally, they could nail you as an accessory, Terri—"

Her eyes widened behind the glasses and she leaned forward as if she were going to attack me. "Bullshit! I didn't have nothing to do with nothing, man. You think somebody's gonna trip me up with that shit, man? I'm not the Lone Ranger. I'm not going to take a fall for anybody."

"Don't tell it to me. It's strictly between you and The Man." I watched her. She looked a little shaken up now after that last accessory bit. She stared out the windshield, trying to regain her composure.

"Who paid you to keep Fein occupied?" I asked.

She smiled stiffly. "Uh-uh, man. No way. I want some bread for that."

"What kind of bread are you talking about?"

She hesitated. "Five thousand."

"Who's going to give you five thousand bucks?"

She gave me a calculating stare. "Fein's old lady should be willing to part with a measly five grand to nail the guy who killed her husband."

"Your bargaining position is a little weak to be asking for money," I told her. "You know what you can get as an accessory to murder?"

"Fuck accessory to murder," she said, her voice whiny now. "I don't even want to talk about that bullshit. I want five thousand bucks, otherwise I'm going to split town and you'll never hear from me again, I guarantee it."

"Why did you call me? Why didn't you call up Mrs. Fein and lay all this on her?"

"Because her number isn't listed and yours is. Besides, you're working for her."

"I *was* working for her," I corrected her. "I'm not working for anybody anymore. I'm off the case."

She did not seem to know quite how to take that. Her mouth opened silently, then she grimaced as if she were in pain. She tossed a hand in the air at nothing and said: "You can give her the message. You just tell her if she wants to find out who killed her old man to be ready to cough up five grand. I'll call you tomorrow morning at ten-thirty. She'd better have the money ready by then, otherwise I swear to God I'm going to disappear and you'll never find me."

She said it as if she were trying harder to convince herself than me.

"If you try to disappear, Terri, the D.A. is going to be on your ass so fast it'll make your head swim. You'd be a perfect candidate for accessory to murder then."

"Don't you worry about me."

"But I do. I can't help it. I'd never forgive myself if anything bad happened to you."

"You can cut the smart shit," she snapped. "It's not funny anyway."

I had to admit she was probably right. "Mrs. Fein isn't going to just hand you five thousand bucks for a few names, Terri. You could throw out any names you wanted and it wouldn't mean a goddamn thing. She's going to want to see some results for that money, like somebody convicted for murder. She's going to want to see you stand up in court and point that pretty finger of yours at somebody."

"I'll work that out with the D.A.," she said. "*After* I get that money." Her mouth tightened into a hard frown.

"You're really too damn money-conscious, did you know that?"

"Goddamn right," she sneered.

I didn't expect it to work in a million years, but I thought I'd give it a try anyway. "Where can I get in touch with you in case something goes wrong?"

"You can't," she said. "I'm staying with friends." She bit her lip worriedly as if she had already said too much. "I'll call you tomorrow morning. You just have that bread ready."

She grabbed the door handle. "Who paid you, Terri? D'Augustino?"

She turned back toward me, a look of genuine puzzlement on her face. "Who?"

"Nick D'Augustino."

"Never heard of him," she said firmly.

"Tortorello?"

Something quivered behind the glasses. She must have felt it because she turned away and pulled on the door handle. She got out of the car and bent down and stuck her head through the open window. "Tomorrow," she repeated. "And don't bother trying to follow me."

She started back to her own car. She walked quickly and I watched the two hard, rounded hemispheres of her ass bounce in time to the sharp clacking of her wooden heels on the pavement.

She started up her car, slammed it into reverse and laid a small patch of rubber backing up. Then she put it into drive and shot out of the parking lot, nearly running over an old lady pushing a shopping cart. The old lady yelled something at her and shook her fist, but Terri didn't seem to notice. She made a left on Olympic and squealed out into traffic.

I killed my motor and locked up the car and went inside the market to look for a pay phone.

· 18 ·

AN EMACIATED-LOOKING GIRL with scraggly hair stood on the curb with her thumb out. About twenty feet farther on, her long-haired boyfriend stood with his hands in the pockets of his Army jacket trying to look casual, watching out of one eye for any sign of a car slowing down. That was true love for you, pure selfless dedication. Pick you up on the way back, girlie.

Jim watched them as we drove up Sunset, then said: "It was a cerebral hemorrhage on the right occipital. He got hit with something good and heavy."

"They have any idea what?"

"No," he said. "They didn't want to make an estimation. That's what's got me worried."

"What?"

He sighed. "You know anything about blunt force injuries?"

"A little."

"You know what a contrecoup injury is?"

"Can't say that I do."

"Well, when somebody falls and hits his head, the brain tends to compress on the side the head hits and tear away from the skull on the other side. A lot of times, there's more damage on the side away from the injury than around the injury itself. But if a person gets clubbed, the hemorrhage is almost always directly below the injury. Occasionally, you'll hear some pathologist claim he's got a case where a guy got hit with a board or something and wound up with a contre-coup fracture, but most experts tend to discount it."

"I think I lost something in the translation," I said. "What are you trying to say, that Fein fell down and hit his head?"

"It's a possibility. I mean, it's a possibility that he *was hit* and then fell down and hit his head. Which means that as far as proving intent goes, it's going to be a bitch to try. The defense will dig up its own experts to give all sorts of highly technical testimony that the injury was the result of a fall and all that garbage. I tried a similar case once. The jury was so confused by the time all those fucking doctors got through with them that they wound up hung, eight to four for con-viction. I had to try the whole thing again."

"Did you win it?"

He frowned. "No."

"Well, I wouldn't worry about it at this stage. It's a little premature to be thinking in terms of a trial, don't you think? I mean, we don't even know who killed Fein yet—"

"I'm always thinking in terms of a trial."

"I know," I said. "What was the time of death?"

"Between ten P.M. of the twenty-ninth—that was Thursday, the night Fein left home—and five A.M. of the thirtieth."

"That's a lot of leeway."

He shrugged. "They can't pin it down any closer. The de-composition of the corpse was too advanced."

The light up ahead turned yellow and I began to slow down. "Were there any other signs of violence on the body?"

"He had a deep laceration and contusion above the orbit of the right eye," he said. "Looks like he got slugged with something from the front first, then hit from behind after he went down. Or maybe he just fell backwards and hit his head. That would explain all the contrecoup bullshit."

"It doesn't sound like a mob hit," I said, stopping for the light. "It's not exactly their style. If they wanted Fein executed, why not just take him out and put a few bullets through his head?"

He kept staring out of the windshield. "Maybe it wasn't supposed to be a hit."

"What do you mean?"

"I mean, maybe Gierak or somebody was sent to have a nice friendly chat with Fein and clue him in that he was behind in his payments. Maybe Gierak's sadistic streak got the better of him and he overdid it a little."

"And stuffed him in the trunk of his car so the Gardena P.D. would think it was another mugging case—"

"I'm not saying it was like that," he said, "but it could've gone something like that."

"You've talked to Marinko, right?"

He nodded solemnly. "Yeah. I called him and he drove up and discussed everything."

"What did he have to say?"

"Just what I told you he would say. He was tickled pink we were coming in on the case. He's going to handle things from that end, interviewing everybody in the casinos who might have seen Fein that night, and we're going to dig around up here."

The light changed and I took off. The road curved and dipped smoothly past a grassy schoolyard whose baseball diamonds stood deserted in the afternoon sun. "Something he didn't tell you—" Jim said.

"Who?"

"Marinko."

"What?"

"They found Fein's checkbook in the glove compartment of the car. His bank account was bone-dry. He'd even written a few bum checks during the last couple of days before he was killed. The checks hadn't cleared yet, and I guess he figured he'd have enough in by the time they did to make them good. He'd apparently become quite expert at that. The guy's cash flow was really something. During the past year, five, six grand a month, in and out, which means either he was winning some as well as losing—which is doubtful—or he'd been sucking Supreme Packing dry. I'd sure like to get into those books and see what's been going on."

"Any names on the check record?" I asked.

"No. Everything was done in cash. Marinko went over and talked to the bank manager and they went through the records together. Almost all the deposits were made in cash and the checks were all made out to 'Cash.' "

We passed the Pacific Palisades city limits sign and as the grade sharpened my engine started pinging noisily. I eased off the gas. "This is the same car you had three years ago, isn't it?" Jim asked.

"Nothing like a little non sequitur," I said. "Yeah, it's the same one. Why?"

He pointed out the windshield. "I didn't think you could have two with coat hangers for radio antennas."

"On a clear night I can pick up Salt Lake City with that coat hanger," I said.

"Terrific. I'll come by some night. I've always wanted to hear the Mormon Tabernacle Choir singing through a coat hanger."

"Have you checked out that Cee Jay broad I told you about?"

He nodded. "I've got her address, but I haven't sent anybody over there yet. In case Terri is staying over there, I don't want to spook her. I just want to let her do some talking tomorrow and then we'll rip them all. Until then, I just want to give her a lot of room to breathe so that she thinks she's home free. I want her to feel good and cocky. No pun intended."

I signaled and made a right and started up the hill toward Mrs. Fein's house. Jim fell into a thoughtful silence, looking out the window at the passing parade of plush lawns and sprawling houses that lined the street. I pulled into the Fein driveway, backed out and parked on the street.

Mrs. Fein opened the door. Her blonde hair was pulled back away from her forehead and tied. She wore no makeup and her face had a drawn, pinched look to it. Her nose didn't look so out of place now. She was wearing a simple green print cotton dress.

"Hello, Mr. Asch," she said. She smiled without showing any teeth.

"Mrs. Fein," I said, "this is Jim Gordon, from the District Attorney's office."

They shook hands and she invited us in. The three of us went into the living room and after Jim and I had sat down, she said: "I have some coffee made. Would you like some?"

"Please," Jim said.

I took the Fifth, silently.

She went into the kitchen and neither of us spoke as Jim eyed the place admiringly. Mrs. Fein came back out with the same tray she had served me from the last time. The coffee was a repeat performance, too.

Jim took a sip. "Good coffee," he said, his face betraying nothing.

Goddamn lawyers, I thought. Nothing but a bunch of frustrated actors.

"I guess Jake explained the situation to you on the phone," he said, holding the cup and saucer in the palm of one hand.

"Yes," she said. "At least all he was able to. Do you really think this Terri whatever-her-name-is knows who killed David?"

"I don't know," he said with a meaningless flourish of his free hand. "I think it's altogether possible. It's also possible she doesn't know anything and she's just trying to shake you down for five thousand dollars. But it's no gamble—I mean, there's no danger of losing the money—that I can guarantee. I'll give you a signed receipt for the cash and we'll arrest her as soon as she puts her hands on it. We'll have four cars covering the meeting. Jake will be wired up with a tape recorder, and we'll be monitoring their conversation the whole time. No matter what she tries to pull, she'll never get out of there with the money."

She nodded, but her face held a faintly puzzled expression. "I realize I'm dense in these matters, but why don't you just go to wherever she lives and arrest her now?"

He took another sip of coffee and put the cup down on the table in front of him. "Number one, we don't know where she is. She's moved out of her apartment. One of my investigators was over there this morning. She told Jake this afternoon that she's staying with friends. We could pursue that, but before we make any moves in that direction, I want to see what she has to say. Once we get her down on tape and she even mentions the word murder, we'll rip her for obstruction of justice. That'll give her a little more incentive to turn state's evidence, if she really does know something. We can even nail her as an accessory, depending on what she says."

"Do you think she had something to do with David's death herself?"

"I don't know," he said. "Actually, I know very little about the girl. Just what Jake told me about her and that's about all."

"What if she doesn't know anything?" she asked.

He shrugged. "Then we'll nail her for extortion. All our bets are covered. Once she says anything at all, she's had it."

Mrs. Fein turned and looked out the window at the fig tree. The slanting rays of the afternoon sun threw long shadows over the brick patio. "Mr. Asch seems to think there's some chance Mr. Tortorello was involved some way in what's happened. Is that what you think, Mr. Gordon?"

Jim looked at me woodenly, then turned back to her. "We're looking into that angle, Mrs. Fein. That's about all I can tell you right now. Tortorello seems to have certain connections with known underworld figures. Just what those connections are, I'm not sure at this point. I don't know if he had anything to do with your husband's murder or not."

She took a cigarette out of the case on the table, and Jim,

gentleman that he was, sprang forward out of his chair and lit it for her. She leaned back and wrapped one arm around her waist, balancing the elbow of the arm holding the cigarette on it. She exhaled smoke and said: "I can get the money tomorrow morning."

If Gordon was relieved by her answer, he didn't show it. He just nodded and said: "Where is your bank?"

"Union Bank in Westwood," she said.

"I'll have one of my men drive you to the bank in the morning," he said. "The girl is supposed to call Jake at ten-thirty. As soon as she calls and we set up the meeting, I'll radio the car you're in and he'll drive you to us, or we can drive to you, depending on where the thing is supposed to go down."

She blinked and looked at me. Her green eyes caught and cooled the dying sunlight streaming in through the windows. She looked away, took another drag off her cigarette, and said: "What denominations should the amount be in?"

"Twenties would probably be the best," he said.

"What time will your man be up here in the morning?"

"I'll have him pick you up at nine-thirty."

"I'll be ready," she said.

Jim smiled. There wasn't much in it. It was just a smile. He slapped his knees and stood up. "Well, I guess that's it then."

She laid her cigarette in the ashtray without putting it out, and Jim offered her his hand again. "Everything will work out fine, I'm sure," he said. He was still smiling, but the smile had a slightly frozen look to it, as if he realized what he had just said, that it couldn't be fine for her for a long time, no matter who was pinched.

She accompanied us to the door. On the porch she touched my arm gently. I stopped while Gordon went down to the car. "I want to thank you for all the help you've been, Mr. Asch," she said. Her eyes were a different color now, almost blue in the light, and there was a relaxed gentleness in them.

"I know you didn't expect to get caught up in anything like this when you took on the case. I know that retainer I paid you didn't cover all your expenses. If you'll just send me a bill, I'll mail you a check."

"I'm on my own time now, Mrs. Fein," I said. "I'll send you a bill to cover everything up to yesterday. The retainer took care of most of it."

She nodded and smiled weakly. We said good-bye and I left.

On the way down the hill, Jim took a cigar out of his shirt pocket and noisily removed the cellophane wrapper.

"If you're going to smoke that goddamn thing," I said, "crack the wind wing."

He stiffened indignantly. "You don't know a good cigar from horseshit," he said in a hurt tone.

"Yeah, I do. Horseshit smells better."

He grunted and opened the wind wing and lit up. Most of the smoke was siphoned out through the window, but the little that wasn't filled the inside of the car with a heavy odor. I rolled down my own window and asked: "What do you think?"

"I think you don't know a good cigar from horseshit."

"You're probably right," I conceded, just to get over that point. He was very sensitive about his cigars. "What time are you going to be over at my place?"

"Nine should give us plenty of time to set up," he said. "The phone will take the longest time. Getting you wired up will take two minutes. The recorder is about the size of a pack of cigarettes. All we've got to do is pick an inconspicuous spot on your lovely body and tape it on."

The light was green at Sunset and I made a left. "You going to let Marinko in on this?"

He nodded and took the cigar out of his mouth. It looked like a burning log between his fingers. "I'll give him a call when I get back to the office. What the hell, it's his case."

"Who else are you going to bring over?"

"The sound guy, Marinko, and that's it."

"Who are you going to send to pick up Mrs. Fein?"

"Capek," he said.

I nodded. We passed a series of eucalyptus trees and the sunlight flashed strobelike through their leaves. We drove past the schoolyard and I asked: "You haven't gotten any line on Tortorello yet?"

"No," he said. "I made a couple more calls. I was waiting for an answer back when you called and told me to meet you."

"I just wish to hell I knew what was going on at Supreme," I said.

He rubbed the back of his neck. "Yeah."

The girl with the scraggly hair and her boyfriend with the Army jacket were gone now. That's all it takes to get by, I thought as we passed the spot where she had been. Just true love and a lot of perseverance.

We drove in silence the rest of the way back to the Holiday Inn where Jim's car was parked.

· 19 ·

I DIDN'T FEEL like going home so I drove into West-wood. I had a spinach salad and two glasses of rosé at Yesterday's, then walked up and down the streets of the village, watching the people and trying to let my mind relax. The attempt was a dismal failure. My thoughts kept chattering away about the case, the way it had gone so far and the way it could go tomorrow, until I finally gave up and went back to my car.

It was quarter to eight by the time I pulled into my space at the apartment and parked. I was out of the car and locking the door when the two men stepped out of the shadows, sending a surge of adrenalin through my bloodstream.

The .38 looked almost small in Gierak's meaty hand. He had a different friend with him this time. The pug from the massage parlor stared at me mindlessly from beneath his calloused brow.

"I guess my advice didn't take," Gierak said, grinning.

I didn't think there was much I could say to that, so I didn't even try. My head snapped around, looking for an exit, but there was nowhere to go. I was hemmed in between two cars and the wall of the garage.

"Somebody wants to see you," Gierak said.

His words brushed against my face like a bold breeze.

"Oh yeah?" I asked. I took a deep breath in an effort to control my thrashing pulse. "Who?"

"You'll find out when you get there."

"Where is there?"

He waved the gun at the car. "Just shut up and put your hands on the roof of the car."

I tried to think, map out a plan of attack, but as quickly as I'd form a plan, it would dissolve like sugar in hot water. Maybe the pug had absorbed enough punches in his lifetime to cut down his reaction time, but I'd already had a sample of Gierak's reaction time and found it to be fine, thank you, just fine. I turned and spread-eagled against the car.

The pug stepped up behind me and patted me down. He found my car keys in my coat pocket and pulled them out. "Okay," he croaked. "Turn around."

The pug went around and unlocked the trunk of my car. He took out the jack and a tire iron and put them on the cement floor by the wall. Then he jerked his thumb toward the trunk and said: "Get in."

A jolt of fear ran through me. "What gives?"

"Nothing gives," Gierak said. "We just want to make sure you don't get any cute ideas, like trying to jump out of the car or something."

"What if I promise to be a good boy?"

Gierak's lips contracted into a threadlike line. "Just shut the fuck up and get in."

I looked at the gaping trunk and felt immediately claustrophobic. The last time I had been in the trunk of a car had been in high school, sneaking into the drive-in, but high school was a long time ago and there had somehow not been the sense of urgency about it then as I felt now. Then I had known somebody was going to let me out.

Gierak stepped forward and rapped me hard on the elbow with the barrel of the gun, sending an electric shock down to my fingertips. "I'm not going to tell you again, asshole. Get in."

I rubbed my elbow and grimaced against the pain. I told myself to calm down, that I'd get my chance later, sometime. Maybe. And with that maybe the anger had gone and the fear was back. I climbed into the trunk and the lid slammed down over me. I was in total darkness.

I could hear their muffled voices outside, but couldn't make out what they were saying. Then the car door opened and slammed; the ignition wheezed and we were moving.

The car backed out, then dipped into the street and made a turn and we picked up speed. I remembered an old Steve Cochran movie I had seen on television in which he had been kidnapped by labor racketeers and blindfolded so he wouldn't know where he was going. But good old Steve was too damn smart for those guys. He memorized the bumps in the road, the turns and the sound of the railroad crossings, and after he was released, he led the cops right back to the bad guys' hideout.

I tried it for a while. Stop, start, left turn, stop, start. We really picked up speed and I decided we were on the freeway. But which freeway? Then the air in the trunk started to become stale, hot and steamy, and I forgot all about the turns, trying to fight down the panic that was creeping up from my gut.

I made a conscious effort to slow down my breathing, but the terror I was feeling made it difficult. Every cell in my body was alive and screaming for air; and my thoughts raced. The sonsofbitches were lying. They weren't taking me to see anybody. They were just going to drive me to some desolate, uninhabited spot in the middle of the desert and leave me locked up to suffocate and bloat in the hot sun like David Fein. Jesus Christ, I thought. Control yourself, Asch. Don't lose your cool. Not now, for God's sake.

And then we were slowing down; we were in traffic once more, stopping and starting. More bumps, tar in the road, and then a series of dips and the car turned right and then left and we stopped. The door opened on the driver's side and there was another sound, that of a metal gate being opened; then the car door slammed shut and we drove a few more yards before the engine died.

The lid sprung open, and I gasped involuntarily as the cool, fresh air rushed against my cheeks and tumbled down my throat like ice water. The crushing weight of panic momentarily left my chest, but it returned as I saw Gierak standing a few feet from the rear bumper, the .38 steady in his hand. "Out," he said sharply.

I climbed out stiffly. The amorphous, blocky mass of Supreme Packing stood dark and brooding against the night sky.

My legs had cramped in the trunk, and I began hopping up and down to get some feeling back into them. Headlights swept the courtyard and a car pulled in and parked beside us. The pug stepped out and said: "Everything okay?"

"Beautiful," Gierak said. "Get the gate."

The pug nodded and went back to padlock the gates. While he was doing that, Gierak pointed toward the alleyway that ran between the buildings and said: "Okay. Move your ass. Let's go."

We went through the welding shop, and when he motioned me to the right, I knew where we were headed. The killing floor.

My hands were trembling violently now. I needed time to think, a few seconds to figure out some kind of strategy. I stopped suddenly and bent over. "I—I think I'm going to puke."

That really got his sympathy. The pain from the gun barrel that was jammed hard into my back straightened me up. "Move."

"I'm sick, I'm telling you, goddamn it!"

"And I'm telling you to shut the fuck up and move," he snarled.

I took a halting step forward, trying to map out my moves, not really having any hope that they would succeed, but laying them out in my mind anyway, knowing that whatever I was going to do was going to have to be soon, before the pug came along.

We went up the steps leading to the killing pen; he reached

over my shoulder and opened the door and we went up onto the concrete walkway. I looked down at the empty cattle shoot, then doubled over again. "I'm going to puke."

He pushed me toward the cement wall. "Puke over the side, then, not toward me."

He moved up behind me and the hairs on the back of my neck stood up as if they'd been charged with static electricity. I felt—not saw, but felt—him point the gun at the back of my head. It was now or never.

I put everything I had into the mule-kick and I felt his knee go. The bullet from the exploding gun whined by my right ear. I whirled, grabbed his legs and wrenched upward as hard as I could and he slammed backward against the wall, hitting his head. The gun clattered to the floor.

I charged him with my head down like Billy Goat Gruff and butted him in the stomach. That bothered him a lot. It was more like hitting a bridge than a troll. He grabbed me around the neck and got me in a chokehold and started to squeeze. My head was against his chest and I could see the gun on the floor below me, but I knew that in a few more seconds I wouldn't be seeing much of anything. I clawed at his fingers but it was like trying to force apart the jaws of a vice, so I grabbed his nuts and squeezed as hard as I could. He shrieked and as his grip around my neck loosened, I punched him twice in the crotch, hard, and he let go completely.

I bent down to pick up the gun, but he brought his good knee up, snapping my head back, and I staggered back against the low wall, my vision blurred by tears.

His face was chalk white now, covered with beads of sweat. He bent down to pick up the gun, but he was in slow motion. I charged again, knocking him off balance, but before I could get the gun, he kicked it away.

It stopped sliding about fifteen feet away and I started after it. He grabbed the back of my shirt to stop me so I used my forward momentum to carry him around me. I threw every ounce of my one-hundred-and-eighty pounds into it and he hit the concrete wall backwards and went over the side. I pulled the lever on the pen and the back fell away and he rolled unconscious onto the killing floor.

Hurried footsteps were coming up the stairs now, and I knew I wouldn't have time to get the gun. I vaulted the wall, dropped down into the pen and scrambled out onto the killing floor.

The floor was slippery; my feet went out from under me and I went down on my can. I got up with a second effort and when I looked at my hands, I realized what I had slipped on. Blood.

"Hey!" I heard the pug yell from the other side of the pen, but I didn't stop to see what he wanted. I turned to run and bumped into something large and heavy and pale.

Terri wouldn't be making it tomorrow. She was completely naked but there was no sex in her now. She was hanging upside down from the chain attached to the ceiling and her long black hair nearly touched the bloody floor. Her eyes were glazed and half-shut as if she were fighting a losing battle with sleep. The back of her head had been blown away and her throat had been cut from ear-to-ear.

I turned away, wanting to vomit, only my growing terror keeping me from it. I ran down the floor beneath the now-still conveyor line and heard the pug land behind me with a grunt. There was a blast and a bullet whanged by my head and bit a chunk out of the cement wall in front of me.

I rounded the corner and ran down the assembly line, dodging behind pieces of equipment in an effort to make myself as unavailable a target as possible. A meat hook lay on a stainless steel table—a thing of pure beauty—and I scooped it up and kept going. I didn't know what good a meat hook was going to do me against a gun, but it felt comforting in my hand.

At the wash tank, I looked back and saw the pug make the corner. He spotted me, took aim and fired. The bullet ricocheted off the metal tank and he took after me at a dead sprint.

I looked around frantically, but there was no place to go. A huge metal door stood about twenty feet away. There didn't appear to be a lock on it and the path to it was clear, sheltered from the pug's line of fire by a series of machines. I ran to it and pulled it open and ducked inside. I was in the cold box.

The room was huge but there was barely room in it to move. Sides of beef hung from the ceiling on chains, wrapped in wet cheesecloth like the cocoons of monstrous insects. I froze in my tracks for a second, awed by the sight, then heard the footsteps behind the door and plunged ahead.

I breast stroked my way through the sea of meat and behind me I heard the cooler door open and shut again. And then, nothing. Nothing but the ringing in my ears from the exploding gun and the steady, monotonous drone of the refrigeration compressors.

I dropped down on all fours so I could see beneath the hanging meat and looked back toward the door. The pug's legs were moving about ten yards from me, slowly, cautiously. Lucky for me a few of his brain cells had died in the ring. At least I had that advantage.

I stuck the meat hook as high as I could reach into the side of beef beside me and pulled myself up, grunting, until I got a good grip on the chain. Once I got myself positioned, I was about four feet from the floor. I estimated the direction he would be coming from and brought the meat hook back into striking position. Then I coughed just to let him know where I was.

I waited. The seconds dragged by. My hand was starting to cramp on the chain.

There was a scraping noise on the floor a few feet away, behind me. He had circled around! The punch-drunk sonofabitch had gotten smart one time in his life and it had to be with me! I could only manage a backhand from the position

I was in and it would be a clumsy backhand at that. I couldn't shift my hold on the chain now. He would hear it and that would be that. Bye, bye, Asch.

I cursed him silently. The side of beef next to mine swung slightly. Or did it move at all? Yes, it was being shoved to one side and the barrel of a .38 poked through and then his head. He wasn't looking up. I swung the hook.

It hit him in the neck, and he threw the gun with a spastic motion and went reeling backwards, taking the hook with him. He made a strange, gurgling sound deep in his throat and fell, clawing wildly at the wooden handle, trying to pull it out. He writhed violently on the floor, his legs thrashing as if he were trying to kick someone. It couldn't have been me. I wasn't even close. I dropped off my perch and located the gun and bolted for the door.

The air on the killing floor hit me like a blast furnace. I stumbled out of the cold box and slammed the door and started out of the place. I didn't get far.

Pain bit into my shoulder as the hook glanced off my back, taking a piece of my sweater with it. I screamed and dropped the gun, accidentally kicking it as I ran forward to get away from the hook which was coming down again, this time at my head. The gun clattered underneath a table out of reach, and I ran out into the center of the floor and whirled around to face Gierak. He was coming at me in a semi-crouch. He looked better. He'd gotten some of his color back and he was grinning.

I backed up, my eyes scanning the area around me for some kind of weapon, any kind, and I cursed myself for dropping the gun. My foot hit something on the floor—the nozzle of a steam-cleaning gun someone had left lying around—and I stumbled. Gierak bellowed like a wounded water buffalo and charged.

I bent down and picked up the steam gun and pulled the trigger. He was almost on top of me when the white blast hit him square in the face and he screamed and grabbed his eyes.

He staggered backwards and his heel hit the edge of the corkscrew-trough and he fell. He reflexively put his arm out to break his fall and it disappeared into the trough. He began screaming. I dropped the steam gun and ran over to him, trying to pull his arm out of the turning corkscrew, but I couldn't budge it. He kept screaming until I thought my nerves were going to snap, and then he passed out from the pain.

I found a piece of rope and used it as a tourniquet around his shoulder and then stumbled outside. I kicked in the door of the superintendent's office and used the phone to call the police.

I WINCED PAINFULLY as I tried to get more comfortable in the hardwood chair. To add insult to injury, my right buttock was asleep. It began to tingle as the blood flowed back into it.

"How's the arm?" Jim asked.

"I'll live," I said. The truth was that the procaine was starting to wear off and it was throbbing like hell, but I didn't say anything about it. I counted myself lucky. If I had been coming out of that cold box just a little slower, it would have taken a lot more than four stitches and a tetanus shot to set things right.

I took out the brown plastic bottle of pain pills the doctor in emergency had given me and shook one out into my hand. "Got some water around here?"

Jim turned to one of the cops at the table, a young detective from Robbery-Homicide named Heller, who looked like an ad for the Dry-Look. "Get him some water."

Heller stood up and left the room, leaving Jim, myself, and the other cop to stare at each other. The cop's name was Sergeant Emerson and he was from C.C.S., L.A.P.D's Criminal Conspiracy Section. He was a stocky man in his middle forties. He had blonde-gray hair and a broad, ruddy face seamed with deep lines. The pale and polished oak table we were sitting around was in a starched, brightly illuminated interrogation room in Parker Center. The clock on the wall said 12:47.

Heller came back carrying a tiny white paper cup filled with water. He walked slowly and kept his eyes on it, obviously afraid he was going to spill it. He seemed relieved when I took it out of his hands. "Thanks," I said, and downed the pill.

He nodded and resumed his place at the table.

"I may be obtuse," I said after putting the pills back into my pocket, "but I still don't get it. Why the hell would they want to kill me?"

Gordon took a sip of coffee from the Styrofoam cup in front of him and said: "Heller here talked to that Cee Jay broad a couple of hours ago. She's in the County Hospital. They pushed her face in pretty good. From what she says, Terri was trying to make a double-payday. Tell him, Heller."

Heller took a breath and said: "Terri had a big mouth. She couldn't keep secrets, especially around her friends and I guess Cee Jay was a pretty close one. They used to share an apartment together last year before Terri moved out and got her own place. Anyway, Terri told Cee Jay she was planning to shake Tortorello down for twenty grand. She was going to collect from both him and Mrs. Fein and then split town with the bread. She must have gone through with the plan because this afternoon, Gierak and his buddy, the bouncer at the New World, came by Cee Jay's place wanting to know where Terri was. Cee Jay wouldn't tell them at first, but then they started punching her around and burning her with cigarette butts and she came up with the name of a motel in Redondo Beach."

"How did I get into the picture?" I asked.

"They must have gotten to the place right as Terri was leaving, to meet with you," Jim interjected. "The time fits. They must have seen her talking to you and reported back to Tortorello and he figured you were in on it."

"How the hell could Tortorello figure I was in on it?"

Jim shrugged. "Maybe he figured he couldn't take the chance, that you knew too much and it was probably safer to get rid of both of you while he was doing it."

"All because Barbara Fein has an unlisted number," I mused. "Remind me to have my number taken out of the fucking phone book."

Emerson guffawed.

"You're sure about Terri trying to shake down Tortorello?"

"That's Cee Jay's story," he said.

"Terri mentioned Tortorello by name?"

"Sure," Jim said, making a face. "Listen, Cee Jay and Terri used to go to some of Tortorello's parties. He'd give them a couple of Cs a piece so they'd make sure everybody had a good time. Cee Jay says she was even in the Crow's Nest when Terri met Fein. She said the whole thing had been set up by Tortorello to make it look like they were just meeting accidentally."

"Yeah, that's the story Terri told, too," I said. "How did they happen to meet Tortorello in the first place?"

"Arthur Browne from the New World took them to one of the parties one time. It started from there. Whenever Tortorello needed some broads, he'd call up Cee Jay and Terri. She said he was always well mannered and was generous with the green stuff."

"I'll bet he was real well mannered when he ordered her butchered, too," Emerson chimed in. "He probably said please and thank you and observed all the social graces."

"That's one thing I still don't get," I said. "Terri wasn't stupid. How could she possibly think in a million years she could get away with trying to shake down Tortorello? She had to know he was connected, for chrissakes."

"From what Cee Jay says, no. Neither of them did."

"Who did they think was running the New World, the Salvation Army?"

"Terri knew the massage parlor was run by a couple of shysters who employed some punk hoods, but that's all she knew. She had no idea she was in the middle of the big leagues. She had no idea who Tortorello was. She thought he owned a restaurant and was a friend of Browne's, but Browne had a lot of friends. Look, the guy is educated and polished and has been through business school. He doesn't look or act like a guy who's plugged into the mob; he seems like just another horny businessman who's loose with his money."

"She had to figure something was up when he asked her to keep Fein busy—"

"Why? She may have had some idea that Tortorello was planning to rip Fein off, but so what? That was no skin off her nose. Things like that happen all the time in business. People screw each other all the time. It's the world's favorite pastime."

"But what about when Fein turned up murdered? It must have dawned on her that something was up."

He leaned back and sighed. "According to Cee Jay, Terri never really believed that Tortorello had anything to do with killing Fein. She just thought she could shake him down by threatening to bring his name into it." He caught my doubting look and said: "Look, she was a hooker with a hooker's brain. She figured she could make a nice killing and split town. End of story. Only she really read it wrong and the end of the story was a lot different than what she'd planned."

The door of the room opened and a uniformed cop stuck his head in. "Sergeant Emerson, telephone call for you."

"Thanks," Emerson said and went out.

The three of us stared at each other silently, then I said: "So why do you think Tortorello had Fein bumped off?"

"That's one I'd like an answer for," Jim said. "My guess is we'll find the answer in Supreme's books." He tilted his head downward and gave me a professorial look over the top of his glasses. "I did a little research since I talked to you last. The profit margin in a packing house is very small—only about one percent—but the volume in dollars and cents is incredible. Supreme is a comparatively small operation. It's only capable of slaughtering about nine hundred head of cattle a day." He paused and wiped off his glasses with a handkerchief which he brandished from his pocket, and went on. "The average side of beef weighs around 350 pounds. The market price right now for undressed sides is about 73¢ a pound. You figure it out. At full operating capacity, an outfit like Supreme kills and disposes of about $460,000 worth of meat a day. It's true that a packer only has a couple of days to pay off a grower for a shipment of beef, but hell, all Tortorello would have to do would be get away with four days' kill and he'd have almost two million bucks. Not bad for a $75,000 investment. If anything was ever invested at all. That $75,000 Tortorello says he paid Fein might have just been a bookkeeping entry. In the end, after he'd drained off the money, Tortorello could just walk away and Supreme would be bankrupt. Not only would he have the cash he's siphoned off, but he'd have a nice deduction for his income taxes."

"Yeah, but if Supreme went bankrupt, there would be an investigation. How the hell could Tortorello get away with that kind of money without having the law come down on him?"

"Who's to prove anything? Listen, a guy like Tortorello, who's been through business school, would know just how to dribble the money away in bits and pieces so that nobody would be able to pin down where the hell it was going. Supreme is an old firm and has a good line of credit, that's why he probably picked it. The first thing he'd do is expand its credit base by extending its list of suppliers. If Fein was dealing with two suppliers, Tortorello would contract with five or six. He'd pay on time for a while, keeping them all happy, and when he was ready, he'd start juggling the money around —pay one off a few days late, stall off another one, but always paying off so that they wouldn't revoke his credit. Every week he'd pay off one day later, but the suppliers would be lulled to sleep because they always got their money. Pretty soon, he'd have four or five or six days credit from five suppliers instead of two days credit from two. Then, one morning, he'd file bankruptcy papers and walk off with six or seven million dollars."

"Is that what you think those extra shipments of beef were all about?"

"Could be."

"But how could he get away with it, that's what I want to know. How the hell could he convert that kind of money to cash without somebody getting wise? Granted, I'm no financial wizard, but—"

"Any number of ways. Look, Jake, it's done all the time. He could have a retail outlet of his own he ships beef to with dummy invoices. He could have a kickback scheme worked out with a couple of growers, overpay them and get the cash back. He could set up some dummy corporation and sink a chunk of Supreme's money in it. He could start drawing money out of the bank and enter it on the books as officers' loans. He could arrange a fake theft. Any goddamn thing. Listen, there are ninety-nine ways to catch a thief, but there are a hundred ways to steal."

"Tortorello could claim that Fein had gambled away the money," I said. "If he was dead, nobody would be able to say any different."

"That thought crossed my mind. Or he could have guessed what was happening and threatened to go to the cops. Or he could have just been in the way."

"One thing bothers me," Heller cut in. "If Tortorello had his boys hit Fein, why didn't they just grind him up into hamburger like they were going to do with the girl? Why lock him in the trunk of a car and leave him around where he'd be found?"

I looked at Jim. He rubbed his chin and said: "Maybe we'll be able to get the answer to that one from Gierak and his buddy." He turned to me. "The pug's name is Robert Carcinero by the way. You did a nice job on him. He's on the critical list."

"I'm sorry," I said. "I should've asked them if I could make one phone call before they strung me up and cut my throat. That way you could have had them both intact and you could've gotten them on three counts of murder instead of just two."

He didn't say anything to that. He just frowned. He took a cigar out of his pocket, snipped off the end and lighted it. I didn't say anything. I knew my entreaties would fall on deaf ears. "How is Gierak, by the way?"

He looked at me impassively. "He'll live. That tourniquet of yours saved his life."

Heller sneered. "You should've let the asshole bleed to death. It just would've meant one less on the street."

"He isn't going to be on the street for a long time," Jim said. "Besides, he'll only be half a problem. He'll only have one arm."

"Between the courts and the goddamn doctors today," Heller said, "they'll probably turn him loose with a bionic arm or something and we'll have the Six Million Dollar Man running around, twisting people's heads off like bottle caps."

The door opened and Emerson came back in with a strange smirk on his face. "That was Catalano from the F.B.I. I called him at home earlier and he contacted some people in St. Louis. Guess what?"

Jim took the cigar out of his mouth. "Surprise me."

"Tortorello is D'Augustino's nephew."

Jim came forward in his chair and slammed the palm of his hand on the table. "Shit! Those fucking bastards!" His face was livid. "I talked to Catalano this morning. He said he'd never heard of Tortorello."

"He says he hadn't this morning," Emerson said. "He claims nobody bothered to notify him because as far as anybody knew, Tortorello was clean. He owned a restaurant in St. Louis before he came out here and that's all. Apparently, he's never been within a hundred miles of anything dirty."

Jim waved his cigar in the air. "He knew, the lying sonofabitch. Those Feds will come in and take everything out of our files, but ask them for something and all you get is a line of bullshit."

Emerson sighed and nodded, then went over to the coffee maker and poured himself a cup. "Think we have a chance of getting D'Augustino tied up in this?"

"Hell," Jim spat out, "we'll be lucky if we get Tortorello. It all depends on those two assholes in intensive care. If we crack them, we've got a chance to nail him. If not, I doubt it." He turned to me and stared. "I'm going to put you under protective custody, starting tonight."

I looked up sharply. "What for?"

"Because you're the only eyewitness against those two."

"All I'm a witness to is my own kidnapping. I didn't see them kill Terri. Besides, Tortorello isn't going to be worried about me. He's going to be worried about those two gorillas turning state's evidence."

He looked at the wet end of his cigar, then back at me. "That's right. And if the pressure is off those two, there's a lot less chance they'll turn state's evidence. You are their main source of pressure right now. You and Cee Jay. And we've got her under guard at the hospital."

"I don't want any protection," I said.

He studied my face as if to determine my resolve. "I can lock you up as a material witness."

"You could lock me up until my lawyer got me out," I told him. "Look, it's going to be eight weeks before you get a trial date and then Tortorello's attorney will get it postponed fourteen times after that. I spent six months in stir once and I'm not going to go through that again. Not for you, not for anybody."

He turned up the palm of one hand. "We'll get a hotel room. You won't be in jail."

"No."

He leaned back and raised one eyebrow. "I could book you for assault with intent to commit murder."

We stared at each other. I shrugged but inside I was seething. When it came down to it, I knew he would not do it, but even the fact that he would throw it in my face made me mad. "Take your best shot, Jim. Do whatever you have to do, but I'm not going to be locked up in any fucking hotel room or anywhere else for three months."

He sighed loudly and threw up his hands. "All right, all right. I'll give you a phone number you can call in case you get into trouble."

"If I get into trouble," I said, "I have a feeling I won't be able to get to a phone quick enough for it to do me much good."

He looked at the others and said laughingly: "What the hell are you going to do with a guy like this?"

Nobody answered him. Jim was smiling easily, but the strain still hung in the air between us, thick, like his cigar smoke. "We'll get complaints drawn up tomorrow. You'd better go home and get some sleep. You look like the wrath of God."

"Thanks," I said, and stood up. I felt a little light-headed from the pill. Jim must have noticed it, because he asked in a concerned voice: "You want me to have somebody drive you home?"

"I can make it."

He looked at the others again. "See what I mean? What the hell are you going to do with a guy like this? Stubborn as a fucking mule."

I didn't think that needed any amplification from me, so I didn't attempt it. I didn't attempt to shake hands with anybody, either. My arm hurt too badly.

The drive home was lonely. The goddamn world was lonely. When I got to my apartment, I took a shower, taking care to follow doctor's orders and not get my stitches wet and taking care to disobey doctor's orders by downing two stiff bourbons.

That sent the room spinning. I got into bed and tried to

sleep but it wasn't because of the arm that I couldn't. I kept seeing Terri hanging upside down above me like a side of beef, the wound at her throat gaped at me like some obscene, leering smile. Finally, I got up and turned on the tube and watched the end of some dumb western.

It was almost two-thirty when I got the bright idea to call Mrs. Fein. I don't know what prompted it—maybe the combination of the booze and the pills. I know I was pretty far gone, but I started thinking, hell, she's got the right to know what's happened. She'd want to know who killed her husband. Hell yes, she would. I picked up the phone and dialed her number.

After four rings, a man's voice said sleepily: "Hello?"

I was listening through a gauze-wrapped fog, but it seemed to me the voice was that of Mark Fein. I've dialed the wrong number, I thought, and sat with the phone in my hand, not saying anything.

"Hello?" he said again. I put the receiver gently back on the hook.

The room was really spinning now and the last thing I needed was another drink, so I went into the kitchen and fixed myself one and took it to bed with me.

By the time I had finished it, Terri was gone, but I went to sleep with the lights on, just in case she came back.

· 21 ·

IT HAD BEEN three weeks and according to Jim everything was cool, at least as far as I was concerned.
The day after the Supreme incident, he and a couple of boys from the Federal Strike Force had visited with Mr. D'Augustino in his Bel-Air home and dropped the subtle hint that they didn't think it would be such a good idea if Cee Jay or I got hit. Otherwise, a lot of doors might start getting kicked in that Mr. D. and some of his associates would rather have remain shut. Jim had reenacted the scene for me in his office, taking the part of D'Augustino, rolling his eyes and expressing in soft, persuasive tones that to his knowledge there was no plan afoot to eliminate anyone named Asch from the face of the earth.

Gierak and Carcinero stood indicted on one count of murder (Terri) and one count each of assault, kidnapping, and attempted murder (me), and although Jim had hopes of using some of the time facing them as a club to get them to finger Tortorello as the man who had given the orders, as yet he was having no success. There was no physical evidence that could pull either of them into the Fein murder yet, so that file was still open. Tortorello had not been charged with anything due to the lack of hard evidence, but the homicide boys were working on it, trying to dig up something they could make stick.

Jim's assumptions about what was going on at Supreme were turning out to be true. Since Tortorello had taken over as general manager, the number of outfits supplying cattle to Supreme had gone from three to five and Tortorello had applied for credit with two more. During the past month, a little over $200,000 had been converted into cash and mysteriously disappeared. Proving just who had waved his magic wand over the money and made it disappear, however, was going to be another matter, especially with David Fein dead.

The funeral service for David Fein had been held nearly three weeks before, at Hillside Mortuary. It had been sparsely attended. Tortorello had been diplomatically absent. Barbara Fein had worn a dark gray dress and her face had had a pale, gaunt look that added an appealing fragility to her beauty. I'd wanted to say something to her, utter some deep and meaningful truth that would immediately lighten her load of grief, but all I'd managed to come up with was my usual silver-tongued, "I'm sorry. If there's anything I can do. . . ." Not that it mattered. From the looks of things, she was being adequately comforted by Mark Fein, who had stood throughout the entire graveside service with his arm wrapped around her shoulders like a shawl.

The funeral had been the last time I had seen or heard from anyone involved in the case, (except Jim, of course, with whom I checked in periodically, out of curiosity and a well-developed sense of self-preservation), and to tell the truth, I had sort of purposely shoved the entire thing to the back of my mind. Every time I thought about Tortorello running around unscathed by the whole affair, my blood pressure went up twenty points, so I tried not to think about it.

I was currently working for an attorney, running a background check on a man who was suing his writer-client for libel. I was downtown running a D & B on the clown when I decided to check my messages.

"7712," Penny said.

Every time she answered the phone, I went through a

period of agonizing indecision. I was still trying to decide whether to ask her out for a drink. "Hello, Penny dear. This is Jacob Asch, private eye. Any messages?"

"Let me see. Yes, Mr. Asch. One call from a Mr. Zimmerman. He left a number. 349-0891. He said it was important."

"Thanks, Penny. And we've known each other long enough for you to start calling me Jake. Mr. Asch was my father."

"Ooooohh, I couldn't do that," she whispered, "Mrs. Cranston would fire me."

"That old bitch? Never mind about her. We'll have to get together for a drink sometime soon and talk about that—"

"Anytime," she said quickly.

I felt a twinge of nervousness. Had she jumped so fast out of sheer desperation? Did she sit home every night because she weighed three hundred pounds and had pimples?

"We'll definitely do it," I said, regretting it the minute it was out.

The number Penny had given me belonged to some outfit called Coastline Wine and Spirits. I had no idea what Mr. Zimmerman's position there was, but it was enough of one to warrant his own office and secretary.

Zimmerman's voice was old, but firm, with a thick Jewish accent. He thanked me for calling back so promptly and then asked me to meet him for lunch. He said he had a confidential matter he would like to discuss with me. He suggested Perino's at noon.

Perino's is probably L.A.'s finest restaurant. It is also probably the stuffiest and the most expensive, which is why people have not exactly broken down its doors to get in. It has only managed to survive by the good graces of the Chandlers and the Otises and a few other of Los Angeles' First Families who have generously subsidized the operation to insure that they had a place to eat.

Benjamin Zimmerman must have eaten there quite often because he knew the maitre d' and the chef by their first names. He also knew his food and his wines, so I let him do the ordering for both of us. He started with a wilted lettuce salad and graduated to veal piccata with a side of fetuccini and a bottle of some vintage white wine I couldn't even pronounce, not being able to speak French. And he did it all without batting an eye, even though the bill would come to around fifty bucks.

He was a small, wizened little man who looked as if he had shriveled inside his blue suit that appeared almost as old as he was. It had wide lapels and padded shoulders that made him look as if he had forgotten to take the hanger out. He had a narrow, hooked nose and deep-set, penetrating eyes and a small, ascetic mouth with thin lips that were almost blue in color. His hair was white and extremely fine, spread across his parched scalp like spun glass.

He took a bite of salad, then raised his wine glass in a salute to me. "L'Chaim."

I mirrored the salute and took a sip of wine. Zimmerman smiled and turned to the head waiter, who was hovering obsequiously over the table. "Excellent," he said.

The waiter nodded stiffly and moved away from the table.

"You have a very good reputation, Mr. Asch," he said, wiping his mouth with a napkin. His hand motions were like his speech, slow, but very steady. There was no trace of a trembling in his fingers, even though he must have been in his seventies. "That's the reason I called you. I was assured you could handle this little matter, er, shall we say discreetly?"

I waited for him to go on and when he didn't, I said: "What matter is that, Mr. Zimmerman?"

He looked at me and smiled paternally. "First of all, may I call you Jacob?"

"Sure."

He nodded. "My brother was named Jacob. The name has an Old Testament strength to it that appeals to me." He stopped and touched me lightly on the forearm with his right hand. The back of his hand was pale, crisscrossed with a network of blue veins. "You're a Jewish boy, aren't you?"

"Half," I said.

He raised his eyebrows and smiled, as if to say, ah well, half is better than none. "Your father married a Gentile girl?"

"Yes," I said, trying to hide my annoyance at the meandering conversation.

"You go to Temple?"

"Not as regularly as I should," I lied. The last time I had been was ten years ago, at Yom Kippur, and then I'd only gone to make my father happy. When he had died, I had no one to make happy, so I had not bothered to go back. But I didn't want to burst Zimmerman's bubble, so I said nothing.

"Where did you grow up?" he asked, after a pause.

"Here. L.A."

He leaned back in his chair. "A native. You don't find many of them out here. I've been on the coast myself for about thirty years. I'm originally from St. Louis."

His eyes sparkled as they studied my face, waiting to see how I would take that. I was not taking it well—there was a little alarm bell going off in the back of my mind—but I concentrated on keeping my face as blank as I could.

"Tony Tortorello—Steven's father—has been a dear friend of mine for many years. We used to work together in St. Louis. When the distillers we both worked for opened a subsidiary out here, I came out, but Tony stayed back there."

I was suddenly very sorry I had said he could call me Jacob. I still didn't say anything.

"Yes, it's a shame about what's happened to Steven," he said, shaking his head. "It's really broken Tony's heart. He had hopes for the boy, you know how it is with a father. He called me from St. Louis last night and poured his heart out to me. He's an old man now, in his late seventies, and he hasn't got much longer left. Maybe a few years. He's really sick about this whole thing. It's really upsetting him. Steven's basically a good boy, a good son. He's got his faults—he's a little wild—but that comes from being young. Tony asked me to see what I could do to help Steven out. You can understand his concern."

"The D.A. hasn't pressed charges against Tortorello yet."

"Tony wants to make sure that doesn't happen."

"Then tell him to talk to the D.A., not me," I said gruffly. "I'm not the foreman of the Grand Jury."

"I realize that, Jacob," he said in a soft voice. "But you see, Tony can't believe his son had anything to do with the murder of that fellow—what's his name? Fein. He feels that they're going to try to railroad Steven for it."

"I doubt that. He'll get a fair trial. If he ever goes to trial."

He sighed regretfully. "I wish we could be sure of that. Unfortunately, our system of justice isn't infallible, as you well know. People get overzealous. Things happen. Innocent men do get convicted. You've probably handled more than one case in which you've saved an innocent man from false charges. Tony is worried about that. You see, he feels that Steven is going to have his hands full with legal matters in the next few months without having that hanging over his head, too."

I watched him carefully. His eyes burned like a banked fire in the old skull. "What do you want, Mr. Zimmerman?"

He tapped me on the arm with two fingers. "Bear with an old man, Jacob. I realize all this must be hard for you to understand and I know youth must be served—"

"Frequently smothered with mushrooms," I said.

"Pardon me?"

"Look, Mr. Zimmerman, let's get one thing straight: I don't care if Steven Tortorello takes the Big Pill or not. He's not one of my favorite people. He ordered me strung up and butchered like a goddamn steer without the benefit of a rabbi there to make sure it was done kosher-style. Whether that's ever proven in court or whether his father believes it or not, I don't give a shit. I know it. So you can't really expect me to sympathize with his plight right now. As a matter of fact, I hope they throw the book at him and make it stick."

He smiled understandingly. "You've got to realize I'm just an innocent party in all this. I know nothing about what happened to you, although I'm sure from what you've just said that it must have been a traumatic experience. I'm just doing a favor for a friend. I owe him that much."

"What kind of favor is that? You still haven't elucidated that point yet."

He shrugged. "The boys around the office have taken up a little collection. A lot of them used to work with Tony, too. So what are you going to give an old man for a present? We've sort of put together a little defense fund and we decided to hire you."

I must have looked stupid. My mouth was hanging open. I closed it. "To do what?"

"To find out who killed David Fein."

"I don't get it. If Steve Tortorello wants to offer me a bribe, why the hell doesn't he just come right out and do it? Why send you to blow good money on an expensive lunch? Hell, we could've eaten at the Golden Steer, except I'd have probably felt a little uneasy, if you want to know the truth. I wouldn't have been sure just who I was eating."

The words poured out rapidly. I was feeling slightly manic.

"Steven didn't send me, Jacob," Zimmerman said quietly. "To my knowledge, he doesn't even know his father contacted me. Like I said, Tony and I are old friends—"

"Sure. Okay. Old friends. I love old friends. If you're going to have friends, old ones are the best kind to have. You can go back and tell your old friend, Mr. Zimmerman—and the 'boys in the office' while you're at it—that I don't have to dig around because I already know who killed Fein. Steven Tortorello killed Fein. He paid a couple of grand to his trained animals and said, 'Kill,' and that's just what they did, they killed. They were kind of messy about it, too. They strung Terri up by her heels and slit her throat and caved Fein's head in and left him in the trunk of his car. Ever smell a body after it has rotted in the trunk of a car for four days, Mr. Zimmerman? It's a smell that is beyond a smell."

I had hoped to spoil his lunch, but he gave no outward sign that my soliloquy had affected his appetite. He took another forkful of lettuce and gazed at me steadily. "If that's what your investigation turns up, you'll still be paid. I wouldn't expect you to compromise the truth. I know too much about you. But, Jacob, Tony is convinced Steven is innocent. He and others."

"What others?"

He smiled, but didn't say anything. He twirled the stem of his wine glass slowly, between his thumb and a gnarled index finger.

"Maybe Tortorello is giving his father a snow job."

"No," he said definitely. I did not like the certainty in his voice. It made me doubt and I did not like to doubt. Not about what he was talking about. "Steven had no real motive for killing Fein."

"A couple of million dollars is a hell of a motive. He could have pulled that much out of Supreme within a month without any problem at all once he started things rolling full steam."

He gave me a disappointed look. "Let me ask you this, Jacob, because I know you're a bright boy—a thinker, I can tell by your eyes—if you were going to bankrupt Supreme Packing, would you kill Fein, or would you use him as a cover?"

"What do you mean?"

"Simple. I mean, as long as Fein was around, you could drain the business dry and claim Fein was taking the money to cover his gambling debts, couldn't you?"

"And with Fein dead, nobody would be able to prove any differently."

He held up a finger and his eyes twinkled. "From a logistical standpoint, I'm willing to grant you that that might be a good move to make. But would you make it before you'd finished what you were doing or after?"

His eyes probed mine, greedy for the answer. Instead, I answered him with a question. "And as long as we're speculating, what if Fein discovered what I was doing and threatened to lower the boom? I'd almost have to kill him, wouldn't I?"

He shrugged. "Not necessarily. But assuming you did, once his body was discovered, the boom would be lowered anyway, wouldn't it? The police would start poking their noses around looking for a motive and whatever you had planned would have to be put off indefinitely. Which brings us to another logistical problem: Say you, an intelligent capable young man, were put in a position where you had to murder Fein. Would you leave his body around where it could be found, or would you dispose of it so that it would never be found?"

"You mean, à la Terri?"

"You're talking about the girl they found in the packing-house?"

"Yes," I said. "The girl your good friend's son used to get to Fein."

The remark bounced off him like a rubber bullet. He seemed preoccupied with other thoughts. "That's precisely what I mean."

I didn't tell him that that thought had already been brought up within the hallowed walls of Parker Center by a couple of cops working the case, and returned his stare, deadpan. If he was going to score any points, I didn't want them to show on the tote board. "Tortorello was the only one with a motive for wanting Fein out of the way, Mr. Zimmerman."

He smiled and brought up from his lap a manila envelope. I had noticed it when he carried it in, but had forgotten about it since then. He handed it across the table to me.

I bent open the metal clasps and pulled out the contents. It was a Xeroxed copy of a life insurance policy made out to David Fein. The company was Aetna Life and Casualty and the amount was $250,000. It was dated February 2, 1971. The beneficiary was Barbara Fein.

I picked up the envelope and shook it, once. "Where'd you get this? Insurance information is classified stuff."

"I have friends," he said.

"Yeah, I know. Old ones. That routine's getting old. Let's drop it." I put the stuff down on the table in front of me and said: "So what's it supposed to mean?"

"$250,000 is a lot of money. Especially considering Fein had mortgaged everything he owed to pay off his gambling debts."

"A couple of million is a lot more," I said.

"That's true," he said. "And I didn't mean anything by showing you that, except that there are other people who might have had a motive to kill Fein. At least you have to admit that perhaps it should be looked into before Steven is condemned for a crime he didn't commit. We assume in this country that a man shouldn't be presumed guilty until all the facts are in, don't we?" He raised an eyebrow and watched me craftily. "For example, Fein's brother—the doctor. He is recently divorced."

"That's a crime?" I asked. "Everyone I know—including myself—is divorced."

He shook his head sadly. "That's one trouble with the world today. Too many divorces. Young people today are flighty, they don't share the old values, family and the home—"

"What about Mark Fein?" I cut in. I was not in the mood to hear a lecture on the old values, especially from him.

He shrugged helplessly. "I'm not one to spread gossip, Jacob, I'm really not, but from what I hear, he is very friendly with his sister-in-law. For recently being widowed, she spends a lot of time with him. Too much, maybe. I realize they're family and it's a time when families pull together and comfort one another, but people are starting to talk."

"You've made your point, Zimmerman," I said. "You seem to already have somebody doing work on this. Why not just let him continue. Why come to me with it?"

"I don't have anybody working on it in the sense you mean. Some friends have made some inquiries for me, that's all," he said in a tone that was meant to be casual. "They are just people who know other people. What Tony would like is a professional on the job. You're the most logical person. You've already been digging around in Fein's past. Besides, like I said earlier, you've got a reputation for tenacity."

"My tenacity nearly got me made into a bunch of Jacob Aschburgers," I said. "But that isn't why you want me on this job."

He raised an eyebrow. "No?"

"No," I said. "You want me on it because one, you know I've got an open line into the D.A.'s office, and two, if Tortorello is my client, I wouldn't be likely to testify against him."

He smiled proudly, as a father would smile at a son who just came home with a straight-A report card.

"I don't take bribes," I said. "And I don't take money from hoods."

"Tony is not a hood," he said sternly. "He is just a father very concerned about his son. Surely you can understand his feelings—"

"I'm tired of hearing about Tortorello's feelings. I don't give a shit about his feelings."

His expression never changed, the smile still lingered on his lips. "Someday, Jacob, you'll be a father and you'll know what he's going through."

"That's probably the reason I never did become a father. I was afraid my son would turn out to be a big disappointment to me. I don't think I could handle it if he turned out to be a slimeball like Steve Tortorello. It'd be just too much of a trauma for me to bear."

He touched my hand again, knowingly, and said: "The boys around the office have chipped in generously, Jacob. We're going to pay you double your normal rate, plus a substantial bonus—say, five thousand dollars?—if you come up with Fein's killer—"

"No."

He sighed and leaned back in his chair and shook his head.

It was probably an illusion—everything the man did was an exercise in the Stanislavsky method—but the regret in his eyes seemed deep and real. "Well, then, I'm prepared to offer you something else. Something that I'm sure will mean more to you than the money."

"What's that?"

"How old are you, Jacob?"

"Thirty-five. Why?"

He smiled and patted me gently on the shoulder. "I'm going to offer you your thirty-sixth birthday."

· 22 ·

M R. BENJAMIN ZIMMERMAN WAS a mystery to everyone. Jim had run his name through the FBI and it had come back clean. Ostensibly, at least, he was who he said he was. He had been working for Coastline Wine and Spirits for the past twenty-two years, and for fifteen of those he had been the vice-president in charge of sales. He had not been lying when he said that he and Tortorello had worked for the same outfit, either. A call to St. Louis confirmed that before he retired, old man Tortorello had worked for Trans-National Liquor Distributors, the corporation that owned Coastline.

A check on Tony Tortorello had come back negative, also. He was clean. His son was clean. Zimmerman was clean. It was a very hygienic crowd. That made me feel good. At least if I was going to be offed, it would be by *clean* people.

During lunch at Perino's (of which I did not each much; I had suddenly had a loss of appetite), Zimmerman had said he would give me a couple of days to think about his offer. It had been a couple of days and I still hadn't heard from him, which was all right, because I still had not decided what the hell I was going to do. Jim wanted to put a bug on my phone and get Zimmerman on tape when he called, but I vetoed that idea. A lot of my clients called me at home and I didn't think it would go over too big with them if they found out that the D.A. was monitoring all of their conversations. That upset him, but he was no more upset than I was. He wasn't the one who was going to be blown away.

If Zimmerman had been a six-foot-six, three hundred pound thug, it wouldn't be bothering me as much as it was. But when you got to be as old as Zimmerman was in that business, you didn't make idle threats. People don't bluff in the Syndicate and live a long time. But there was something else about Zimmerman that bothered me, perhaps even more than his vague allusions to my possible impending execution unless I played ball. A lot of the things he said made a hell of a lot of sense, and they kept running through my mind, over and over, keeping me awake nights. What if he was telling the truth? Were the police so sure Tortorello was guilty they were blinding themselves to every other possibility? I kept flashing on that call the night of the Supreme incident and Mark Fein's voice answering the phone . . . I had to constantly keep shuffling my thoughts around to keep the seeds of doubt he had planted from sprouting to the surface. Hell, the whole thing was probably just what I'd told him it was, a bribe to make sure I didn't get up on the witness stand and point a finger at Tortorello.

In the meantime, I was still working on the libel case for my attorney friend. The plaintiff in the case was a hotsy-totsy real estate developer my friend's writer-client had done a rather derogatory magazine piece on. I had spent the afternoon in the County Assessor's office digging into some old land deals the developer had been involved in and had come up with some things I was sure would tickle the attorney's fancy. I was on my way home, fighting the rush-hour freeway traffic, thinking about nothing except how good a hot shower was going to feel.

The twilight was blackening quickly into night and the taillights of the cars ahead merged into one along the concrete glacier that ran down the pass to the San Fernando

Valley. The Santa Monica Boulevard exit finally loomed up ahead and I signaled and started to edge over toward the ramp. I glanced in my rearview mirror and noticed a Ford station wagon pulling up fast on my left, his right blinker flashing madly. Lucky I did and braked, because the wagon roared by and cut in front of me, nearly taking off a piece of my bumper. I caught a glimpse of the lone driver as he shot past—a heavyset man with long hair and a beard, dressed in an Army flak jacket.

I swore and hit my horn. That must have made him mad because he instantly put his foot on his brakes and began slowing down, just to show me who was boss. He slowed down to twenty miles an hour as we headed down the ramp, then ten, then five. The smart-ass bastard.

I leaned on my horn. That didn't seem to bother him a bit. We were barely crawling now, at five miles an hour. I was still leaning on the horn when the back window of the wagon began to roll down automatically. What the hell . . . ?

I watched in mute horror as a man in a gray ski mask and an Army flak jacket like the driver had on sat up in the back and levelled a pump-action twelve-gauge shotgun at my face. The bore on the gun looked as big as the Black Hole of Calcutta.

The whole thing from beginning to end took place in no more than five seconds, but each of those seconds was segmented in my mind into separate and distinct eternities. I glanced up in my rearview mirror and saw the grill of a Mack truck riding up my tail pipe, then jerked my head from side to side, looking for a place to go. Nowhere. Jesus. There was a steep concrete embankment to my left and to the right was a high curb on the other side of which was a patch of ice plant.

I probably would have picked the ice plant if I had had time, but I didn't. The shotgun roared and I caught a yellow flash of the flame as I fell sideways in my seat. Pellets rained off the windshield like hailstones and when my foot left the gas, the truck rear-ended me, pushing the car up the curb and onto the patch of ice plant.

I scrambled to the door on the passenger side, keeping my head below the line of the windshield and jumped out. As I crawled on all fours to the back of the car, the tires of the station wagon screamed, and I popped my head up just in time to see it hanging a right on Santa Monica Boulevard and taking off.

I stood up. Up to that point, there had not been time to do anything else but react blindly, instinctively, but suddenly everything caught up with me. My diaphragm started pumping like a bellows and I started shaking and my knees turned to water. Using the car for support, I made my way to the open door and sat down. I looked at my face in the rearview mirror. It was the same face, paler now, but there were no white hairs I could see. You never could tell, though; there might be a delayed reaction with these things. Maybe I would wind up with a swath of white cut down the center of my scalp like Humphrey Bogart in the *Return of Dr. X*.

The driver of the Mack truck had stopped in the middle of the ramp and was out of the cab. Traffic was backing up the ramp onto the freeway and the din of angry horns was swelling. I barely heard them. I felt slightly nauseous.

The trucker ran to my car and put his hand on my shoulder. "You okay, buddy?"

He glanced at me with rapid, nervous eyes.

I nodded dumbly.

"Fuck, those guys tried to kill you," he said in an excited tone.

I nodded again.

"I'll call the CHP."

I didn't nod to that. There didn't seem to be any need.

He bent down and looked at me searchingly. "You okay, buddy? You don't look so good."

"I'm okay," I said. My voice was a whisper.

"You're sure?"

I nodded.

"You stay here," he said, backing away. "I'll call the CHP."

I can't do much else, I thought, as the clamorous noise of the horns rose in my ears. There's no place else to go.

The world was just one lonely little island of ice plant and I didn't care if I ever left it. . . .

"**B**IRD SHOT," JIM SAID, staring in amazement at the little copper BB he rolled around between his thumb and forefinger. "I don't even believe it. The assholes used bird shot."

"Lucky for him they did," Emerson said gravely. "It didn't even crack the windshield. If it'd been a standard magnum shell, it would've taken his head off."

We were in Parker Center again, sitting around a different table that looked the same as the other table in a different interrogation room that looked the same as the other room. I was only half-listening to what they were saying. I was half in the bag from the bourbon-laced coffee I had been drinking for the past half hour. Jim had thoughtfully stopped off on his way over and picked up a half-pint. I looked at the hand holding the ubiquitous Styrofoam cup. It had stopped shaking.

"Maybe they were trying to give me a warning," I said.

Jim shook his head. "They already gave you a warning. They told you what was going to happen. They don't give out warnings like this. No, these guys were just assholes." He shook his head in disgust. "Bird shot. Jesus Christ. One day I'm going to sit down and write a best seller about the myth of the Mafia hit-man. The guy in the sharkskin suit with the attaché case with the silencer and the rifle with the telescopic sight inside. Most all of these guys are just losers—small-time slimy creeps who are looking for some extra bread to pay for their old ladies' dental bills. Hell, just last month, there was a case where two guys went to hit some biggie in New York. They ran up along both sides of the car, stuck their guns in the windows, and shot each other—real Charles Bronson types."

Emerson chuckled at that one. "No shit? I didn't hear about that one."

"Yeah," Jim said. "It happened just last month. In Queens, I think—"

"Okay, you two," I butted in. "The anecdotes are really amusing and all that, but I'm not really in the mood to hear them right now. What I want to know is who the hell tried to have me blown away and why?"

The smiles died and Emerson said: "We've got an APB out on the car and we're running your description of the driver through every source we've got. We're pulling in all our snitches to see if any of them have seen anybody around who looks like that. We should get something back pretty soon."

"So the guy cuts his hair and shaves," I said. "Then where are you?"

"I doubt he grew a beard just for this job," Emerson said.

"I want to know who ordered the fucking job and why," I repeated.

"Don't you think I'd like to know the same thing?" Jim asked. "Look, Jake, I've had my ear to the ground for three weeks and haven't heard a word of anything like this going down—"

"Somehow, I'm losing faith in your information network, Jim. First, nobody's heard of Tortorello and then Tortorello turns out to be D'Augustino's nephew. Then nobody's heard of Zimmerman—"

"I've got something on Zimmerman," he said.

I sunk my teeth into the edge of the Styrofoam cup and said: "What?"

He made an expository gesture and said: "Well, not exactly on Zimmerman, but on Coastline Wine and Spirits. You remember I told you Coastline is owned by Trans-National Liquor Distributors, the company old man Tortorello worked for in St. Louis? Well, get this: Trans-National is the exclusive distributor of Royal Bagpiper's Scotch. The reason it's the exclusive distributor of Royal Bagpiper's Scotch is because it's owned by the Royal Bagpiper's Distillers of Edinburgh, Scotland. Royal Bagpiper's Distillers is owned by a company called Allied Distributors in New York, which is owned by another New York corporation, Mary Ellen Confectioners." He paused meaningfully and one eyebrow became a question mark. "Guess who owns Mary Ellen Confectioners?"

"For shit's sake," I said. "My head nearly gets blown off and you want to play the $25,000 Pyramid—"

"Arnold Gelson," he said.

I felt as if an ice cube had just been shoved up my ass. Arnold Gelson. The financial wizard of the Syndicate, sometimes called the Computer because of his lightning-quick mind and his prodigious facility for mathematics. A man, who at seventy-eight, had survived all of the gangland vendettas and emerged as the unofficial head of organized crime in America. And he had accomplished it all being a Jew, without even possessing a vote on the council of the Unione Siciliano. He had managed to survive because he was tough and ruthless, but more importantly, because he was indispensable. He had just made everybody too damn much money to get gotten rid of.

"Jesus Christ," I shouted. "You mean to tell me I'm going to have Arnold Gelson on my ass unless I start working for Zimmerman?"

He held up the palms of his hands in an attempt to calm me down. "I don't mean that at all. I'd lay a hundred to one Gelson has never heard your name and probably never will. You don't think he has time to worry about what the hell's happening to the punk nephew of D'Augustino, do you? This whole thing is going down at a very low level, I'd lay money on it—"

"I'm not asking you to lay money on it," I said, waving my hands wildly. "I just want some assurances, that's all. I thought you said you talked to D'Augustino."

"I did. He says he didn't know of any contract being put out on you. He didn't seem to think his nephew was in any kind of trouble his attorneys couldn't handle."

"Well, somebody sure as hell passed some bucks to somebody," I said.

"The question is who."

"Why don't you pick up Tortorello and ask him?"

He shrugged. "We could do that. But he wouldn't give out any answers. He'd just call his lawyer and that would be that."

"You've got to be able to charge him with something and make it stick," I said. My voice sounded frustrated, probably because I was feeling frustrated.

He looked at me steadily. "What? You tell me."

"How about murder for starters?"

He came forward in his chair and put his hands palms up on the table. "Whose? Terri's? Prove it. Gierak and Carcinero aren't talking. Trying to prove anything without their testimony would be a nice job. All we've got tying them to Tortorello is the fact that they had access to Supreme— Gierak had a set of keys on him to the back gates—but we can't prove how he got the keys. We've got no proof that either of them were working for Tortorello or ever worked for Tortorello."

"What about Cee Jay? Terri told her about Tortorello—"

"That's hearsay," he cut me off sharply. "It's inadmissable in court. How are you going to prove Terri wasn't just throwing out a name to Cee Jay? There was no record of that call being made from the switchboard of the motel she was staying in, which means she probably made it from a pay phone." He paused and drummed his fingertips on top of the table.

"There isn't one goddamn shred of physical evidence tying Tortorello to Terri's murder or Fein's murder. So now, you tell me what to charge him with."

I shook my head. "I wouldn't try to tell you anything. You're the attorney. You know all the rules of the game, and that's all it is—a game. All I know is that I'm sick and tired of hearing about the technicalities of law and debating Robert's Rules of Order with a bunch of two-bit hoods. I've had it, Jim." I stood up and looked down at both of them. "You know what's coming, don't you? I hope you do, because you'd have to be pretty goddamn blind not to. You can't stop these people. Justice doesn't mean a damn thing in the system anymore. It isn't who's telling the truth that matters, it's who can twist the facts and make them sound better to a jury. A guy like Tortorello makes ten times what you do in a year. You can hire an awful lot of legal talent for that."

He looked at me as if I were some homeless pathetic animal in the pound. "You really believe that?"

"You're damn right I believe that. So do these assholes. They've got to if they keep on winning. And it's finally going to reach a point where they start thinking they're God and can get away with anything. They're going to start hitting D.A.s and cops and your whole precious adversary system is going to come tumbling down around your ears. It's going to boil down to vigilante committees—death squads like they had in Brazil a few years back—and then people like Gierak and Tortorello are going to start turning up in alleys with the back of their heads blown off. And you know something, Jim? It's going to be hard to cry about the breakdown of law and order when it comes."

He frowned. "I'm going to send Capek and somebody else over to your place to make sure nothing happens until we find out what's going on."

"Bullshit," I said. "I'm not living with any cops for a couple of weeks, while you guys run around in circles. I'm sick of cops and I'm sick of police stations and I'm sick of rooms like this and I'm sick of being threatened and beaten up, getting my ass shot at and I'm even sick of you, Jim. You guys can round up all your snitches and put out your APBs and do whatever the hell you do to justify your jobs to yourselves. I'm going home. Alone."

I knew I was not being fair when I said it, but I was having too much fun with the scene to care. It felt good to release all the aggressions that had been building inside me, even if I was displacing it on them.

"What are you going to do?" Jim asked.

"I'm sick of third parties. I'm going straight to the horse's mouth."

His expression turned mean. "What do you mean by that?"

I smirked at him and waved at Emerson. "Thanks for the bourbon, Jim. I'll see you guys."

I turned around and Jim's voice said from behind me: "You're not going anywhere."

I wheeled around. "And who's going to stop me?"

Jim turned to Emerson. "This man is in no condition to drive. I think we'd better put him in the drunk tank—"

A wave of terror passed through me. The thought of being confined within the four bare walls of a cell—even for a few hours—made my skin crawl. I had done that number for six months once and still bore the mental scars. "I swear to God, Jim," I snarled, the animal quality of my voice surprising even me, "I'll never forgive you. I'll come after you, I swear to God I will."

He studied me calmly, then said: "I'll make a deal with you. If you promise to go home tonight and stay there, you can walk out of here. In the morning, you can do whatever the hell you want to do. But if you tell me you're going to go out and start looking for people tonight, I'm going to have you locked up." He waited and said: "What's it going to be?"

We locked stares. His eyes were deadly serious and about

as yielding as a concrete sidewalk. "All right," I said. "I'll give you my word. Tonight I go home and stay. Tomorrow, no guarantees."

He nodded, never taking his eyes off me. "Hopefully, we'll know something by tomorrow."

I turned around and started for the door once more.

"I'm sorry it has to be this way," Jim said.

I stopped, but didn't turn around. "Yeah. I am, too."

I went out the door without saying another word.

· 24 ·

THE SIGN on the front of the restaurant said: OPEN 5 P.M. The doors were locked, so I went through the parking lot to the kitchen entrance.

Huge barrels of fat stood by the back door, stinking in the sun. Thick clouds of flies buzzed above them like miniature tornadoes. I pulled open the door and went up a concrete ramp into the kitchen.

The kitchen was a long room with white brick walls and filled with stainless steel ovens, sinks, refrigerators and tables. I asked a Filipino cook who was standing over a wooden chopping block, cutting up a New York strip with a curved knife the size of a scimitar, where I could find Mr. Tortorello. He gave me a black, beady glare and waved the knife toward a pair of swinging doors. I went through them like John Wayne coming into a saloon.

The place was not quite as lively as John Wayne was used to walking into. There was something oppressively morbid about it, as there was with all restaurants in the daytime. The dining room was haunted by the ghosts of last night's dinner crowd. The stale smells of cigarette smoke and spilled alcohol still hung in the air and clung to the backs of the leather booths. The usually dimmed lights were turned up to full brightness to allow the maintenance men to work, and the naked light glaringly displayed every chip in every formica top of every table in the room. The feeling of the place was contagious and I began to feel lonely and abandoned.

Two long-haired young men were pushing vacuum cleaners over different sections of the crimson carpet. I asked one of them where I could find Tortorello. He shouted over the whine of the Hoover motor that he might be in the office and directed me through a brick archway.

I found myself in a darkened cocktail lounge. The only light was that flowing under the archway from the other room. I could make out the dim outlines of a long, padded bar and a lot of small cocktail tables, and I had stopped in the middle of the room, trying to figure out where to go, when a voice behind me said: "What can I do for you?"

I turned. The man stepped into a stray shaft of light.

He was a caricature from a Damon Runyon story. He was no more than five-foot-six and was built like a pickle barrel —all neck and chest and quite a bit of belly, too. He had black hair with a few gray streaks in it, slightly bugged eyes and a loose, fleshy mouth. His nose had a sizeable knot in the middle of it and was pushed slightly to one side of his face. A fist could have done that, or even a piece of pipe, but on him it looked natural, as if that was the way his nose should be.

"I'm looking for Mr. Tortorello," I said.

"You got an appointment?"

His accent sounded Chicagoese. Eastern accents were beginning to get on my nerves. "No, but I think he'll see me."

"What's it about?"

"It's personal."

"It's personal," he said, turning away slightly, as if talking to someone standing beside him. He turned back, his fat lips parted in a friendly smile. I had the feeling that his routine never varied, that he always started out with the same friendly smile, even when he was making overdue collections. Just a smile and a love-pat across the face with an open hand. ("Jeez, bub, why didn't ya show up today? Y'know I waited and waited and ya didn't show up. Where's the money? Y'know I hate to do this, don't ya?") And then the smile fades and the sickening sound of snapping bones starts. "What's the name?"

"Jacob Asch."

"Just a minute." He went through a door behind him. I waited in the dark, listening to the whine of the vacuum cleaners in the other room, and then he poked his head through the door and said: "This way."

I followed him through the door and then through another one and into a windowless office. The office was not large, but it was large enough. Besides the big executive desk which dominated the room, there were assorted filing cabinets, a small leather couch, two matching leather chairs, a small portable Sony television set on a brass stand, and a cocktail table well stocked with various quarts of liquor, all good stuff. On the desk was an adding machine, a typewriter, a telephone, a large brass ashtray, and a stack of last night's dinner checks, neatly encircled with a rubber band. It looked as if business was good. Behind the desk was Tortorello.

He was sitting in a high-backed swivel chair, holding both ends of a pencil in his hands. He was wearing a brown imitation leather sports jacket over a beige-and-yellow print shirt. The shirt was open at the throat with the collar spread over the lapels of the coat. His eyes were as small and black and emotionless as I remembered them.

"Before I offer you a seat, Mr. Asch, you don't mind undergoing a little search, do you? It's a customary formality around here."

"I'm not carrying a gun," I said.

"It isn't a gun I'm worried about. My private office is just that—private. I intend for it to stay that way."

I shrugged and lifted my arms. The Pickle barrel did a quick but efficient frisk and backed off.

"This is Johnny, by the way," Tortorello said lightly. "Johnny, Mr. Asch."

Johnny pushed out his short, stubby hand. His fingers looked like sausages. I tried not to wince when they closed around my hand. It was like being caught in a grape press. I was sure he had done that for effect. At least I hoped he had.

"Pleased to meetya," he said.

A self-amused smile spread across Tortorello's lips and he waved the eraser of the pencil at the chair in front of the desk. I sat down, and Johnny leaned against the wall behind me and folded his arms.

"Drink?" Tortorello asked.

"No, thanks."

"Coffee?"

"Nothing, thanks."

"Not nothing," he said. "You came here for something."

"A couple of assholes tried to kill me last night."

"Really?" He said it casually, as if I'd just told him my grandmother jars her own strawberry preserves.

"As real as you can get," I said. "They were driving a late-model Ford station wagon. Green. I couldn't make out the shooter—he was wearing a ski mask—but the driver was kind of fat and had a beard and long hair and was dressed in an Army flak jacket. Know him?"

He looked surprised. "How would I know him?"

"I just had a wild hunch you might. Believe me, you wouldn't want to know either of them anyway. They're real fuck-ups. They used a twelve-gauge shotgun, but they loaded it with bird shot shells instead of magnums. The stuff just bounced right off the windshield."

He didn't say anything. I went on. "I realize the help situation is bad nowadays, but you'd think with all the unemployment in this country, you'd be able to find competent people somewhere."

He shook his head and laid the pencil down on the desk. "I think you're laboring under some sort of misconception about me, Asch. I'm just a businessman—"

"Sure," I cut him off. "And your uncle is just a real estate developer and Ben Zimmerman is just a liquor salesman. Now that we've gotten that out of the way, let's talk. Your office is private, remember? There's nobody here but us chickens and none of the chickens are wired up. So let's cut out the bullshit and get down to it."

"Get down to what?"

"I want the contract out on me cancelled."

We stared at each other, trying to read each other's thoughts. I hoped he could not read mine, although they were probably stamped clearly on my face like a USDA seal. I felt helpless, slightly sickened with myself, like a native coming to the village witch doctor to have a curse taken off that he had put on in the first place. "I don't have any contract out on you," he finally said.

"You know Ben Zimmerman," I said.

"Ben is an old friend of my father's."

"That's what he said over lunch the other day. He also said your father contacted him and asked him to see what he could do for you. He seems to have some crazy idea you're going to be railroaded for the murder of David Fein. He wants me to do some poking around and come up with a different answer, one that will satisfy the D.A. He told me in so many words that if I didn't play ball, I was going to be blown away."

"I didn't have anything to do with that fiasco last night, Asch. Neither did Ben."

"Who did?"

He curled his fingers and studied the ends of his nails. "It's just pure speculation on my part, you understand, but those two thugs who broke into Supreme and tried to kill you— what are their names? I read about it in the papers, but I've forgotten—"

"Gierak and Carcinero," I said obligingly.

"Yeah, that's right. Well, I started thinking about it and it's possible they could have pooled their money together into a common defense fund and hired somebody to try to eliminate you as a witness."

"You know that for sure?"

"I don't know anything for sure," he said. "Like I said, I'm just a businessman. It just seems to me that they'd be the two most likely suspects, since you're a big source of their current problem."

"I want the contract cancelled."

"And I ask you again: Why come to me?"

"Because you can get it cancelled."

He picked up the pencil again and tapped the eraser absently against his chin. After a few seconds of that, he said: "I know what you think, Asch. You think I ordered David Fein murdered. Just for the record, I didn't. I had nothing to do with it and neither did anybody else I know. Fein was of use to me alive. Dead, he's caused me nothing but trouble."

"And Terri? I suppose you had nothing to do with that, either?"

"Ah, poor Terri. We went out once or twice, but I suppose you already know that. She came to a couple of parties I threw. Again, I could only speculate about it. From what I knew of Terri, I'd have to say that she set herself up for what she got. She was a very hard-nosed girl. She was too hungry for her own good."

"How about a little speculation about what almost happened to me?"

"You mean the reason why?"

I nodded.

"You're a badger, Asch. You ever see a badger work? He finds the burrow of a ground squirrel and he starts digging. The ground squirrel can hear him coming and tries to dig its way out, but the badger digs faster and finally catches up with his prey. Your digging could upset a lot of business deals, Asch. You could cause people to lose a hell of a lot of money."

I looked over at Johnny. He put a hand up to his mouth and yawned. The scene was boring him. It was starting to bore me. "Somehow I think you've got your metaphors mixed up, Tortorello. Me a mean old badger and you a poor innocent little ground squirrel? Come on."

He smiled. "I didn't know anything about Ben coming to see you. As a matter of fact, when I heard about it, I got kind of pissed-off at dad for sticking his nose into this whole thing. But the more I thought about it, the better I liked the idea. I respect Ben's judgment. It's hard not to. He's been around a long time and he's been right about things like this in the past." He paused and said: "I think maybe you should take him up on his offer. Fein's murder has gotten me intrigued now. I'm getting anxious to find out how it's all going to come out. It's kind of like watching a whodunit and trying to figure out who did it."

"It was done by Professor Plum in the conservatory with the lead pipe."

The line of his mouth hardened. "Save the smart-ass remarks for somebody who appreciates the humor. I don't care much for it."

Johnny unfolded his arms and came away from the wall. He was going to be ready in case anything started. I had no intentions of starting anything and we both knew it, but he just thought he'd be ready. A good boy, that Johnny. His ears were always tuned to his master's voice.

"What if I turn down Zimmerman's offer?"

Tortorello shrugged. "Like I said, Ben's been around a long time. He was around when things were a lot rougher than they are now. If Ben makes a promise, he keeps it. You understand what I'm saying?"

"I think you're saying if he sends somebody, there won't be bird shot in the gun."

"You have a clear, concise way of putting things."

"Yeah. Me and Hemingway." I thought for a few seconds and said: "I don't have a hell of a lot of choice, do I?"

"No," he said. "Not a hell of a lot."

"One thing, Tortorello—"

"What's that?"

"Zimmerman said that if I dig around and find out you ordered the hit on Fein, I could use it to nail your ass."

He said in a serious tone: "If you dig around and find that out, I'll hand you the hammer."

"What about the jokers in the station wagon?"

"That will be taken care of," he said. "Slobs like that shouldn't be allowed to have access to guns anyway. They could wind up shooting each other."

"I hear a couple of guys in New York already have that act," I said and stood up. "If this kind of thing keeps up, you people could find yourselves facing a credibility gap."

"Somebody will be in touch," he said, frowning. His eyes were shiny and depthless, like two flat black buttons. "Johnny, show Mr. Asch out."

· 25 ·

I WAS NOT SURE that was what was bothering me. And it was not just a rationalization to justify my own position. I *wanted* it to be Tortorello. I really did. If I had not gotten lucky, Rodney Allen Rippy might have been eating me on nationwide television right now. I wanted it to be him and I wanted to tell him to go screw himself, but I couldn't because deep down, a little voice kept nibbling at my thoughts saying, *What if he's telling the truth, goddamn it! What if he's telling the truth!*

The voice kept repeating the question all the way to the L.A. County Superior Court.

Mark Fein's divorce papers told me that his ex-wife's name was Elaine and that she lived at 601 Roxbury Drive, Beverly Hills. She had been the one who had served the papers on her husband, on February 19, 1975, at the same Roxbury address. The reason stated for the action was the only one stated anymore in California, "irreconcilable differences," which could mean almost anything and usually did. Mark Fein was listed as the party "living apart," and his address was given as 536 N. Beech Street, West L.A., Apartment 71. The Feins had been married twelve years and there were two children from the union, a boy, Bill, and a girl, Janet. Elaine Fein had been awarded custody of the children, the house, one of the cars, and alimony and child support payments totaling $2,500 a month. A nice nut for the good doctor to crack. Two more appendectomies and a gall bladder operation a month.

When I looked at cases like Fein's, I counted myself lucky. I'd gotten off easy. No kids, the woman had remarried almost immediately. As a matter of fact, the entire process would have been almost totally painless if it hadn't been for the fact that I'd loved the woman.

The Computer Credit Corporation was only a few blocks away on Hill Street. I gave the female clerk there Mark Fein's name, his ex-wife's name, his office address, and $1.50, and she gave me a computer print-out that went back to 1963.

From the surface appearance of the report, Mark Fein's financial affairs seemed to have been in pretty good shape until about eighteen months ago. Since then, he had taken out several bank loans and the repayment code for two of them was "Slow Payment." There were also several retail items in the last few months—credit card purchases—with the same "Slow Pay" code. There was one legal item, a lawsuit for $620, brought against Fein by a garage called Bavaria Motors. I took down the date the case was filed and the docket number and went over to L.A. Municipal Court.

There was nothing much in the case. Fein had gotten his car transmission repaired at Bavaria and had stopped payment on the check because he claimed they had done faulty work. Bavaria had sued and Fein had lost and had to make the check good.

It was after five when I stopped at a coffee shop on Olympic and chewed things over with a grilled cheese sandwich and coffee. The sandwich was greasy and tasteless and I only ate half of it. The voice was still there, nagging a little louder now. Nothing I'd found out meant much, of course, except that whoever had done Zimmerman's preliminary research was on the money so far. What I wanted to find out was how long the streak was going to hold up. It was already dark when I paid my check and left.

I stopped by the apartment on the way to prepare myself

for the evening. I took a mini-white and wrapped another one carefully in a piece of toilet paper and put it in my pocket. I made a pot of coffee, filled a thermos with it and changed clothes.

I congratulated myself for bringing my own jacket. The night up at the Palisades was wet and dark. A thick fog had rolled in from the coast and the street lamps were soft, diffused halos of light in the mist. I passed the house slowly. The Mark IV was alone in the driveway and the living room lights were on. Up the block, I U-turned and parked.

It was seven o'clock. I unscrewed the cap of the thermos and poured myself a cup of coffee. I hadn't put enough sugar in it and it was bitter, but at least it was hot. The pill was starting to work now and my eyes felt as if they were being held open by toothpicks.

I turned on the radio, soft. There were no games on, so I tried music, but got bored with it after ten minutes or so. I found a call-in show and listened to that for a while, but soon the intellectual level of both the callers and the commentator began to drag me down and I turned it off.

Several cars came up the street, but none of them stopped at the Fein house. Then, at eight-fifteen, a pair of headlights burned through the fog and turned into the driveway. It was Mark Fein's BMW.

They came out of the house together about fifteen minutes later, got into his car and drove off. I waited until they got a little ways down the hill, then followed.

At Sunset, Fein made a left and drove toward the beach. The fog was like soup on the Pacific Coast Highway and I had to close the gap between us to keep his taillights in sight. Just before Malibu, he turned into the parking lot of a seafood restaurant called the Navigator. As I slowed down, the parking attendant was opening the door for Barbara Fein. I pulled off on the dirt shoulder and waited until they had gone inside before I drove down the highway to a bar I knew. I figured they would be awhile and there was no sense being cold and miserable in the car; I'd be doing enough of that all night.

I killed the next hour sipping bourbon and water and watching the fog roll across the black surf and hug the windows of the bar. At quarter to nine I was parked outside the Navigator watching Fein's BMW, which was parked on the edge of the lot. My watch ground out another twenty-five minutes.

When they came out of the front doors, Fein had his arm around Barbara Fein's waist. With his free hand, he signalled the valet who ran for the car.

At the Sunset turnoff, I got the message that they were not going back to the Palisades. The BMW followed the Pacific Coast Highway onto the Santa Monica Freeway. Fein kept it at a leisurely fifty all the way to the San Diego Freeway, then swung north. The fog was patchy here and I had no difficulty keeping them in sight.

At Wilshire, Fein signaled and exited. He made a left, then a right at San Vicente. Beech Street was a small street lined with expensive apartment buildings just off San Vicente. Fein turned into the underground garage of one of them, a three-story complex with huge iron gates guarding the courtyard.

I parked across the street and killed my lights. The two bourbons I had consumed in the bar had done nothing to diminish the action of the pill I had taken earlier and I felt wide awake. To occupy myself, I poured another cup of coffee and sipped it in the dark. I had a feeling it was going to be a long night.

I was right. They didn't leave the apartment until ten after three. I didn't bother to follow Fein after he dropped her off at her house. I just went on home.

When I got home, the television was on next door. I tried to ignore it, but I wasn't in the best of moods anyway, so after about half an hour of staring at the ceiling, I said, "Fuck it," out loud and got up.

I put on a bathrobe and leaned on the buzzer next door,

and when nobody answered, I picked the lock and went in. The television was a portable Sony color set and inside it, Gary Cooper and Katy Jurado were riding on a covered wagon, discussing somebody they both knew who had just been killed.

I went into the kitchen, filled up a glass of water and came back out. I poured the glass of water down the back of the set. There were some sparks and a minor explosion inside the casing and Gary Cooper and Katy Jurado faded into oblivion. I put the glass back in the sink, wiped it off with a dishrag and went back to my own place. I felt a little better after that. It was the first thing I had done that I could feel proud of since I had gotten involved in this whole affair.

I drifted off into a dream-filled sleep. Although I don't remember what the dreams were about, they must not have been that pleasant, because the sheets were a tangled mess when I woke up the next afternoon at twelve-thirty and I felt as if I'd been reamed, steamed, and dry-cleaned.

· 26 ·

AFTERNOON SHADOWS striped the front lawn of the house. It was one of those two-story Beverly Hills homes that had been built thirty-five years ago to last a hundred. The architecture wasn't exactly Spanish, but then it wasn't exactly not, either. It had thick white plaster walls and a terra cotta tile roof and some of the windows were arched, but a wooden balcony ran across the front of a row of French doors on the second story, messing up the hacienda image. Two large olive trees stood guard on either side of the driveway, messily shedding leaves and black olives on the asphalt.

Attractively dumpy would be about the best way I could describe Elaine Fein. She had big shoulders and was heavy in the hips and thighs, and although she dressed to minimize the fact, in dark baggy slacks and a loose-fitting plaid top, the attempt was a dismal failure. She was around forty somewhere and had an intelligently lined face and dimpled cheeks and large, cowlike brown eyes, bordered with long lashes. She had short brown hair that was flecked here and there with patches of gray, and a wide mouth that looked hard but which turned soft when she smiled. Her eyes said she had not done much of that lately, however.

I told her my name and gave her a quick glimpse of my photostat—too quick, I hoped, for her to see what was on it

—and said I was an investigator currently working with the D.A.'s office on the David Fein case. I didn't feel too badly about the lie. It wasn't enough of one to really bother my conscience.

She gave me a quizzical look and said: "I already talked to one policeman a few weeks ago. A detective. I can't tell you any more than I told him. I don't know anything about what happened to David."

"This is just routine, Mrs. Fein. I'm just double-checking some things and I'd like to ask you a few questions if it wouldn't be too much of an inconvenience."

"I don't—oh, all right. I suppose so. Come in."

She showed me in and we went through the entrance hall in to the living room. It was a large, quiet room filled with substantial pieces of furniture, all polished wood and warm fabrics the colors of autumn and rust. I sat in a chair that was one of several clustered around a central hexagonal coffee table and she sat down in another across from me, looking uncertain of what either of us was doing there.

I looked around appreciatively. "You have a beautiful home."

"Thank you," she said stiffly.

"Did you decorate the place yourself?"

"Yes. Well, most of it."

"It shows," I said, smiling profusely. "It has a lot of warmth. Many of the homes I've been in are cold and impersonal. You can always tell they had some interior decorator come in and do it for them. They don't even look lived in half the time."

None of that seemed to do much to put her at ease. She sat rigidly in her chair, her eyes tense. I decided to try again.

"You have any children, Mrs. Fein?"

"Two."

"A boy and a girl?"

She looked at me as if I were clairvoyant. Maybe I was. "Yes. How did you know?"

"A lucky guess. How old are they?"

"Ten and twelve."

"Are they in school now?"

She looked at her watch. "Yes. They should be home any-time."

I shook my head in admiration. "My hat's off to you, Mrs. Fein. You must be something to be able to handle two kids and keep up a house like this at the same time. I can't imagine it. I have two, also—a boy and a girl, too—and, let me tell you, I've got my hands full, and my house isn't half the size of this."

"It's a job," she said.

"I'm just finding out what kind of a job. I've only had them by myself for a year and sometimes I think I'm going to go out of my mind. My girl is seven this month. She's an angel. It's the boy—he's the one. A real devil. Always into something." I paused and added with just a jigger of bitterness: "I got custody of them when my wife and I split up. The man she left me for didn't want them, so I took them. But even with all the extra work, I can't say I regret a minute of it."

Her mouth seemed to soften and she smiled sympathet-ically. Now we had a common ground of communication—we were two divorced people who had been hurt and loaded with our own burdens of responsibility. Misery loves com-pany. I hoped hers would love mine. "What did you want to ask me, Mr.—"

"Asch," I said. "Jacob Asch." I took out my notebook and flipped it open to a blank page, just to make it look official. "Like I said, this is strictly routine and I'm sure I'll be cover-ing some of the same ground you covered with the detective who interviewed you, but you never can tell when we'll find something that will help that we didn't think was important before."

"I understand."

"Can you think of anyone who might have had a motive to kill your brother-in-law, Mrs. Fein?"

She shook her head. "No. I never really knew David that well or the people he associated with. He and my husband never saw that much of each other. David and Barbara would come over here for dinner maybe three or four times a year, or we would go over there, but that was about it. David had a whole different circle of friends than us."

"Why didn't your husband and his brother see each other? Didn't they get along?"

"Not really."

"What was the problem there?"

"I don't know. They just never did. When they would get together, it seemed as if things would always wind up in an argument."

"What did they argue about?"

"Nothing. That was what was so stupid about it. They seemed to look for things to argue about. They, I don't know, they always seemed to be competing with each other. . . ."

Her voice trailed off. I pursued it. "How do you mean?"

She shrugged. "Like if David said something funny, Mark would always try to top it. If David bought a new car, Mark bought a more expensive one. Things like that."

"Why do you think that was?"

"If you want to know the truth, I think Mark was always kind of jealous of David. Even while David was having all of his trouble with the gambling, I think he secretly envied him."

"How was he jealous?"

"David was always their father's favorite," she said. "That was always a sore point with Mark, even though he'd never admit to it." She started to say something else, but then caught herself and bit her lip as if she had already said too much.

"Did they ever get violent with one another? Did any of their arguments ever come to blows?"

She fiddled with the seam of the seat. "Why are you asking these questions?"

"Like I said, Mrs. Fein, it's just routine."

Her expression said she didn't quite believe me but that she didn't have the courage to disbelieve me, either. "No, I never saw them fight with their fists."

Something in the way she said it, a slight hesitation, made me press the point. "Do you know if they ever got into a fight when you weren't around to see?"

"I don't know."

She was starting to clam up. I had to spring the big one on her now. It would either open her up all the way or close her completely, but if I kept on this way, she would close up anyway. "You said the two of them were in competition with one another. Were they competing for the same woman, too?"

Her cheeks reddened and her body stiffened as if I'd just slapped her face. "What do you mean by that?"

"Why did you sue your husband for a divorce, Mrs. Fein?"

Her hand flew up to her throat. "What's my divorce got to do with anything?"

I ignored the question. "Was it because of Barbara Fein?"

Her fingers fiddled nervously with the buttons of her collar. "Before I answer any more of your questions, I want to know why you're asking them."

"I told you. I'm just double-checking some things—"

"You can't be double-checking," she said flatly. "The other detective never asked me questions like this." She squirmed in her chair and thrust her arm out stiffly, the palm of her hand up. "I'd like to see your identification again, please. I didn't get a good look at it the first time."

I reluctantly pulled out my wallet and showed her my photostat. Anger boiled to the surface of her face as she read it. "You're not from the District Attorney's office."

I was already hearing the chewing-out Gordon was going to give me after the woman called him up screaming like a banshee. "Not exactly. I'm a private investigator. I've been working in conjunction with the D.A. and the police on this case—"

"*She* sent you over here, didn't she?"

"She?"

"Barbara."

"No," I said, locking stares with her.

"I heard she hired a private detective to look for David."

"That's right. That was me. But I'm not employed by her anymore. I'm on my own. What I told you is the truth. I'm working in conjunction w——"

"I think you'd better leave," she cut me off. Her voice was quiet and final.

"Mrs. Fein—"

She stood up without saying another word. She didn't have to. Her eyes said it all.

As I drove into Beverly Hills, I thought about the woman's reactions. She had been on the verge of spilling it but had pulled back. Maybe if I had handled it a little differently she would have opened up completely, but then you can always look back and whip yourself with a lot of if's. As things stood, I was not too displeased with the way things had come out; her paranoid allusion to Barbara Fein had told me a lot. I did still want verbal confirmation of my suspicions, however, and I could think of only one person who might be both able and willing to give it to me.

I pulled into a gas station on Little Santa Monica and used a pay phone to call Fulton Packing. I caught Nate just as he was getting ready to leave his office and told him there was something important I wanted to discuss with him. He gave me his home address and said he would be there in about an hour.

The house was in Studio City in the foothills just off Coldwater Canyon. It was a one-story, brick and stucco house surrounded by a clump of large elms. There were brick planters out front, but all the flowers had been pulled up some time ago. A FOR SALE sign was stuck in the front lawn telling interested buyers to contact Coldwater Realty and giving a telephone number.

"Come in, Jake," Bloom said, pulling open the door.

The living room was warm and cozy, dominated by a large brick fireplace that was now filled with cold gray ashes. The furniture was solid and timeless. It could have been bought thirty years ago and probably was, but it still had a modern look to it.

"So what's been happening?" he asked. "I thought you were going to keep me up to date on everything? The last time I heard from you was two weeks ago when they arrested those two goons."

"I'm sorry, I haven't been in touch," I said. "But I haven't been working on the Fein thing at all. I've been doing some other things."

He nodded. "Sit down. How about a beer?"

"Sounds great."

I sat down on the couch. He disappeared around the corner and I heard him banging around in the refrigerator.

"Don't bother with a glass for me," I shouted.

"You're sure?"

"Yeah."

There was some more noise, the sound of a cupboard being opened and closed and he came back around the corner holding a glass of beer in one hand and a can of Ole in the other. He handed me the can and sat down in a thickly stuffed chair. "I really like your place, Nate."

"Thanks. You've never been here before, have you?"

"No."

"I've got it on the market."

"I saw the sign out front."

"There are too many memories tied up in the place," he said. "I thought I could handle it, but it's started to get to me. I come home and just sit and stare at the walls. There's no movement, no noise, but the memories of all the movement and noise are intact. It makes it hard."

I nodded. "How long have you lived here?"

"Fourteen years," he said. He stared out the window and his eyes grew watery.

"That's a long time."

"I guess. It doesn't seem so long, though. It seems like a couple of days ago. But that's what happens when you get old—the years slip away from you. You just look around and they're gone."

He took a sip of beer, then pried his eyes away from the window and looked at me. He forced a smile and said: "One good thing: Property's gone sky-high in fourteen years. The value of the house has tripled since then, which is nice. I can use the money. The bills for the doctors and the hospital for Vera drained off a lot of the money we'd saved, even with the insurance."

"You're probably better off selling," I said.

"Sure," he said halfheartedly. "What do I need it for anyway? The place is too damn big for a single man. It's a pain, really. I have to have a woman come in twice a week and clean. I'll wind up getting an apartment closer to work. It'll be more convenient all around." He crossed his legs and raised his glass to toast the walls. "I take it you aren't out here to discuss buying the place."

"You take it right. I want to ask you some questions about David Fein."

"I thought you said you were working on other things?"

"I was. But certain things have started to bother me about this whole Fein affair. There are a few points I want to clear up before I drop it completely."

"What points?"

"I just got through talking with Mark Fein's ex-wife. You know they're divorced?"

He nodded gravely. "Yeah."

"Did David Fein ever mention anything to you about it?"

"About Mark's divorce?"

"Yes."

He shook his head. "No."

"He never mentioned the reason for it, then?"

"No. Why?"

"Mark and Barbara Fein are having an affair."

He seemed stunned by the revelation. "I don't believe it."

"It's true, Nate."

"How do you know?"

"I followed them last night. She spent the night at his place."

He rubbed the back of his neck. His face seemed to pale. He bowed his head and mumbled something, but I couldn't make it out.

"What I'd like to know is whether they've been carrying it on for some time and whether or not it was the cause of Mark Fein's divorce. I'd lay a nice bet that it was, but I'm trying to get some confirmation on it."

His head snapped up and he said: "Well, I can't give it to you. What difference does it make anyway, even if it's true?"

"It could make plenty. A year ago David Fein started gambling again. Why? You told me his love for his wife was what had made him stop before. With that reason for holding back gone, Fein might have just said to himself, 'To hell with it,' and let his old compulsions take over."

"You think he found out about Barbara and Mark?"

"The timing fits," I said. "Elaine Fein served papers on her husband right around that same time."

"So why are you asking me about it?"

"You worked with him every day. You were close. I thought he might have talked about it to you. Those kinds of things you need to talk to somebody about, if you don't want to go crazy."

"He never mentioned anything," he said. "He didn't talk over his personal problems with me. He never did much, but especially lately. We were closer before his father died, for some reason. I don't know what it was. Maybe he thought I was his father's ghost hanging over his shoulder or something." He paused and looked at me questioningly. "Anyway, I thought you said you already talked to Elaine herself?"

"I did."

"Why come to me now then?"

"She wasn't very communicative. I thought you might know something about it."

"This is the first I've heard about any of it." He began rubbing his forehead with two fingers. He stared at a point on the carpet for a few seconds, then his head came up and there was something in his eyes, far back, worried and nervous. "You're not thinking Barbara and Mark had something to do with David's murder—"

"I'm not thinking anything."

"I know you better than that, Jake—"

"All I know, Nate, is that this case isn't over. Not yet it isn't."

He gave me a probing look. "I thought Tortorello had Dave killed to get him out of the way—"

"Tortorello is still suspect number one, but there are some other things that should be looked into."

He sat silently for a few seconds, with a brooding expression, then leaned forward in his chair intently and said: "Why don't you just let it alone, Jake? Why stir up all this *drek?*"

I shook my head. "I can't."

"Why not?"

"Because I can't, that's all."

"Why not?"

"Because there's something else there. I can feel it."

"You don't know that."

"No. I don't."

"Then let it alone. Let the cops handle it."

"Cops suffer from tunnel vision sometimes. After an arrest is made, the whole focus of an investigation changes. They're so glad when they get something on someone like Tortorello, they spend all their time trying to dig up evidence to bury him with—"

"So what?" he said, his voice shrill. "Why do you think they do that? Because they know the sonofabitch has committed a dozen serious crimes he'll never be brought to trial for, that's why. So even if he didn't do this one, which isn't likely, so what? Let them nail him on it. What difference will it make? It'll be doing society a favor."

"I can't play it that way."

"Why not?"

I just shook my head. What could I tell him? He wouldn't understand it, because even I didn't, not completely. It wasn't Tortorello or Zimmerman or any vague threats of execution that were driving me; it was an obsession and obsessions were not explainable, at least by the people who were possessed by them. My life had always been dominated by facts—facts and the truth facts told. Facts had always come first, they had been my primary passion, and people had always run a poor second, which was probably why I was living alone in a studio apartment staring at the ceiling nights. I had asked too many people in my life "why" when I should have just let things slide. That was the way things were, but I couldn't really say I was sorry about it. Words like "sorrow" and "regret" have no relevance when there is no free choice. It was just the way I was.

"It doesn't make any sense," Nate said. "Mark's divorce was final months ago. If Barbara didn't love Dave—if she loved Mark—why didn't she just divorce him and get it over with? She didn't have to kill him to get rid of him."

"Fein left a life insurance policy behind worth $250,000. He didn't leave much else, except a lot of debts. He'd mortgaged everything to pay off his gambling debts."

"No matter what you say, you won't get me to believe that," he snapped. His entire posture was becoming increasingly defensive.

"What about Mark Fein? What was his relationship with his brother like? From the impressions I've gotten, they didn't like each other much."

"I wouldn't say that. They argued, but there was never much behind it. They didn't hate each other, if that's what you're getting at. There wasn't enough passion between them to motivate a murder."

"Passions get buried sometimes," I said. "They have a tendency to come up at inconvenient times. What about his finances?"

"Mark's?"

I nodded. "You know if he's gotten into trouble lately? Made some bad investments maybe? I know he used to dabble in the stock market—"

"I don't know anything about Mark's private life," he said curtly. "It's none of my business."

The implication was clear he didn't think it was any of mine, either. "You like Barbara Fein a lot, don't you?"

"Yes. I like her a lot. And I'll still like her no matter what you say, so I suggest you don't say anything more at all."

I nodded and finished the beer. I squeezed the aluminum can for no reason at all other than force of habit and stood up.

"What are you going to do?" he asked.

"Go," I said. "Thanks for the beer."

I went into the kitchen, located a wastebasket in the corner and dropped in the crumpled can. He was standing by the front door when I came back out into the living room. "You're making a mistake with this," he said.

"It won't be the first and it won't be the last. See you, Nate. Sorry I bothered you for nothing."

I went down the walk past the barren flower beds. They suddenly seemed terribly symbolic to me, but I tried not to think about that. I had enough to think about. Too damn much.

· 27 ·

THE CAR WAS against the curb across the street from my apartment building. It was a drab-green Plymouth four-door sedan about as nondescript as it could be. It might as well have been black and white with running lights.

I pulled in and parked, then walked out the driveway and across the street. Capek looked at me blankly from the driver's side. There was another man I did not know sitting next to him in front. He had a long face and a lot of Brylcreamed-hair that was parted conservatively along the right side and a pencil-thin mustache.

I leaned my forearms on the window and said: "We've got to stop meeting like this, Frank. People are going to start to talk."

He grunted.

"If you're going to stake out my place, I wish you'd get a hat or something. There could be a serious accident here. The glare from your head nearly blinded me when I came down the street."

"Very funny," he said. He turned to the man next to him: "Wasn't that funny?"

"That *was* pretty funny," the other man said, grinning. Capek gave him a dirty look, but that didn't seem to bother him much. He kept right on grinning.

I sighed. "I thought I made it clear to Gordon that I didn't want any protection."

He shrugged. "Yeah, well, after that last incident on the freeway, he thought it might be a good idea to keep an eye on you for a while."

"I've got two eyes myself," I told him. "Some Hindu mystics would even argue I had three—"

"Huh?"

"Nothing," I said. "Look, I appreciate everybody's concern, but if I was really worried about it, I'd get a watchdog."

"Look, Jake, I've got a job, too."

I straightened up. "Yeah, I realize that, Frank. I'm sorry about it. I'm sure you could think of more interesting ways to spend your evenings. I'm just sorry you've got to be stuck out here because of me."

"It sure would be nice to have a tap on your phone," he said.

I looked down at him. His face was still a blank. "Uh-uh."

He made a gesture with one hand. "Listen, it would only take a couple of minutes. Al here is a sound man. Have you met Al?"

I bent down and looked at the long-faced man. "I don't believe I've had the pleasure."

"Al Burnett, Jake Asch," Capek said.

I nodded. "Glad to meet you, Al."

Burnett gave me a polite, tight-lipped smile. "Same."

"How about it?" Capek asked.

"No."

His eyes pleaded with me. "Listen, if that joker calls and says something, even hints at a threat, we can nail him and you'll be off the hook—"

"Sorry. You guys have a nice evening."

I went upstairs, made myself a drink and took a shower and was in my bathrobe, rummaging through the refrigerator, trying to come up with some dinner, when the doorbell rang.

The dyke from next door was standing on the doorstep, shoulders hunched up against her thick neck and fists clenched. She was femininely dressed in a wool sweater, jeans and tennis shoes and her expression told me she'd tried the evening news.

I smiled at her. "Howdy, neighbor."

"You motherfucker—"

I tried to look shocked. "Sticks and stones will break my bones—"

She didn't let me finish. "You broke into my apartment last night, didn't you?"

"I don't have the foggiest idea of what you're talking about."

"You're a liar. You broke in and poured water down the back of my TV set and now it's going to cost me a hundred bucks to get it fixed."

"I'm sorry to hear about your TV," I said. "But I was out last night. When I got in your set wasn't on."

She pushed her face at me. "You're a liar and I want that hundred bucks."

"It shouldn't take you long to make it up. I hear you heavy equipment operators make a lot of money."

"You asshole," she spat. "I'll get you. I'll fix your ass."

"There's nothing wrong with my ass that I know of."

"There will be before I'm through."

I smiled. "Say, I've been wanting to ask you. When you have one of your girl friends over sometime, can I watch? I'd really like to see you sometime when you're all soft and cuddly, whispering sweet nothings in some little girl's ear. I'm a student of personality and it'd really be an interesting change to see. Like Dr. Jekyll and Mrs. Hyde. Or should I say, Ms. Hyde?"

Her upper lip curled under and she snarled, "You god-damn—"

I pointed at her teeth. "You've got a short, blonde curly hair there, stuck in between your two front teeth."

She choked off her sentence and her hand involuntarily went up to her mouth. I smiled and slammed the door in her face.

I waited, but she didn't ring the doorbell again and then I heard her go back to her apartment and bang the door. I went back to the icebox and got out the mayonnaise and some celery and opened a can of tuna. I was just starting to mash up the tuna with a fork, when the doorbell rang again. "Oh for Christ's sake," I said, and went to the door with the bowl of tuna in my hand.

My eyes were levelled down, where the dyke's face would have been, but they landed on a man's shirt collar. I looked up and was surprised to see Mark Fein's face. That was about all I saw. I didn't see the fist that was on its way to meet my chin from somewhere behind him.

I fell backwards and my head hit the seat of a chair. Fein charged into the room like an enraged bull and stood glowering over me, his fists clenching and unclenching, as if to the rhythmic surges of blood through his arteries. "You goddamn sonofabitch," he said through clenched teeth. "You stay away from my goddamn wife—"

"Ex-wife," I said.

"Don't give me any of your double-talking shit, Asch—"

"I'm not giving you any double-talk, Fein. You're not married to the woman anymore. Therefore that makes her—"

"I know what it makes her!" he shouted. His face was twisted in anger and there were red blotches, almost perfectly circular, like half-dollars, on his cheeks.

I shook my head and rubbed my chin at the same time. I had already recovered from the blow and had picked my spot in case he decided he wasn't through being physical. His feet were planted on either side of my right leg and all I had to do was bring up my foot to take the fight out of him. "Sit down, Fein," I said. "Just back off and sit down."

That seemed to make him madder. He bent forward and leaned over me.

"Don't you threaten me, you bastard—"

"I'm not threatening you, Fein, I'm telling you," I said in a quiet, steady tone. "I've given you one punch for nothing. Anything more is going to cost you. Now *relax*."

Maybe it was the self-confidence in my voice that did it, but the red splotches on his cheeks died down to a dull pink and he took a step backward. Keeping my eyes on him, I used the seat of the chair to help me stand. There was tuna fish all over the back of the chair and the carpet. "Shit," I said, picking up the empty bowl.

Ignoring Fein, I went into the kitchen and tore five paper towels off the roll, wet them and then came back and started wiping up the mess. Fein was still standing in the middle of the room, looking lost.

I finished getting up what I could and straightened up.

"I didn't know you and your ex-wife were on speaking terms," I said.

"She called Barbara and accused her of sending you to spy on her."

I nodded. "She seems to have an irrational streak in her when it comes to Barbara Fein. Why is that?"

He blushed and some of the anger came back into his cheeks.

"That's none of your goddamn business—"

"You're right. It's probably not. Except I have a thing about being played for a sucker."

"What the hell is that supposed to mean?"

I didn't answer.

He took a step forward. "I asked you what you meant by that?"

I kept staring at him fixedly. "Where were you the night your brother was murdered, Fein?"

His face screwed up in disbelief. "What?"

"You heard me."

"I—I was home," he said.

"Can you prove it?"

"I don't have to."

"Not yet anyway."

"Are you implying I might have had something to do with David's death?"

"I'm not implying anything, *Doctor*. I just asked you a simple question about your geographical location the night your brother was killed."

"What reason would I have to kill David?"

I shrugged and turned up the palm of one hand. "I could name at least three: his wife, money, sibling rivalry—"

"That's ridiculous," he said, his voice hard.

"If you say so."

He straightened up in an attempt to regain his lost composure and stabbed a finger at me threateningly. "You'd better get this straight, buster: Barbara's been through enough pain without you bringing her more. You stay out of our business or you'll be goddam sorry, I promise you. I've got friends—"

"Yeah, I know," I said. "Like the psychiatrist friend who was ready to see your brother. Only your brother didn't need a psychiatrist. He just needed somebody who needed him back."

"You don't know anything about my brother," he growled.

Old, ugly memories were floating to the surface and I didn't want to look at them again. I felt myself getting mad at Fein for dredging them up again. "You're wrong, Fein. I know a lot more about what he went through than you probably do. I know what it's like to walk in and find your wife with her legs wrapped around some other guy's back. You just stop caring about anything for a while, Fein. If you're strong enough, you get over it, but your brother wasn't strong. He was weak. 'Impressionable,' as you'd say—"

"You sonofa——" He came at me fast, but I was ready this time. I stepped inside his roundhouse right and hooked him in the stomach. He exhaled noisily and collapsed on the floor.

I stood over him while he gasped for air.

"You want to talk about it?"

"Go to hell," he said weakly.

I stood back while he got to his feet.

"No matter what happens, Fein, you're going to have to live with it. You and her."

His eyes clawed at my face. "You just stay out of our way, Asch. I'm telling you. Otherwise, you'll be sorry."

"Why? What are you going to do to make me sorry, Fein? Just what the hell are you going to do?"

He started to answer, but then thought better of it. He showed me some front teeth, then turned on his heel and went out the door. I listened to his footsteps fade down the outside stairs, then closed the door. To hell with it, I thought, I'll go out and get something to eat.

I got dressed and went downstairs. I backed out of the driveway and pulled up alongside Capek and stopped with my engine idling.

"You guys are terrific," I said. "Really great. I feel a lot safer with you two around to watch over me. It's kind of like having a nail file among feeding sharks."

Capek blinked and his face went deadpan. "Why? What happened?"

"Oh, nothing. Didn't you see Fein go up?"

"Yeah, we saw him. What'd he want?"

"He wanted to punch me in the mouth," I said. "He did it, too."

He blinked again and scratched his shiny pate. "Why'd he do that?"

"He said he didn't like me snooping around in his personal life."

"Have you been snooping around in his personal life?"

"A little."

He nodded. "He didn't look so hot when he left. Did you do something to him?"

"Something."

"Nothing too much, I hope."

"Nothing too much."

He nodded again. "What part of his personal life didn't he like you snooping around in?"

"Tsk, tsk," I said, shaking my head. "You know better than to ask a question like that, Frank."

He grunted.

"Look, fellas, I've got some things to do. A few minor errands. I'll be gone at least four or five hours. There's no sense in you sticking around here."

"What kind of errands?"

"I've got to go to the drugstore and pick up some toothpaste, get some groceries, things like that."

"Buying toothpaste takes four hours?"

"You caught me, Frank. Okay, I'll confess. I'm going over to see a dolly I know, and it wouldn't make a good impression on her if you two guys were hanging around in front of her place. You're liable to make her paranoid and blow my whole scene."

Capek gave me a doubtful look.

"Don't worry, Frank. I'll be okay. Nothing's going to happen. I should be back around eleven or so."

"I don't know—"

"Look, you're going to have to leave sooner or later anyway to get something to eat, right? I mean, you can't sit here and starve. I just slipped out on you when you went to get dinner, right?"

He turned to Burnett. "You want to get something to eat?"

Burnett shrugged indifferently. "It's all right with me. Anything's better than sitting here."

"How about Chinese food? There's a place near here, on Sawtelle. I know the owner."

"Okay."

Capek looked over with a friendly grin. "Nice doing business with you. We'll see you back here around eleven. How about the address of the broad, just in case?"

I gave him the address of my old junior high school and he took it down. "Thanks."

"Hell, it's nothing," I said. "Just because we're not going

together anymore, that's no reason why we still can't be friends."

"Huh?"

"Never mind, Frank. Just get a hat, for God's sake. I mean, even Kojack wears a hat."

"Kojack's a pimp," he said, his tone suddenly defensive. "I was shaving my head a long time before Telly Savalas ever thought of it."

"I don't doubt it," I told him. "But he's a sex symbol—"

"Sex symbol, my ass. The guy's gotta be a closet queen, sucking on those Tootsie Roll Pops all the goddamn time."

"Break open a fortune cookie for me," I said and drove down the block.

They pulled away from the curb and followed me up to Santa Monica. I hung a right and they peeled off and went to the left.

The freeway traffic was light all the way out to Gardena.

· 28 ·

DURING THE COURSE of any investigation, there is a point at which you start operating on the law of diminishing returns. You go through all the routine procedures—sifting through the physical evidence, checking out suspects for motives and opportunity—and after you've done that and it does not come together, you start looking around for something, a long shot, that will break it open. Most of the time, the long shots don't pan out, which is why there are a hell of a lot of unsolved homicides in police filing cabinets.

The media image of the intrepid police detective solving cases through relentless work **and** brilliant deduction is just that—a media image. The truth is that if a perpetrator is not uniquely identified at the scene of a crime, the chances are a lot better than even that he will not be identified at all. Nine out of ten cases are solved through information provided by a witness to the uniformed cop who first arrives on the scene or by a snitch who drops a dime in a pay phone and calls downtown to his favorite detective-moneyman.

Since I didn't have any snitches working for me and since there were no witnesses to the Fein killing—at least any that I knew about—I was operating on the law of diminishing returns. I had motives and possibly opportunity for at least three people, but that was all I had. I did not like it, but there was not much I could do but start playing long shots and hope one of them paid off.

The Horseshoe Club was as packed at seven-thirty as it had been at three o'clock. The same faces painted with the same anxious desperation stared across the green-felt tables waiting for an emptying chair.

There were four phone booths in the entryway, the inside of each decorated with a large composite design of the four jacks, queens, kings, and aces of the deck. I took down the number of each phone then used the aces booth to call the local office of the Rapid Transit District. The female clerk who answered the phone told me that there was a bus that ran up Western Avenue and that with one transfer, I could get to downtown L.A. She said it stopped running between midnight and five in the morning.

I hung up and phoned the Gardena P.D. Marinko was in for a change. I told him I was coming right over and asked him to wait.

The detectives' room had a dry, official, but not quite clean look to it. The walls were lined with filing cabinets and its floor space was filled by eight or nine desks which were lined up at perpendicular angles to one another to economize on space. The bright overhead fluorescents sent down a shower of stark, white light that seeped into every nook and corner, making one feel lonely and pursued. That was probably how one was supposed to feel.

Only three of the desks were occupied now and Marinko was one of the occupiers. The top of his desk was covered with reports and he was leaning back in his chair, looking over one of them, a cigarette dangling loosely at the corner of his mouth. He squinted painfully against the smoke, looked up, and said halfheartedly: "Hello, Asch."

"Hello, Sergeant," I said. "How's it going?"

He scowled. "How's what going?"

"The battle for the streets."

He took the cigarette out of his mouth and crushed it out in the ashtray on his desk. "The battle is going okay. It's the war that worries me. What do you want?"

"A little help."

"What kind of help?"

"I'm working on the Fein case—"

"What for?"

"For myself," I half-lied. "Are you still handling it?"

"No," he said firmly. "I've turned everything I have over to the D.A.'s office. They can handle it. They've got a bigger staff to work with than we do. I can't handle what I've got as it is."

He tapped his fingers on the edge of the desk nervously. "What do you mean, you're working on the case for yourself?"

I shrugged. "I'm just trying to answer some questions that have been bothering me about the whole thing, that's all."

"Why bother?" he pressed.

"Because somebody asked me some things that aroused my curiosity, that's all."

"A client?"

"Not really. I don't have any intention of getting paid for it."

"Who is it?"

I thought that one over before answering it. Somehow, I didn't think he would understand if I told him I was looking into it for the Syndicate, and I didn't feel like going into any long, drawn-out explanations.

"I'm sorry, Sergeant," I said, trying to invoke a helpless quality in my voice. "I'd really like to tell you, but I can't. The person doesn't want his name mentioned."

He leaned back in his chair and made a face to show his disapproval of that.

"It could save me a lot of time duplicating work you've already done," I went on, "if you could give me some information—"

"What makes you think I'm interested in saving you time?"

I've often wondered what it was about some cops that made them try to get me to jump through hoops. Maybe it was just professional jealousy, the rankling thought of an "amateur" invading their field of competence, the fear that they might be shown up or some extension of the territorial imperative or maybe it was just my personality. But when I did run into it, I usually got hot because most of the time it was unprovoked on my part. Marinko's attitude was a perfect example, and I felt myself getting hot. "I'm not some hotshot asshole trying to dig into this muck just to make you look like a fool, Sergeant. Believe it or not, I've got better things to do. Whatever I come up with, I intend to give it to you, for chrissakes, so if you don't want to help me out, just let me know and I'll take a walk. There's no need for that other crap."

"All right, all right," he said, waving a hand in the air. "It's been a rough day. What do you want to know?"

I handed him the slip of paper on which I'd scrawled the pay telephone numbers at the Horseshoe. "Did you check out the calls made from the pay phones at the Horseshoe on the night Fein was killed?"

He nodded. "I checked them out."

"And?"

"There were no calls made from any of those phones to anyone connected with Fein. Or with Tortorello. Why, what are you thinking?"

"Remember what the security guard said, that Fein said he was going to go get some money and come back?"

"So?"

"So, suppose he did just that? Suppose he went to see someone about money?"

"So?"

"He could have been killed somewhere else, somewhere outside Gardena."

He rubbed the back of his neck, then shook his head. "It doesn't make sense. Why would somebody haul the body all the way to the parking lot of the Normandie?"

"Maybe whoever did it knew where Fein had been and figured it would look like he never left the city limits."

"You ever heard of Occam's Razor, Asch? Never add more complications than you need."

"Occam's Razor often doesn't cut it when it comes to human behavior," I said. "People are complicated. It's all speculation, I know, but there isn't a shred of evidence to prove that Fein was killed in Gardena. The car was clean. The only evidence of blood was in the trunk where the body was. That means he was either killed on the street or in the parking lot of one of the clubs, which isn't likely, or somewhere else."

"What's your point?" he asked. "I know you've got one."

"Okay. Say he was killed somewhere else. How would the murderer get back to wherever he'd come from?"

His eyebrows were coming alive now, as if warming up after a cold frost. "What do you mean, how would he get back? He'd drive."

"How? If he was driving Fein's car and he left the car at the Normandie, how would he get back?"

"Gierak never worked alone," he said testily. "He always had a partner with him, if you remember. And you should, since you experienced a little of their persuasion firsthand."

"What if it wasn't Gierak?"

"What do you mean?"

"Just what I said. So far, Gierak is denying the whole thing. So is his partner. What if they're telling the truth and they had nothing to do with it?"

He put both of his hands flat on the surface of the desk and leaned forward. "Who the hell else would it have been?"

"That is a good question."

"Who've you got in mind for it?"

"I don't," I said.

He hesitated, then said: "You're lying."

"I've got nobody in mind for it," I said positively. "I'm just throwing a lot of shit on the wall and hoping some of it sticks."

His mouth turned down at the corners unpleasantly. "Yeah, well some of the shit has already stuck—on Gierak."

I shrugged. "It's possible Gierak had a hand in it. I'm not trying to say he definitely didn't. But, suppose he didn't. What if it was somebody else, somebody Fein knew—"

"Who, for Christ's sake?" he blurted out. "Who else had a motive to kill Fein?"

"I can name you two people," I said. "His wife and his brother."

His eyes searched mine. "What about them?"

"Come on, Sergeant. You have to know about the insurance policy. You must have checked on that. It's standard procedure in a homicide case to determine who benefits financially from the death."

"Okay, so I know about the policy. That policy was taken out four years ago. There's nothing suspicious about that."

"No. But Fein wasn't getting along with either his wife or his brother lately. He'd quarreled violently with both of them."

"So what? I fight with my wife too. That doesn't mean anything. Listen, those insurance companies have investigators looking up people's assholes, for God's sake. If there was anything wrong with the Fein murder, you think they'd pay off? Not a chance."

"There are other things," I said.

"What other things?"

"I'd rather not get into it. Not yet, anyway."

He made a faint clicking sound far back in his throat and sat back with a smug smile on his face. It was almost a leer.

"You don't care whose side you're on, do you? One minute the broad is your client and the next you're ready to turn her in—"

"I'm not ready to turn anybody in, Marinko," I said, trying to keep the anger out of my voice. "I do what I have to do and I don't need any lectures on professional ethics from you."

The tension stretched between us. "Exactly what do you want from me, Asch?"

"Just an answer to a simple question. Supposing Fein did see somebody else that night and supposing the killer worked alone and had nobody to drive him back, how would he get there?"

He rolled his eyes impatiently. "Jesus Christ. He'd take a bus."

"The buses stop running between midnight and five. The outside time the coroner fixed Fein's death was five A.M. of the thirtieth."

"So he'd take a cab—"

"Have you checked out the cab companies in town to see if they picked up a fare around the Normandie that night?"

"No."

"What do you say we do that?"

The suggestion seemed to astound him.

"What the hell for? This is all a bunch of bullshit, Asch. Listen, I'm up to my ass in cases already; I don't need another one. I just got rid of that turkey and I don't want it back again. Let the D.A. handle it."

"It may be bullshit, Sergeant, I'm willing to grant that. It may all turn out for nothing. But, it'll take half an hour at the most to check out and at least we'll have eliminated one possibility—"

"*We?*" He came forward in his chair. "*We?* Where do you get this we business? I don't have to eliminate any possibilities, Asch. That's what I'm trying to get across to you. The D.A. seems to be satisfied that Tortorello used Gierak to do the job and I'm willing to accept that. If you want to go around jerking yourself off on some wild goose chase, go ahead. I've got better things to do. Hell, you could make up a thousand different possible solutions to that killing and spend the rest of your life checking them out."

I waited until he had finished, then said calmly: "You know, I don't understand you, Sergeant. One day you're giving me a lot of crap about, 'This is police business now, Asch. Don't get any bright ideas about working on it alone,' and now you're telling me to do whatever the hell I want to as long as you don't have to get off your fat ass and do any work yourself. Your attitude isn't very consistent."

That got to him. His face darkened and he opened his mouth to say something. He never said it, not what he had originally intended to say, anyway. The anger drained out of his face suddenly as if somebody had pulled a plug and he sighed loudly. "So what do you need me for? Why don't you just check it out yourself?"

"I could, I suppose, but you'd be surprised what worlds a flash of that shiny badge of yours opens up. No dispatcher is going to show me his logs without giving me a huge hassle. I could maybe get to him with a bribe, but if he didn't take it, I'd just have to come back to you. And if he did, it would be just another blow to my blind faith in human nature. You wouldn't want to live knowing you'd contributed to the making of a hard-bitten cynic, would you, Sergeant?"

"Jesus Christ, Asch, you're really something, you know that? All right, but this is it. If nothing turns up this time, I don't want to see your face around here again. Understand?"

"Understood."

He sighed again and stood up wearily. He plucked his Robert Hall Madras sports coat from the back of the chair and said: "Let's go. I want to get this over as fast as possible."

· 29 ·

GARDENA WAS SERVICED by two cab companies: Star Cab and Checkerboard. They had different phone numbers, but both were subsidiaries of Yellow Cab and both worked out of the same building, to save on costs, I assumed.

The building was a huge, hangarlike garage located at the dead-end of a narrow, unlighted street that ran off Artesia Boulevard. Inside, several dozen cabs, predictably painted with stars and black-and-white checkered squares, sat resting, waiting for their shift to begin. There were empty parking spaces for at least three dozen more.

We walked past two gas pumps to the glass-enclosed office where two drivers loitered in the doorway, listening to the dispatcher. The dispatcher was a thin, nervous-looking man with red-brown hair and a bloodless triangle of a face, like a wedge of pale cheese. The sleeves of his white shirt were rolled up to the elbows and the front of it was covered with several large reddish stains. The source of the stains—the remnants of a meatball sandwich—was on the desk in front of him on a bed of waxed paper. Behind him, at another desk, a not-half-bad brunette sat answering the phone and sending out addresses over a microphone in a strident, nasally voice.

The dispatcher looked up at one of the drivers, a long-haired blonde kid and said: "Marston, you take 283 tonight. Gas up."

The blonde kid nodded and walked away. The dispatcher eyed the remaining driver, an older, sallow-faced man. "You take 135, Wall."

"Okay," the man said and started to move away. He was stopped by the dispatcher's voice calling after him.

"I've been hearing reports about you, Wall," the dispatcher said. "Some of the guys say you've been snatching their fares. We don't go for that shit around here."

"They're full of crap," Wall shot back.

"The logs bear them out."

"They don't like it, tell them to get their asses in gear. The call goes out and if I get to a fare first, that's tough shit. It's survival of the fittest."

"Not in my cabs it's not," the dispatcher growled. "You must have been driving like a bat out of hell to get to some of those fares first. You're not going to stack up one of my cabs just because you're hungry. If I hear anymore about it, I'm canning your ass. You got it?"

Wall mumbled something, stuffed his hands deep down in his pockets and stalked off. The dispatcher's eyes were still fixed on his back when we stepped into the office. The man looked up at us sharply. "Yeah?" His tone was not exactly friendly.

"You the owner here?"

"Night manager."

"What's your name?"

"Irv Watson. Why? What do you guys want?"

"I'm Sergeant Marinko from the Gardena Police Department." Marinko flipped open his wallet and flashed his badge. The man's face softened immediately. He even tried on a smile. It was not much of one—his teeth were badly stained by nicotine—but it was still a smile.

"Sorry, I snapped at you there, Sergeant. I get aggravated having to cope with jerks like that guy."

"I understand," Marinko said.

"What can I do for you?"

"I'm working on a homicide case and I'd appreciate a little assistance if you would. I'd like to see your logs for the night of November twenty-ninth through the morning of the thirtieth. I need to know what fares were picked up on those dates around the vicinity of the Normandie Club."

"No problem," Watson said. "Just a sec and I'll check." He seemed surprised, then pleased by the rhyme. "Hey, that's not bad. I'm a poet and don't know it, eh?"

I was going to finish it for him—but your feet show it, they're longfellows—but I kept it to myself. You never know where things like that can lead.

The chair creaked loudly as he pushed himself out of it. "We like to cooperate with the police one hundred percent, Sergeant. Anything you need." He went to a filing cabinet on the other side of the brunette's desk and pulled open the second drawer.

"See?" I said, nudging Marinko in the ribs. "I told you. A little flash of gold and nothing but cooperation."

Watson came back holding a long white sheet and sat down at his desk. "You wanted the Normandie, you said? Let's see, that's 14808 South Western. Cab 451 picked up a fare from the Normandie at eight-fifteen—"

"This would be after ten o'clock," I said. "Probably after midnight."

"After midnight, eh? Okay." He ran his finger down the page. "Let's see. Cab 209 had a fare there at ten-twenty—"

"Where to?"

"1900 Gramercy Place."

"Where's that?"

"Gardena."

"No," I said. "We're looking for something that would've been out of town."

"Out of town . . . Cab 120 had a pickup from the Normandie at twelve-fifteen of the thirtieth that went to Hawthorne. 22350 Rosecrans."

He looked up and I shook my head. He went back to his

logs. "Cab 117 had a fare at two-twenty A.M. that went into Hollywood. But that wasn't from the Normandie. It was from 14185 South Western—"

"Where in Hollywood?"

"To the Hollywood Bowl."

"Go on."

There were five more fares from the vicinity of the Normandie, but three of them were local and the other two had gone south, one to Long Beach; the other to Torrance. None of them looked too promising, but I wasn't going to give it up completely yet. I was here and I was going to give it my best shot.

"Who was the driver on that fare to the Hollywood Bowl?"

"McBride."

"Is he on tonight?"

"Yeah. I just sent him out a little while ago."

"Can you get him in here?" I asked.

"Why? Is it important?"

"It may be," I said.

He shrugged. "Yeah, I can get him in. Rose, send out a call for McBride. He's in 104. Tell him to come in."

Rose nodded and put it out over the microphone. Marinko tugged my sleeve and said: "I'd like to talk to you outside for a second."

When we got outside the office door, he said: "What gives? What the hell's at the Hollywood Bowl?"

"Nothing," I said. "It's the off-season." Before he had a chance to react to that, I said: "If you'd just killed someone and dumped his body, would you get in a cab and drive directly to your house?"

"You're reaching now," he said. "You were reaching before, but now you're really reaching."

I couldn't help but think he was right, but I wasn't about to let him know it. "Maybe. But we're here now. It's worth checking out."

"And if it doesn't check out?"

"Then, it will be logical to assume that the killer had a partner who picked him up."

"I don't get it. If the guy got dropped off somewhere and picked up another cab, who's to say he didn't go to Torrance or Long Beach to do it?"

"Nobody is," I said. "I've got to check them out, too. I just thought I'd start with the Hollywood Bowl fare. At least it was headed in the right direction."

His face reddened. "You mean you're going to interview all those drivers? You said this was going to take half an hour. I haven't got the time to stand around here with this shit for the rest of the night—"

"So go back to the station," I said. "I'm not keeping you here."

"Right. After you used my badge as a wedge to get in here—"

I smiled. "What are friends for?"

· 30 ·

"Yeah, I remember the fare," McBride said. "I wouldn't normally, but I don't get fares that far very often. And the guy seemed kind of weird. Spaced-out. I figured he was probably senile."

McBride was chewing gum which he snapped about every fourth or fifth chew. He had a round face dotted with freckles. One of his eyes—the left—had a slight tic in the lid.

"Why'd you figure he was senile?" I asked. "Was he old?"

"Old enough to be senile."

"How old?"

He shrugged. "Late fifties, early sixties. It's hard to say."

"How was he spaced-out?"

He shifted uncomfortably in his chair and screwed up his face. "He didn't, uh, I don't know. It was like he was in another world, you know? I tried to talk to him—I like to talk with my fares, you know? It kind of makes the time pass faster and people usually like it when a driver's friendly. It builds your tip. Oh, you get some that don't, that tell you to shut the fuck up and drive and crap like that. But this guy, he didn't seem to hear a word I was saying. He just sat in the back and stared out the window like he was in another world. After awhile, I gave up trying and just drove."

"And you drove him to the Hollywood Bowl?"

"Well, right near there. There's a market right across the

street on Highland, a Ralph's or something, I don't remember. But, he asked to be dropped off right there. Right next to a pay phone. I was kind of surprised, you know, because it's close to three in the morning and there's nothing there, just the market and that's sure as hell closed. So I ask him if he's sure he wants to be let off right there and he says, 'Yeah, right here,' so I say okay and let him out."

"Did you stick around at all afterward?"

"What should I stick around for?"

"No reason," I said. "I was just wondering if you did."

"No."

"What'd he look like?"

He shrugged. "He was short. Kind of wiry. Gray hair, receding a little in front. Jewish-looking guy. Sounded Jewish, too. It was more in the way he said things, y'know? But, he didn't say that much."

"Remember what he was wearing?"

"Naw, it wasn't nothin' strange, otherwise I'd a remembered."

Something stirred in my gut. "Did you notice the color of his eyes?"

He stared at me incredulously and his left eyelid twitched. "Are you serious?"

"No, I suppose not. Where did you pick him up?"

"That's another reason I remember the guy. He was waiting for me in front of the Satellite Club. It's a bottomless bar and a rough one, too. I wondered what an old geez like that would be doing in the Satellite. When he got in the cab, I said to myself, 'Jesus Christ, I got myself a real hardcore dirty old man.' "

"Would you be able to identify him again if you saw him?"

He snapped his gum. "Yeah, sure."

"Can you remember anything else about him?"

"Yeah," he said. "He was a lousy tipper."

"Okay, thanks, McBride. That's all for now."

McBride left the office and I stood up. I may have teetered

a bit. I was feeling a bit unsteady. "I think that's it." I said.

Marinko looked at me questioningly.

Watson flashed us both a smile and thrust out his hand. "Like I said, we always like to cooperate with the police. I just hope you found out what you wanted to know. Who was it who got killed by the way?"

"A man named Fein," Marinko said.

"Oh yeah. I remember reading about that. They found him in the parking lot of the Normandie, didn't they?"

"That's the one," Marinko said.

"You know who did it?"

"We think we do," Marinko said. "Thanks for your help, Mr. Watson."

I walked out of the garage ahead of Marinko and he had to hurry to catch up with me. A half moon was climbing away from the horizon silently, with slow, sad steps. The sky was cold and starless.

"Okay," he said, "let's have it. Why didn't you have him call in the other drivers?"

"I've just decided you're right," I said. "This is stupid."

He regarded me with suspicion. "Then why all those questions in there? Why'd you pump that guy?"

"I decided it was stupid while I was pumping him, okay?"

"No, it's not okay. When he described that guy, your face nearly hit the floor. You know who he was talking about."

"That description could match a hundred people I know."

"But only one that killed David Fein—"

I started to walk away, but he grabbed my sleeve. "You're lying, Asch—"

I pulled my sleeve out of his grasp and said: "That's twice you've called me a liar, Marinko, and I'm not sure I like it."

I especially didn't like it because he was right. But I needed time to think things out. I had to be sure. "What I said before still stands. Whatever I get, I'll give to you."

"You'd goddamn well better," he snarled.

· 31 ·

THE PORCH LIGHT went on and there was a fumbling at the peephole and an eye peered out at me. The door opened and Bloom was standing there in a striped bathrobe and slippers. He blinked at me blearily and said: "Jake. What are you doing here at this hour?"

"Can I come in, Nate?"

He looked at me uncertainly. "Yeah, sure. What—well, here, come in." He closed the door behind me and asked: "What's happened? What's the matter?"

I watched him silently for a few seconds, then said: "Sit down, Nate."

He pushed his hands into the pockets of his robe and sat down on the couch. I took one of the easy chairs in front of the fireplace. "I talked to the cab driver, Nate. He can identify you."

Apprehension flickered darkly across his face. "What cab driver? What are you talking about?"

I felt totally drained, exhausted. "Jesus Christ, Nate. What the hell happened? Why did you do it?"

He drank silent thoughts, then bowed his head and sighed heavily. "How did you know?" he asked finally.

"I didn't. It was a hundred to one shot. I didn't really expect anything to come of it. If anything did, I expected to get a description of Mark Fein."

He nodded. "I was going to tell you anyway. I want you to believe that. As soon as you told me you suspected Mark and Barbara, I knew I was going to have to tell you. I couldn't let them take the blame for it."

"There wouldn't have been any physical evidence to tie them to it anyway," I said. "They both had motives, but other people did, too. The D.A. never would have filed charges against them."

"I would've told you anyway."

His voice carried a hopelessness in it, a complete surrender, that repelled me.

"Okay."

He slouched back in the chair and waved a hand weakly in the air. "It was an accident. Really it was. I didn't mean to do it. I just lost my temper, that's all. He made me so damn mad coming over here like that, that I—I guess I just exploded." He paused and said, "It's actually kind of ironic. I didn't know anything about Mark and Barbara until you told me this afternoon. If I had—when Dave came over—I probably wouldn't have gotten so worked up. Part of the argument was about Barbara. I can understand now what he was going through. I didn't know then."

He shook his head, then leaned forward with his elbows on his knees and covered his face with his hands.

"How did it happen?"

He brought his hands away and stared at me. His blue eyes seemed to penetrate my thoughts, but only, I soon realized, because there was nothing behind the eyes. It was like looking into a void; only a reflection of myself came back. "He came over to borrow money. He said he was broke and needed a loan. Isn't that a laugh? The sonofabitch fires me after twenty-one years of pouring everything I had into Supreme and then he comes to me for a loan to bail him out—"

"You mean to bail out the business?"

He nodded. "He poured it all out to me, how Tortorello was Mafia and how he'd used Dave's gambling debts to muscle in on Supreme. He said he hadn't wanted to fire me, that Tortorello made him. He said he thought Tortorello was planning to suck the business dry and then walk out. He wanted to raise the money to buy Tortorello out before that happened."

"What made him think Tortorello would have been willing to sell?"

He shrugged. "I don't know."

"He couldn't expect you to have that kind of money—"

"Of course not," he said, smiling dryly. "He wanted a gambling stake. A few thousand, he said. He was *sure* he could build it into a hundred thousand with a little luck. He was always sure of that. Only he never had any luck. Not that kind, anyway."

My mind had ceased forming coherent phrases and thoughts; I shook my head and said: "What, did he think you'd have a few thousand just lying around in cash?"

He rubbed his eyes. "I don't know what he thought, Jake. His eyes were wild. He was pretty far gone. I'd seen him throw fits before, but I'd never seen him that bad."

"What'd you tell him when he asked for the money?"

"That I didn't have it."

"What did he say to that?"

"He called me a liar. That's when I started thinking about what he'd done to me, to everyone around him. The more I listened to him, I don't know, the more he made me sick. He blamed everyone else for his troubles but himself. He always did. He could never accept responsibility for his own actions. That was always a sore spot between him and Leonard. I told him that that night. I told him to go back to Barbara, that he should be ashamed of himself the way he was treating her. He flew into a rage then. He started calling her a whore and ranting and raving. That's when I told him to get out. I wasn't going to listen to that kind of crap in my house. Then he started calling me names. He said we were all a bunch of Judases and we could all go to hell. I told him to shut his mouth and one thing led to another. He tried to take a swing at me, and, I don't know, I vaguely remember picking up an ashtray—it was a heavy pewter one with sharp corners—and hitting him with it. Anyway, the next thing I knew, he was lying with his head on the bricks by the fireplace, bleeding. I tried to revive him, but he was dead."

"Where?"

He pointed to a spot on the bricks in front of the fireplace. I went over to it and bent down to examine it. I could vaguely make out the outlines of a darker spot on the bricks and some stained sections that had been cleaned out of the carpet. The lab would never be able to make an identification of blood from that. "What about the ashtray?"

"I threw it away."

I spread out my hands toward him. "Why the hell didn't you call the cops?" I asked in a harsh voice. "You could have pleaded self-defense, for God's sake. No jury in the world would have convicted you. Now it looks bad."

He rubbed his head. "I don't know. I just don't know. I got panicky, I guess. Then I started thinking about what Dave had said about Tortorello and I thought that once the police started digging into what was happening at Supreme, they'd think Tortorello did it."

I put my hand on the mantelpiece and stared across the room at him. "And you dropped a few hints to me to make sure."

"I didn't figure he'd be any great loss to society. Everything was okay, until you started coming up with that stuff about Mark and Barbara."

My stomach was sour, and the taste of it was creeping up into my mouth. "Why did you take the body all the way back to Gardena?"

He shrugged. "I wanted to get him as far away from here as I could. That's all I knew. Then I thought people would have probably seen Dave out there earlier—people who worked in the clubs and knew him—and the police would think he never left there. It was pretty stupid, I guess."

"No," I said. "It was pretty good figuring. The whole thing was pretty good figuring, right down to taking two cabs home."

He smiled weakly. "The only stupid thing I did was recommend you to Barbara."

I felt an incredible heaviness inside me. I found myself wishing I was someone else, far away from here. "I'm sorry, Nate. I really am."

"Don't be. It's not your fault, kid. Actually, I'm glad it's over. When I said the whole thing was stupid, I meant that my trying to muck it up was stupid. It was all survival tactics on my part and that's what's funny, because survival doesn't mean anything to me anymore. Vera and Supreme Packing were my life. They were the only things that really meant anything to me. When they were gone . . . I don't know . . . I just don't seem to give a damn about anything anymore. I'm just tired. Old and tired. . . ."

"I wish I'd have listened to you, Nate. I wish I'd let it alone. I really do."

He shook his head. "You couldn't. There wouldn't have been any way you could have."

I stood, thinking about what I was going to do. There was nothing to think about, really, but I went through the motions.

"I've got to take you in, Nate."

He nodded heavily. "I know."

"A good attorney will still probably be able to get you self-defense. I have some friends who are specialists. They'll cost you, but they'll do a good job for you."

"Yeah, sure," he said, as if it didn't really matter.

"I'm sorry it's me, Nate."

"I'm not, I'm glad. I wanted to tell you about it before. I just couldn't seem to, I don't know why."

He looked down at the toe of his slipper and his gaze grew distant and hazy. I went to the phone and called the Gardena P.D. The girl on the switchboard said Marinko had gone home and I told her sharply to get him at home then, because I was coming in with a prisoner. I hung up and turned to Nate, who was still staring at his slipper.

"You got any booze around here?"

He waved a hand at a cabinet on the far wall. "In there."

"You want a drink?"

He stared at me, then his eyes focused and he nodded. "Scotch."

I fixed him a double Scotch and myself a double bourbon and we drank without saying anything. While he got dressed, I made myself another one and waited in the cold and pressing silence that filled the house.

· 32 ·

S ARAH OPENED the door a crack and squinted through
 the slit with one sleepy eye. "Jake . . . Jesus Christ.
What time is it?"

"I don't know exactly. After two. I wouldn't have come
over but I really need to be close to someone right now,
Sarah. . . ."

I started to go on but faltered, knowing I would just
stumble over the words, that they would mean nothing to
her.

She opened the door and touched my arm. Her expression
turned instantly solicitous. "You're shivering."

She pulled open the door and stepped aside to let me in.
She was wearing her Bobby Womack T-shirt again and nothing else. I grabbed her and pressed her close in an attempt to
absorb some of her warmth. She stroked my hair tenderly
and said: "What is it, Jake? What's wrong?"

"I just need a refuge," I said in a shaky voice. "Some place
to hide for a little while. I'm so damn cold."

She took my face in her warm, soft hands and looked
deeply into my eyes. "I'm glad you came here. I really am."

We went to bed and made love and she was all air and fire
in my arms. After the third time, some of the chill had
passed, enough so that I was not shivering anymore. In between, we talked—or rather, I talked, I talked like a madman,

and she listened—and sometime before dawn, I looked down and realized she was asleep against my chest.

I lay there, watching the few stars bold enough to burn through the canopy of city lights fade and the sky pale with the approaching dawn. A lonely restlessness crept up on me, a feeling of utter isolation, and I realized that whatever feelings of sanctuary I found here in the night had fled with the light. I slipped out of bed without waking her and left her a note that I would call tomorrow.

I arrived home at six-forty. I trudged up the outside stairs and put my key in the lock when I noticed the jimmy marks on the door frame beside the handle.

The hairs on the back of my neck stood up and my organic alarm system went off, banishing my physical exhaustion. I turned the key in the lock, took a deep breath, flung open the door and charged into the room.

The apartment was deadly silent. I stood in a crouch in the middle of the room for a full ten seconds taking everything in, soaking up every sound, but there was nothing except the faint and steady drip-drip-drip of the leaky faucet in the kitchen. I searched the bathroom and the closet, then came back out into the living room. Then I noticed the television set. The back had been taken off and all the wiring pulled out.

"Shit," I said, then started to laugh. I laughed until I cried, then took off my clothes and fell into bed and fell into an exhausted sleep. I dreamed I was in an underwater bicycle race, tied for the lead with four thousand other helmeted riders. Although I never knew what the first-place prize was, it must have been a big one, because we all peddled away at a furious pace and all somehow stayed neck-and-neck. I never found out if I won or not because I was startled out of the dream by the sound of the doorbell.

There was a sour taste in my mouth. The clock by the bed said 11:46. I yelled, "Just a minute," and pulled on a pair of pants and went to the door.

Johnny the Pickle barrel smiled at me crookedly. "Hiya, bub." He inspected my condition and said apologetically: "Sorry. I didn't mean to wake you up."

I rubbed my eyes. "What *did* you mean to do?"

"Deliver this." He took an envelope out of his inside coat pocket and slapped it into my palm. There was at least a couple of thousand in crisp, new hundred dollar bills inside. "What's that for?"

"We heard about the pinch last night," he said. "Mr. Zimmerman was real pleased with the job."

"You heard? You guys must have an in somewhere. It only happened a few hours ago."

"We got a pretty good line on things," he agreed.

I pushed the envelope back at him. "I told Zimmerman once, I don't take money from hoods. You can pass the message on."

That didn't dampen his enthusiasm. "You want to pass on that message, you do it, bub. I'm just supposed to deliver that, that's all. Don't be a jerk. Take it. It's good bread."

I didn't take it. "Let me amend that message." I said. "Go back and tell Zimmerman and your boss Tortorello that I said to go take a flying fuck at a rolling doughnut."

The smile disappeared as if it had been wiped off with solvent. "Mr. Zimmerman ain't gonna like that."

I started to raise my voice, but then I caught a glimpse of Capek coming through the garage into the swimming pool courtyard.

It had been building up in me, I suppose, for the whole case, and now it came rising to the surface in a rolling boil. Everything I detested in the world suddenly came together in the man standing in front of me.

I thought for a second about how he would have handled it, then said in a quiet voice, "You're right. I'm sorry. That's a bad attitude. I guess I'll take it."

He pushed the envelope at me and while he did that, I hooked him in the gut. It didn't have much steam on it, but enough to take the wind out of him. I hit him in the throat, then grabbed him by the front of his shirt and swung him into the side of the plaster wall. His head opened a hole in the wall and I kneed him in the balls as hard as I could and as he doubled over, I pushed him. He went rolling backwards down the stairs and came to rest at the bottom. He managed to get to one knee, then tried to stand, but Capek sapped him behind the ear before he could make his feet, and he fell back down and lay still.

I came down the stairs. "He assaulted me," I said.

Capek nodded. "Yeah. I saw it." He turned to Burnett who had moved behind him. "You saw it, didn't you, Al?"

"Yeah. I saw it."

"You know who he is?" I asked.

Capek nodded. "John Dragesevich. A third rate punk. A collector. He busts up guys for spare change."

Capek grasped the limp hulk by his shirt collar and dragged him to the swimming pool and immersed his head in the water. When that didn't do any good, he took the man's arms and Burnett took his legs and they staggered with him to the car. I followed and when they loaded him into the back seat, I tossed the envelope on top of him. "Don't forget this," I said.

Capek got behind the wheel and looked up. "You did a pretty fair job, Asch."

"I was mad."

He laughed. "How can you let a creep like that get to you? Try and get over that. You've got to master your emotions."

"Have you?"

"Sure," he said. "The day before yesterday. I'll take this asshole downtown and book him for assault. You want to come down later and sign the complaint?"

"I don't think so," I said. "I think I've had enough excitement for one day."

"Whatever," he said. The car took off and I went back upstairs. I popped the tab on a beer and sat down on the rumpled bed and stared for a while at my disembowled TV set and felt a twinge of regret that I had not kept at least enough of that money to pay for a new television.

I felt like calling Barbara Fein and trying to explain, but that, of course, was out of the question. Instead, I dialed the answering service. "7712," Penny said.

"Penny, love," I said with all the false cheerfulness I could muster, "this is Jacob Asch, Number 411. How would you like to go out for dinner tonight?"

"Sure," she said.

"I'll pick you up at seven," I said. "Where?"

She gave me her address and I said good-bye and hung up, feeling as if I'd just slit my wrists and got back into bed with my beer. When I finished that one, I got up and got myself another.

"What the hell," I said out loud. "So I'll bring a paper bag to put over her head." I started to feel better after that.

VINTAGE CRIME titles available from No Exit Press

Fast One – Paul Cain
0 948353 03 1 (hb) £9.95, 04 X (pb) £3.95

Possibly the toughest tough-guy story ever written. Set in Depression Los Angeles, it has a surreal quality that is positively hypnotic. It is the saga of gunman-gambler Gerry Kells and his dipsomaniacal lover S. Grandquist (she has no first name), who rearrange the Los Angeles underworld and 'disappear' in an explosive climax that matches their first appearance. The pace is incredible and the complex plot, with its twists and turns, defies summary.

The Dead Don't Care – Jonathan Latimer
0 948353 07 4 (hb) £9.95, 08 2 (pb) £3.95

Meet Bill Crane, the hardboiled P.I., and his two sidekicks O'Malley and Doc Williams. The locale of the cyclonic action is a large Florida estate near Miami. A varied cast includes a former tragic actress turned dipso, a gigolo, a 'Babe' from Minsky's, a broken-down welterweight and an exotic Mayan dancer. Kidnapping and murder give the final shake to the cocktail and provide an explosive and shocking climax.

Green Ice – Raoul Whitfield
0 948353 13 9 (hb) £9.95, 14 7 (pb) £3.95

Watch out for Mal Ourney: where Mal goes, murder follows. It is on his heels as he walks out of Sing Sing after taking a manslaughter rap for a dubious dame and follows him all the way on the trail of some dazzling hot emeralds – 'green ice'. 'Here are 280 pages of naked action, pounded into tough compactness by staccato, hammer-like writing.' – Dashiell Hammett.

Death in a Bowl – Raoul Whitfield
0 948353 23 6 (hb) £9.95, 24 4 (pb) £3.95

Maestro Hans Reiner is on the podium, taking the fiddle players through a big crescendo. Then something goes off with a bang and it is not the timpani. Reiner finds himself with a load of lead in the back – and a new tune: The Funeral March.

The Virgin Kills – Raoul Whitfield
0 948353 25 2 (hb) £9.95, 26 0 (pb) £3.95

More of the sharpest, toughest writing you will ever read – fast, lean, without an ounce of sentimentality. 'Raoul Whitfield holds up better than Ernest Hemingway.' – Pete Hamill.

If you want to obtain any of these titles, please send a cheque for the appropriate amount, plus 10% for p&p, to: **Oldcastle Books Ltd, Coleswood Road, Harpenden, Herts AL5 1EQ.**